The Alchemist's Prophecy

SULA STANHOPE

First published in the United Kingdom by
Lightenna in 2023
www.lightenna.com/books

Copyright © 2023 Sula Stanhope

ISBN: 978-1-7384-8011-1

DEDICATION

For the all the dreamers. You are the people who take the world by storm, who find quests and magic and laughter in the little things, who see the light and the darkness, who know how to find home again. Wherever you are on your quest, I'm right there with you. Together, we are infinite.

CONTENTS

ACKNOWLEDGMENTS

So little space, so many people I want to thank. Ah, the dilemmas of writers! Firstly, this book would not exist without the authors who have come before: paving the way for us amateurs to follow your inspiring journeys. Without your wonderful stories, I could never have imagined writing my own book, let alone trying to bring it into the real world. The wonderful Alex Stanhope also deserves my thanks for working tirelessly to make that happen. Alex has been a non-stop, constant and supportive publisher, helping me deal with all the finer art of publishing a novel. Not to mention being the best dad in the world! Thank you also to my wonderful mother, Steph Morris, for being the first to read this book when it was nothing more than a mistake-ridden draft, and for always being supportive of my writing, my ideas, the characters, and the story, no matter what. Both my parents have entertained me with stories from a very young age, inspiring me to write my own tales right away. For this, I am forever grateful. Lots of love! Insert virtual kisses!

My family are huge supporters of me and my creative endeavours, but I am also due thanks to my brilliant friends! As an overthinking extrovert, friendship is a key aspect of my life, and the support and kindness you have all shown to me is unforgettable. Whether you're my school friends, putting up with my endless weirdness, or my extracurricular friends who are equally amazing, you all have a special place in my heart, and I am so thrilled to be a part of your lives.

Thank you to my quirky, genius twin sister Delphi, who also adores writing and has put up with my rambles about this book when it was a half-finished idea all the way home from school. For weeks. When we were younger, we were always playing imaginary games, creating imaginary worlds. Without those lovely games, I expect I would not nearly be as good at writing. Thanks for everything, Delphi!

And of course, as a student, I could not forget about my outstanding teachers! In primary school, I was still new to writing, but you all encouraged me and gave me the confidence I needed to go on and pursue my dreams. Thanks to Mrs Coyne, who 'published' my first book in our class reading corner, and who was overall brilliant. Thanks also to Miss Doyle, who dealt with me in year six, continuing to show me kindness even when I was doing my writing in her lessons. Oops!

And now, in secondary school, I have even more teachers to thank! Thank you Ms Hellard, my amazing English teacher, for helping me discover new techniques and vocabulary in writing. Your lessons fly by so fast, but I always wish they could go on forever! Thank you Miss Meenagh, my incredible form tutor, for being supportive of all my creative work and pushing me to be the best I can be. Thank you Mrs Walker, our brilliant librarian! I've always loved talking books with people, and with you especially! On a rainy day, your library is a relaxing and comforting environment where I can delve into a good book, and your recommendations have led me to some of my favourite series! Thank you also to Mrs Ellenthorpe, my year manager. You have always been so positive and so supportive of everything I do, and see the best in me, even when there's not a lot to see. I am so grateful to you and every teacher in my school who's really inspired me along this journey.

Oh! And one last, extra special thank you to anyone along the way who gets what it's like to be a teenage girl trying to do something different. I'm sending you all my love. And I hope that this story, of Avery and her own quest, inspires you to pursue your dreams, wherever they take you.

And last but not least...thank you, my amazing reader! This book is all because of you. Here's to many more adventures to come!

Sula x.

1
SILVER

I'm running for my life. Again.

I can hear the footsteps of the guards behind us, loud and threatening as they yell streams of curses. Hiro's just ahead of me, leading the way through the labyrinth of alleys in this place. The cool square of silver is grasped tightly in my hand, which is slicked with sweat. So much trouble for this thing. It must be worth millions. My heart is banging in my throat and my legs are propelling me forward as fast as they can. The dark cobblestones beneath my feet are nothing but a blur as I run.

Hiro takes a sharp right and pulls himself easily over a grimy wall, blackened with soot. I bend my knees and vault myself over, scratching my knuckles on the way down, but I land smoothly and keep running. I fight the urge to look back to see if Parker's following, because it would slow me down, and chances are he is, even though he's injured. If there was anyone in this city I could call a survivor, it would be Parker.

The life expectancy here is something like three days.

Sure enough, he appears, jumping easily over the wall, swearing as he lands on his injured leg, but soon he's neck and neck with me as we try and keep up with Hiro, who's taller and faster. The late afternoon dusk is blotted out by skyscrapers rising above us and I have to keep one hand along the soot smeared wall to find my way. I can still hear the guards behind us, though they're obviously tired. But police in a place like this don't give up easily. The crime rates are through the roof.

My boots skid in a puddle and I use the extra momentum to my advantage, sliding easily under a couple of wooden beams boarded over a tiny doorframe. It doesn't lead into a building, but rather, a tunnel with sloping walls and industrial lights glowing murky green. Hiro's vanished into the gloom. Parker follows me and we run down the tunnel, boots pounding into the corrugated iron flooring.

The guards yell outside, obviously confused, but then they seem to notice our route and seconds later the footsteps pick up.

"Man, these guys don't quit, do they?" asks Parker breathlessly as the tunnel becomes steeper. I don't have time to answer before the floor drops away. On instinct I curl into the fetal position and roll as I land. Pain shoots up my right arm, making me wince. Somehow I always leave it unguarded when I take this escape route. Never mind, there's time for medical attention later.

Parker groans and pushes himself to his feet. I grab his wrist to steady him and drag him forwards. We're in a murky basement. It's impossibly dark, but I've been here before.

I look up in time to see Hiro vanish through the windows around the top corners. One's open just a crack, enough for us to squeeze through. It's easier for Parker, who's smaller. I climb the crates stacked underneath and pull Parker up, motioning for him to go first.

The second he's through the window I pull out my knife and bang it against the metal drainpipe loudly. The sound will confuse the guards. Then I squeeze through the window and out into the marketplace.

In Zoriana, which is where I live, nobody really cares if you appear from an underground warehouse and start sprinting through the market. Theft is so common that this place is more of a crime hotspot than it is a place for shopping. I push my way through the crowd, one hand clutching the silver thing. I'm about to make it a break for it down a side alley when a hand grabs my arm and wrenches it back. I stifle a cry of pain and kick my attacker hard.

They let go and I glance back to see the guard gesturing wildly and angrily to the others, who lock eyes with me and snarl. I give them a mock salute and dart down the alley as quickly as possible. A gunshot shatters a window above my head and I feel my heart plummet to my shoes. Attempted murder for one silver square? This thing is obviously worth something. And they want it back.

I force my legs to keep running and sprint down another alley, this one so thin I almost have to go sideways. I'm nearly at the abandoned subway now. I just need to get out of the guards' sight, and fast. As long as they have guns, they can aim and fire, and then I'd be nothing but another bloodstain on these walls.

Shallow breathing comes from the building beside me and I

glance up to see Parker leaping lightly between the fire escapes. The guards haven't spotted him yet, though who knows how he scrambled up there so quickly.

I push my hair out of my face and curse as I hit a dead end. The wall in front of me stretches higher and higher, so high I'd have to shield my eyes to see it properly. There's an open window about halfway up, but how am I going to reach that?

The guards' voices become louder and my brain is whirring frantically. There's nothing for it. I'm going to have to climb it. I place the silver square between my teeth and dig my fingers into the cracks between the bricks. With a silent prayer, I start to climb.

My fingertips are slippery and the rough cement is hard to grip, but somehow I'm nearly at the window by the time the guards spot me. With laughs of triumph and yells of anger, they pound down the alley and cluster at the bottom of the wall, glaring up at me.

One of them pulls out a gun and I flatten myself against the wall, hoping that his aim's bad enough to spare me. Luckily, he misses, but the bullet whizzes so close I can feel the heat through my jacket. My pace increases as the bricks become older and older, some crumbling away beneath my feet. I might as well have been climbing smooth obsidian, it's so steep.

Pausing just underneath the window, I take the time to assess the challenge. I can just about reach, I think. Carefully, carefully, I stretch my fingers out, straining for the window sill-

The brick beneath my left foot falls and I lose my balance. I let out what would be a sharp scream, but it comes out as a

4

muffled cry. My other foot skids off the brick and I'm left dangling by one hand off the wall. The other is clawing at the bricks wildly, trying to find a placing. I make the mistake of looking down and my vision blurs.

I'm at least 100 feet above the guards. This is *so* not how I was planning to spend my afternoon. I'm definitely not ready to die. With those thoughts in mind, I scrabble for some kind of foothold and luckily, I find one. My breathing steadies slightly as I find another handhold and stay there against the wall, just for a second, shaking. Then another bullet flies past, hitting the wall inches away from me. It jolts me back into the present. This time, when I reach for the window sill, I manage to hold on.

Carefully, I curl my fingers around it and grab it with the other hand. Arms burning, I pull myself up and through the window, causing even more pain to shoot down my injured arm. Well, that'll leave a bruise.

I push myself to my feet and glance back out the window. The guards are fuming, because they know they can't get me now. I take the silver square out of my mouth and wave at them, "Missing something?"

One of them swears at me loudly. The other calls me something I'd rather not repeat. I laugh at them and pull the window shut before they can attempt to shoot.

I'm in an old, abandoned apartment, the paint peeling off the walls and murky water dripping from a leaking pipe. Grimacing at the smell, I push up the kitchen window with a loud squeak and stick my head out. The sun is low in the sky and Parker's nowhere in sight, but I recognise this area. All I have to do now is get to the abandoned subway before dark.

Yeah. In case you hadn't already figured out, Zoriana is a death sentence at night.

I squeeze out the window and sit on the ledge for a second, mentally visualising the route. With a quick tug on the drainpipe next to me to check it's stable, I wrap my arms and legs around it and slide down.

The street I'm in is basically deserted, which is a relief. Still, I run across the road and back down into an alley before anyone else can try to kill me.

My senses are still on edge, even as I see the familiar subway entrance. It's boarded up, covered in graffiti and drenched in caution tape, but I hack my way through the annoying strands using my knife and descend the stairs into darkness.

My gang has always used these train tracks as our underground escape route. Not a lot of people know they exist, or that there's anything down here worth stealing. Fortunately for us, they're wrong.

Sometimes, if we're not using this place to escape, we'll scavenge old stuff from the broken-down trains. Hiro once found 300 gold pieces hidden under a seat.

"This," he'd said, waving the bag of money in our faces, "Is exactly what happens when you don't hide things carefully."

Then he'd rolled his eyes and grinned, "Amateurs."

I jump over the old ticket barriers and follow a murmur of voices to one of the old platforms.

Hiro's smoking a cigarette, Parker is leaning against the wall looking worried, and Jade has her arms folded, tapping her foot. Hiro hears my footsteps and looks up, frowning, "Who's there?"

"Ahem," I step out from the shadows, grinning, "More defence needed, Hiro. A sniper could have shot you guys dead from a mile away."

Hiro rolls his eyes (he does that a lot) but he looks genuinely pleased to see me, "Avery. You should stop creeping up on us."

"You're just saying that because you're afraid of the dark."

I'm actually really glad to see he, Parker, and Jade are alive, but I still fold my arms and act nonchalant. That's the way we are with each other in this gang. We're there for each other, but we'll be tough with each other. We argue a lot. We're a crazy kind of family.

"Glad to see you're alive. Let's get out of here before more guards show up," says Jade coldly. Everything about Jade Fencer is cold. From her ice blonde hair to her pale green eyes to the sharp dagger at her waist. You definitely do not want to mess with her.

"Split up," orders Hiro, stumping out his cigarette and tossing it onto the tracks, "Parker, Avery, take the west route. Me and Jade will meet you back at base."

This is the way it's always been. Jade's 17, and acts like she's the queen of the world, but Hiro's always had the last say. He's 18 and the leader of this gang. He looks after all of us, especially the younger ones like me and Parker. Granted, I'm 14, so I could probably make it on my own, but Hiro found me, raised me, and taught me everything I know. He's basically my adopted brother.

Gangs here are always turning on each other and going separate ways, but ours is relatively stable. Like I said, we're like family.

Parker groans as we start off towards west route, jogging quickly down the train tracks and pausing at each corner, "My leg is killing me."

"Sorry, dude. Miya will patch you up the second we get back," I say sympathetically, "If it helps, I think I've caused permanent damage to my arm," I add as a joke.

Parker smiles weakly, sweat shining on his dark skin, "Ouch. You leave it unguarded again?"

"Every time," I sigh, swinging back a couple of loose boards blocking a rusted door. Parker shoves it open and we duck through. This part of the subway is darker. It sends a chill up my spine. Footsteps make me freeze and Parker rolls his eyes to the ceiling, exasperated, "Don't tell me they've tracked us into this place?"

"Probably not," I say, sounding uncertain, "But let's check."

I crouch at the corner and keep my eyes peeled. A couple of oil lamps are lit not too far away, and shadowy figures are moving around. Probably not guards, but if they are…

"Avery!" hisses Parker behind me.

"What?" I crane my head around. He's standing in front of a wall, pointing at it frantically. I frown and get to my feet, "what is it?"

I stand next to him and hardly hold in a gasp, "Holy smokes."

In front of us is a wall made entirely of silver. Patterns are engraved in it, weird symbols arranged in a circular pattern, around a…bird? Yeah, it's definitely a bird. An elegant depiction, wings outstretched and beak tilted. Its eye seems to watch us. Grooves form two circles, one inside the other. It's not a wall, I realise, it's a vault.
It seems to draw me in, like somehow I've seen it before. The weirdest thing is there's a square missing, in the middle. I pull the silver square out of my pocket and my eyes widen.

"Parker, look," I say in a hushed tone, and show him the square. He glances between the vault and it, his eyes widening with realisation, "The symbol—"

"—looks exactly like the ones around the bird," I finish.

Then something weird happens. I feel my brain shutting off, darkness tinging the edge of my vision like a vignette. Suddenly I'm not aware of what I'm doing, the only thing I can see is the vault. The bird seems to be winking at me, its silver eye flashing. It's so familiar. I've seen this place before. I know I have. I step towards it, fingers tracing the elegant silver feathers. I can vaguely hear Parker saying my name, but it echoes like I'm underwater.

The silver thing burns cold in my hand, so cold it's like ice. I feel a strange tug of electricity, just a jolt. It wants me to do something. Then I look back at the vault. It's the missing piece.

I slide the silver piece into the wall and the whole thing begins to pulse with a strange golden light. It's only when my breathing catches that I realise it's matching my heartbeat.

The bird's eye flashes open and suddenly I'm somewhere

else.

The first thing I hear is a piercing, rattling, blood-curdling scream, the kind that wipes every thought out of you. The kind that makes you fall to the floor in fright. The sound of murder.

I taste smoke in my mouth. This place is on fire. In front of me stand two girls. One is shimmering, like a ghost. The other is covered in blood. She stares down the ghost girl like she's an old enemy. Her eyes…they scare me the most. Like two hollow shells, but full of bloodshed and carnage. They glow a horrible, evil red.

She doesn't seem to feel the pain of the flames that lap around her feet. She just stares at the shimmering girl, and the spirit stares back. The red-eyed girl raises one pale hand, skeleton fingers clenching. Then she turns slowly to look at me, those evil red eyes boring into my soul. The ground collapses beneath my feet and I fall into darkness.

"Avery!" Parker catches my arm as I stumble backwards, snapping out of the trance.

There's a ringing in my ears and I shake my head, dazed. The world around me comes into focus. Parker looks worried. The silver thing is in his hand.

"Are you alright?" He asks, looking anxious.

"I'm-I'm fine," I say, straightening, "Did you feel that?"

Parker shakes his head, "Feel what?"

I shake my head, "Nothing," but even as I say it, a cold sensation crawls across my skin, like something's watching me. My eyes dart to the left and I scan the shadows. For a second, something shifts. Then there's nothing. I frown. *There's nothing there you idiot,* my brain yells at me. I turn back

10

to Parker, who's looking at me like I'm about to pass out or something.

"What happened to me?" I say, keeping my voice light. Now it's Parker's turn to shake his head, "I can't really explain. You sort of went into this trance and put the silver piece in the wall. Then you just went really pale and stiff. I pulled the silver thing out and then—"

"I collapsed," I finish, and look at the floor, "Right."

Ugh. How embarrassing.

"Uh, should we get going then?" offers Parker, looking spooked. I nod, and give the wall a bitter look, "I've had enough of weird silver vaults for one day."

Without meeting his eyes, I start running my hand down the train track wall, searching for a ladder Hiro apparently showed us a couple of months ago. Sure enough, my hands meet metal rings and I scale the ladder quickly, Parker following. Neither of us speak as I push the sealed manhole at the top open and we climb back into the city.

The bird seems to watch us as we leave.

2
THE NIGHTMARE

The second we step through the door, Hiro knows something's wrong.

"What's up?" He asks, glancing between Parker and me.

"Nothing," I say. Parker nods, and I'm glad he's silently backing me up on this one. It would be so embarrassing for the entire gang to hear I went into a weird trance because of a...wall.

Hiro doesn't look convinced, but he goes along, "All right. Parker, get Miya to fix up your leg. Avery, you can tuck in for the night if you want."

It's not that late, and I don't sleep much anyway, but I appreciate the offer. Hiro knows something happened, like he always does. He knows me too well.

I don't actually go to bed. I just sit by the window, high in the rafters, staring at the stars. The window sill is wide and roughly hewn out of wood, so it's not the most comfortable seat, but the view from up in the rafters is incredible.

Below, Zoriana stretches out in a dark, glittering mass of skyscrapers. *It's a shame,* I think, *that such a beautiful city is so full of death.* And crime. And murder. And darkness. This place is my worst nightmare, but it's my home. And my roots are here, in this bustling, crime-wrecked city.

The murmur of the others' voices are quiet, but at this time of night the city is alive with sound. Not your regular city sounds. Shouting, glass shattering, sometimes screaming, even. But there's the whoosh of traffic, or the occasional jet plane that's forced to fly out here.

And sirens. So many sirens. When I was young, I remember sitting up here with Hiro, back when he was only eleven, and slight for his age, so we could both fit if we tucked our knees. I asked him what the noises were, and why they never stopped.

 I don't remember his exact answer, but I remember the look on his face. Sad, and a little scared. If I were him, I would be. I looked up to him-I still do-but more than that, he was my guardian. He was like an older brother, and an older brother's job is to protect their little sister. Of course, that was hard to do in a city like this.

As the years went on the gang got larger. When I joined, there were five or six of us. Now, there are nearly twenty. Hiro's the oldest, and the youngest is only ten. Her name's Jodi. She's so small it's hard to imagine her being ten. She's got arms and legs like matchsticks. She doesn't talk much either, just sits and watches us with huge brown eyes much too big for her face.

I pity her. This gang is the most amiable in the city (with each other, with other gangs…not so much) but either way, everyone's got it tough. Apart from Miya, none of us know what do if someone gets hurt. And sometimes, some of us get killed.

A year or so ago, we lost a member called Zavier. He was sixteen. He and Hiro went out at night to make a trade with a trusted merchant on the black market. A fire struck that market, killing at least fifty people. Hiro and him got separated, Zavier went back to save a little girl named Katie. He didn't make it. Hiro found Katie later that night, calling Zavier's name with tears down her soot-stained cheeks. He rescued her and brought her back to base.

When he returned we bombarded him with questions. The only thing he said was, "Zavier's gone."

I didn't know Zavier well, but I still bowed my head at his funeral and lit a candle for him. His picture's hanging somewhere, next to an old photo of me, Parker, Hiro, and Jade together.

The worst part was, poor Katie didn't even survive. She was so fragile, only seven, that when she got a lung infection there was nothing we could do. She died a few weeks later. Jade and I sewed flowers for her grave, even though I cannot sew. Miya had to salvage mine, but I imagined Katie was smiling from the afterlife, touched.

I glance down from my perch at the window, where Parker's testing his leg and Jade and Hiro are talking in low voices. The smell of weak, watery soup drifts up and I rub my stomach, which is slightly pained. The hunger's not awful yet, so I'll probably have to give my serving to one of the younger ones. If it makes Jodi's eyes look less scarily big, or puts any muscle on her spindly frame, it'll be worth it.

I catch a glimpse of my reflection in the window and flinch. I always said my hair was brown. But Hiro said that it changed colour sometimes, like it couldn't decide what colour it wanted to be. Nothing dramatic, but in the light, it glows auburn sometimes. Little strands of gold glint in it, especially in warm sunlight. It's naturally straight, but right now it's matted and jagged, courtesy of the streets.

My eyes are…curious, you could say. One's green, like an emerald, or freshly cut grass. The other's crystal blue. Not the kind of blue people usually have. A really intense blue, like a husky. The fact that they're different colours makes people uncomfortable. Usually they try not to make eye contact with me.

Considering I'm usually armed and I've been told I glare a lot, I can see why.

I blink out of my thoughts as Miya appears from the gloomy rafters. I swing my legs down to make space for her and she perches next to me with a smile, "Can I check your arm?"

I nod, and stretch out my arm, "How did you know I've hurt it?"

"Hiro mentioned you were holding it strangely," she replies, "What'd you do to it?"

I sigh, "I fell. Left this side unguarded."

Miya gives me a sympathetic look, "I wouldn't worry. Falls like that won't cause too much damage. Besides, you can get better, right? Some skills take a while to learn."

For some context, Miya's generally like this. She sees the best in everyone, she's quite shy and very sweet, which is probably why she's our medic. She just knows how to make people feel better. Even little silent Jodi can manage a smile with her.

I shrug, "Or some skills just don't stick, you know? If that's the case, I'll be doomed with a useless arm for the rest of my life."

Miya laughs, "Not if I can help it. But don't worry, there's bruising, but nothing much more. You've not fractured anything."

"Alright, thanks anyway," I sigh, and turn my attention back out the window. Miya frowns, "You ok? You have been distracted tonight. Something wrong?"

The same question Hiro asked.

"Nothing," I say, giving her a halfhearted smile, "Nothing's wrong. Just the adrenaline fading."

Miya nods, looking slightly unconvinced, "Alright, well, I'm not eating tonight, so, um if you want my serving then—"

"Thanks," I say, "But it's fine. I'm giving mine to Jodi."

Miya looks slightly pained, "Ah, yes, Jodi," she looks down at her hands. Now it's my turn to sit up, "What is it? Something wrong with Jodi?"

Miya hesitates, then shakes her head, "She's just so small and skinny. It's like this with all the young ones at first, but she's so tiny I'm afraid she won't make it through the coming season."

I give her a sympathetic look, "Like you said, it's like this with every young one. Parker made it, right?" I try to sound encouraging.

Miya shudders at the memory, "Only just."

She's right. When Parker joined, only just turned nine, he was so small and scrappy everyone thought he'd die. I think even Parker thought it at one point. His ribs and shoulder blades jutted out through his chest, and the clothes he wore dwarfed him. His cheeks were hollow and his legs were so weak he could hardly stand.

At the time, I was tiny, too, but I gave him as much of my meals as I could. After all, even by nine I was jacked with wiry little muscles in my arms and legs. A real sprinter.

Everyone favoured him. Miya sang him songs, Zavier made shadow puppets, Hiro gave him piggy backs around base. A girl named Bianca particularly took a shine to him. She always stole extra things for him, went out day after day for extra resources.

Parker grew stronger and even to this day, he owes Bianca his life. She's down there right now, helping Jodi patch up an old rug.

Miya nods, "But you're right. G'night, Avery. Sleep well."

She stands up and makes her way back down to where the others are clustered together eating. I look back out the window as my thoughts turn to the silver vault, and the weird vision.

'Sleep well'. That's unlikely, I think. The girl's red eyes will keep

17

me awake. And sure enough, when I drift off, they stare into my dreams.

I wake up with a start. I'm not in my hammock. I'm still sitting at the window. The moonlight filtering into the room makes my eyes hurt. Carefully, I peel my head away from the uncomfortable window sill, groaning at the pain in my back. Should've brought a blanket.

I sit up and push my hair out of my eyes again. Down below, the others are asleep. The room is filled with the soft sounds of breathing. Parker, predictably, is snoring. Outside, the sirens still drone on, but they're faint now. On the other side of the city.

I'm relieved. Sometimes when they were really loud, when they were fierce and punctuated by screams that could chill blood, we'd all huddle together in here and pray for it to be over. But that's not tonight.

Flashes of my nightmare return and I shudder, rolling over so I'm facing the moonlit window. I dreamt about the ghost girl again. In my dreams she was screaming as the other one, the one with red eyes, laughed manically. Shadows seemed to wrap around her like they were part of her. I blink out of my thoughts. The stars are bright here, tonight. And I can't stand being alone in the dark.

I'm not afraid of the dark. I'm not afraid of nightmares. I'm afraid of that girl, though. And her glaring, pitiless eyes. And the way she stared down the ghost, like she was someone she'd come to destroy. The worst part? She looked a little like me.

There's a rustle down below, and I tilt my head to look down. A pair of grey eyes stare up at me, then seconds later, Hiro clambers onto the rafters.

"Woke up?" I ask, moving to make space as he sits down, barely disguising a yawn.

"Still up," he corrects, "Haven't had a wink. What's up with you?"

"What do you mean?" I sound defensive.

Hiro rolls his eyes, "You've been weird and quiet all evening. What happened?"

"Nothing."

"It's got to be something."

"It's *nothing*, Hiro," I snap.

He scrutinises me, then sighs, "If you say so."

Reverse psychology. Touché. He waits for an answer, but all I'm giving him is an expressionless stare, so he goes on, "By the way, I'm going Hunting in the morning. You coming?"

'Hunting' isn't actually shooting stuff with arrows. At least, not for us. It's me and Hiro's little nickname for when we're going out to trade. When I was younger, I couldn't grasp the whole, 'we trade with dangerous people for money so we have food to survive' concept, so we just called it Hunting.

It wasn't like I was raised with weird moral concepts, by the way. I know right from wrong. Hiro made it perfectly clear that we only did this because we had to, because there was no other way. People from one of the other cities would look at me and think, 'That one's trouble'.

I mean, what kind of kid my age carries a knife?

I've never actually used my knife on anyone. I'll use physical self defence if I have to (there's a punching bag in our base for a reason) but I'd never kill another person. I only ever use my knife for opening locks, or cutting material occasionally.

I shrug at Hiro, "I don't know. Sure."

"We're trading the silver piece you found. That ok?"

"Yeah, why wouldn't it be ok?" I sound defensive again. I don't know how I feel about that silver piece. It's still in my jacket pocket. It's obviously worth a lot of money. Enough for food for a month, maybe two if we get a bargain. I think about little Jodi. She needs that. This is my chance to get that for her.

Hiro blinks at me, then tilts his head, "Yeah, something's up with you? You wanna talk about it?"

"No," I say shortly, not looking at him. Then I glance at him and sigh guiltily, "Sorry, that sounds harsh. I'm just, I'm fine, ok?"

"Ok. Whatever. Just," he hesitates, "I'm here for you, dude."

"That sounds like something you'd say to your mate, not your sister."

Me and Hiro refer to each other as sister and brother sometimes. When I was little I was so desperate for a family that when Hiro said he'd be my big brother I was over the moon. The term's stuck.

"Avery, you know what I mean."

"Yeah, whatever. Anyway," I jerk my head, "You should get a wink. I'll keep watch."

"You know the drill," he says, and bumps his fist against mine lightly, "See ya."

With that he slides down the rafters swiftly and vanishes into the shadow. I yawn and put my hands behind my head, then look back at the stars.

Views like this never get old.

It's a shame the peace doesn't last.

3
HUNTERS TO HUNTED

The next day follows with a fresh bout of screaming. My nightmares tend to end quickly, and I jolt awake with nothing more than a little gasp. Some of the others aren't so lucky.

My eyes fly open to the terrified screams of a little girl. I bolt awake and sit up straight, anticipating an attack. Down below, the others wake up as well. The screaming is coming from Kayla. She's tossing and turning in her sleep, pleading for help and screaming at the top of her lungs. Bianca jumps up and pins a hand over her mouth to muffle the noise. We do this every time. Otherwise we would have been found years ago.

Miya springs up, too and runs to Kayla's side. She starts to shake her shoulders gently. Kayla's green eyes fly open and dart from side to side wildly, still seeing the nightmare. Then her little thrashing body goes slack as she starts to cry. Bianca removes her hand and she and Miya give Kayla a comforting hug, smoothing back her hair and wiping away her tears.

I grab my jacket off its hook and hop down from the rafters. Tears are still streaming down Kayla's face, so when I kneel in front of her I offer her the hem of my jacket. She buries her face in it, bawling. Miya gives me a weak smile of thanks, then stands to go arrange breakfast. Hiro, who's hovering by the door, watching awkwardly nods to me and I stand too, quickly giving Kayla's arm a reassuring squeeze before we leave.

When the door closes, I don't realise then, but it's the last time I'll see base for a long time.

It never gets really cold around here-there's far too much pollution for that-but today the air is crisp and fresh. The streets are quiet, but the remnants of last night's carnage are visible. Buildings that stood there yesterday are no more than debris and rubble now.

A few lone fires still smoulder on the street corners, and me and Hiro have to duck under a few toppled street lights bridging the gap between houses across the road. A few windows are smashed, and there's a dark stain of something across the pavement. Me and Hiro try to avoid it.

I'm used to seeing the city like this. In a couple of hours it'll be bustling and dangerous again. But for now it's quiet. And the air is heavy with tension. For now, it feels like the city's mourning.

We take the subway route again, but this time we don't go the west route. The silver piece is burning cold through my jacket. The shadows seem to watch me.

I jump every time there's a noise. Hiro gives me a curious look, "Hey, what's up? Why're you being so skittish?"

"No reason," I lie through my teeth.

Hiro frowns, "Your nightmare still bothering you?"

"How did you know about that?" I snap.

He gives me a lopsided grin, "Avery, I've known you most of your life. I know when you've had a nightmare."

"Right. Ookayy," I stretch out the word on purpose, trying to make myself sound derisive, "But it's not anyway, so whatever."

"Alright," shrugs Hiro, "We'll go with that answer."

I sigh, "I just, I swear something's watching me? That sound weird?"

"I get it. This place creeps me out," says Hiro, giving the gloomy shadows a sideways look, "But hey, we've got weapons, right? We can protect ourselves."

"Unless they have long range guns."

"Stop nitpicking," he teases.

I raise my eyebrows, "Me? Wouldn't dream of it. I'm just trying to be safe here."

Hiro snorts, "That's wishful thinking."

Hiro's only eighteen, but for a second he looks much older. His grey eyes are stormy and sad. It reminds me that he's lost so many more people than I have. Seen so much. The message is clear: nowhere is safe. Not here.

"Come on," I say, changing the subject and striding forward, "We'll be late."

Half an hour later, we're standing in front of the best place to trade in Zoriana. Or at least, it would be, if it was open. It doesn't look like much: a pale blue shop with peeling paint and faded words spelling *Bilter's and Co* across the top. According to Jade, who discovered this place three years ago, it used to be a tailor's. You can still see the marks where pins have been stuck into the furniture. The grimy windows are cobwebbed and thick with dust, and a mannequin in an exquisite suit is staring down from the window with a haughty expression on their cloth face.

The blinds are down on one side of the window display. Bilter, the guy who runs it, only ever does that with customers. But the sign on the door says otherwise.

"It's closed," I say flatly.

"No, it's not," says Hiro, frowning at it. I tap the CLOSED sign, "You think?"

He peers through a slit in the window, "One second—"

"Are you trying to stalk Bilter now?"

"Shut up," he laughs, then pulls away from the window, "Yeah, they're open. Come on."

I snort, "Jingle must have got the sign mixed up again."

As we step through the door, I'm struck, not for the first time, how much this place contrasts to the prim and proper shop front. Metal benches and tables provide space for negotiations, there's a long wooden bar with red velvet stools, and industrial lighting casts red light onto the whole scene. Candles at the tables are the only other source of light, so it's always dim in here.

And it's loud. Considering Bilter uses this place as a bar half the time, he sells alcohol, which means the noise levels are pretty much deafening. It's just as well Bilter's soundproofed the entire place.

Occasionally guards will poke their heads in to check nothing suspicious is going on. If that's happening, Bilter arranges everything in the blink of an eye, so that the shop looks like nothing more than a tailor's place. He calls it Code Red. Ironic.

Me and Hiro have only been stuck in that situation once. Bilter hissed at us to hide in the wine cellar while he and others flipped the tables, cleared the cards, or whatever people were betting on, and put on their most innocent smiles. As far as the guards know, this is one of the least sketchy places in the whole city.

How wrong they are. I look around, despite myself. Every time I'm here, there's something new. Stuff stays the same, of course, such as the padded booths we love to use to negotiate-Hiro says the comfort lures our enemies into false security- or the golden cage in the corner, always full of shrieking canaries. I think Bilter uses them for messages.

But there's always different people. Today I'm distracted by multiple strangers. There's a man with one eye, glaring at his drink like it's done something to personally offend him. There's a shrivelled old woman knitting, her bony hands moving clumsily and slowly. She's dropping a lot of stitches, but those needles look far too sharp to be regular. I get the feeling she's not one to underestimate.

A weird sensation prickles the back of neck, and I turn to see someone watching me. A lone woman in a hood, sitting by herself in our favourite booth. That's just coincidence, of course, but she's still interesting to watch. The hood's so low over her eyes I can't see her face, just shadows. And she's moving her hands in an interesting way. A bottle of cider is tipped over next to here, and she's…drawing, using the liquid?

Bilter calls out to us at that moment, "Ah, the scrappers are back again! What can I do for you, young Hiro, me lad?"

Bilter's a tough, burly looking guy with a shaved head and tattooed arms, but he's got a soft spot for Hiro. Says he sees himself in him. That's useful for us, because we always get bargains.

Hiro nods to me and we walk over. Bilter snaps his fingers at Jingle, his lanky assistant, who's hovering by the door, "Jingle, my account book please. And for Pete's sake, flip the door sign!" Then he directs his attention on us, "You two have got something special for me today, I can tell. What treasure have my two favourite scavengers found now?"

Hiro smiles and pulls out a shimmering glass gem, "Nicked this from the old jeweller's place. It's not much, but can we get anything for it?"

Bilter scratches his chin, "I can give you a dozen silver pieces for that, I'd say."

Hiro narrows his eyes, "Thirty."

Bilter shakes his head fondly, "Can't fool me with that one, young Hiro. This little beauty's a fake, can't ya tell?"

Hiro persists, "Twenty. Your customers don't need to know that it's fake."

Bilter's eyes twinkle, "You're a mischievous one, you are. Fifteen, no more, no less."

"Seventeen."

Bilter pauses, "You've got guts kid, I'll give you that. Alright, seventeen is," he scrawls something in his account book and hands us the money. Hiro whips it out of sight before we can be seen as a target. He doesn't have to worry, though, as there's no one watching us.

Wait. Hold that. There is.

The lady in the back corner has her hooded face tilted towards us. I can see nothing but the whites of her eyes, staring right at us.

I nudge Hiro, "We got a shadow."

 'Shadows' are what we often call dodgy people who might attack us. It's our way of saying 'yeah…we might wanna run right about now' without making it too obvious. I've been shadowed before, by a couple of weird guys selling weapons and a figure clad all in obsidian, who's movements were so robotic I wasn't sure whether they were android or human.

The creepy lady in black is my definition of a shadow. The way she's staring at us makes my skin crawl.

Hiro's jaw tightens, but other than that he shows no sign that he's heard me. Doesn't want to draw attention. He turns back to Bilter, "We've got one more trade to make. This one's big."

Bilter rubs his hands together greedily, "Go on, then."

I pull out the silver piece and his jaw drops. He reaches for it, but, seeing the look on my face, pulls back wisely. He lets out a low whistle, staring at it, then brings his gaze back up to us with much difficulty. He can't seem to take his eyes off it.

"Now that," he says, "That-that is a really good trade there. What do you want for it?"

I look at Hiro, contemplating the price. His eyes dart away from me and over my shoulder, and then they widen. I don't have time to look before someone grabs me from behind. my arms are pinned behind my back, but not before I can slide the silver piece into my pocket. Reflexes kicking in, I twist around and elbow whoever they are hard.

They let out a cry of pain but don't let go. No one else is batting an eye, but Hiro's face hardens and he launches himself at whoever my second attacker is. They go stumbling back and I use the first thug's distraction to my advantage. I yank my head back and my skull cracks against their jawbone. They let go, startled. When I turn around I almost faint.

Because my attacker is the mannequin.

One empty sleeve hole is clutching at his cloth jaw, but I'm too panicked to freeze for long. I run for the door, passing Hiro, who's fighting a man in black and golden armour. This thug is very much human, and currently being thrown against the wall by Hiro.

"Come on!" I yell at him.

"You go!" He calls back.

I don't look back as I sprint for the door. When my fingers are on the handle I turn, and lock eyes with the lady. She rises to her feet and swishes her fingers. It must be a signal, because three other men in black and gold step forward. She raises one hand, and points at me. I wrench open the door, heart pounding and sprint out into the street. I have to get away.

Who are they? And what do they want with me?

I look back over my shoulder, where, to my immense surprise, the man has let go of Hiro. The mannequin's vanished. The lady's vanished too. In fact, all the fighters have vanished. Hiro spins around wildly, and I'm relieved to see he's unhurt. He sees me and blanches, "Avery, watch out—!"

I should've stopped sooner, but instead I stumble, confused. Then the ground caves in beneath my feet and I fall into darkness.

4
INFINO

When I open my eyes, I'm somewhere else entirely. Sunlight streams through glass archways and refracts off their surfaces, scattering beams of golden light. What I can see of the sky is blue and the clouds are perfect and fluffy and pure white. I'm sitting in a courtyard, the sandstone floor immaculate and smooth, as if it's never seen a day of rain in its life.

As I come round properly, my senses are flooded. The lush green plants blooming from large marble pots rustle tranquilly in the breeze. I can hear wood chimes tinkling somewhere, and the soft tweet of birds.

As I push myself up from where I'm slumped against what looks like a mound of pillows so soft they could have been made of clouds themselves, my eyes struggle to take in what's before me. Golden walkways connect seven glittering golden towers, each one unique in its own way.

One of the towers has what looks like a glass dome for a roof. Another tower has abstract patterns carved neatly into the walls. Another is long and thin, like the shaft of an arrow. The courtyard I'm in is huge, and in the centre sparkles a magnificent crystal fountain: gorgeous, clean blue water cascading down three golden tiers.

My legs feel weak as I stand up, too shocked to do anything but gaze and gaze. How long have I been asleep? Am I dead? Is this heaven?

I never imagined heaven would be so…perfect. So neat, and clean, and sparkling clear. I feel like a speck of dirt on a pure marble painting.

A cool breeze sifts through the courtyard and ruffles my hair playfully. My fingers tingle as the breeze envelopes me, like I'm meeting a long lost friend.

Carefully, I take a step forward, then another. I'm definitely not dreaming. Everything here seems so unbelievable but so…real. The air smells of all different kinds of things: of sea air and roses, and drying paint, and strangely, a hint of something chemical as well. It smells of sawdust and rosemary and burning incense.

Everything's so alive. It's so much to take in at once. Which begs one question: where am I?

My first instinct is to be suspicious after that thought crosses my mind. Nowhere's this perfect, this peaceful, this pure. It must be some kind of trap. And I'm completely out of my comfort zone. The silver piece is still in my pocket: somehow, I know it hasn't moved. But as I look down, I realise I don't even have my knife.

"Looking for your blade?" Asks a voice.

I spin around to see a tall, elegant, beautiful woman walking-no, gliding-across the courtyard towards me. Her long, caramel brown hair is flowing loosely down her back. Her pale grey eyes remind me of peace, of a quiet ocean. It's hard to tell how old she is: her face seems to glow with youth, but at the same time, she looks timeless, like she's been around for centuries.

She's smiling reassuringly at me, but I don't let myself relax. Not just yet.

"My apologies for taking it," she continues lightly, "my warriors will return it. It was just for convenience."

I stay silent. Who is she? What's going on? Where am I? The questions batter the inside of my head.

"You must be Avery," she says, smiling at me.

Her voice is soothing, but that's probably a trap, too. I'm not showing any weakness here.

"Yeah, I'm Avery," I say warily.

She just smiles more, though, "I've heard so much about you. Please, have a seat," she waves a hand, and what I thought were my pillows float and morph into fluffy white chairs. So they really were clouds.

I sit, even though part of me is desperate to run. But where would I run too? I stay silent, even though there's a million questions in my head. The woman only smiles kindly at me, "I must apologise for our, ah, unconventional methods of bringing you here. I promise you that your friend back home was not hurt. My creations would never harm, only restrain."

"Your creations?" I ask warily, then it clicks, "You're the shadow. The lady in the hood. The one who was drawing in the cider…" I trail off, then another idea springs to my head, "You didn't-you couldn't-did you draw those things?"

She doesn't look offended in the slightest, "Yes, I did. And the mannequin. I do hope you didn't find me too intimidating, though. I have never yet brought a new student here myself, and you were a…special case."

I shake my head, dazed with all the information, "Uh, no. Totally fine with getting kidnapped by mannequins. Hang on, what do you mean new student?"

"Well, this beautiful place is Infino Magicki Septem," says the woman, "An education academy for young sorcerers. There are seven towers, one for each branch of magic—"

"Hang on, you've lost me," I interrupt, "Who even are you? Why did you bring me here?"

"Oh dear me, you must think me so rude for not introducing myself sooner!" She laughs: a tinkling, cheerful laugh, like the ocean on a calm day, "I am Lady Tempest, the headmistress of this academy. You are our latest student, and quite an interesting one at that."

I shift, "Uh, no, I'm quite boring actually. Can I go home now?"

I expect her to get angry at that, but she only looks at me sympathetically, "It must feel strange being here. Don't worry, however. You're safer here than you ever were in Zoriana."

"You don't know anything about my home," I say coldly, even though one part of my brain is screaming 'shut up or she'll vaporise you!!'

Lady Tempest looks slightly taken aback, "My apologies, my dear—"

"And where is here?" I ask, "Are we still in Zoriana? Are we still on my planet?!"

Lady Tempest raises a hand and I flinch, but no magic lightning bolts shoot from it so she must be going easy on me, "I shall explain. This is Infino, a school for magic. We are in a special protected place tucked away in the Midlands, which is east of Zoriana. You have been taken here because you are special, Avery. Not only do you have magic, you—" then she presses her lips together like she said too much.

"I what?" I prompt warily. She shakes her head, "A tale for another day."

Then she says nothing.

"And?" I ask incredulously, "You can't just say 'Hey, you're magic' then just leave me hanging! I need an explanation, don't I?"

Lady Tempest blinks, like she's just remembered I was here, "As I said, I shall explain everything. All that you must know right now is that you possess magic, and henceforth you have been brought here to be trained. Now, if you would please come with me, there's a special welcoming ceremony I would like you to attend."

With that she stands. I scowl, "I'm not going anywhere with you. You kidnapped me, brought me here, and started talking nonsense at me. Magic doesn't exist."

But even as I say it, I feel unsure. People have talked about magic before, but in different ways. Some say it's something to be ashamed of, that those who have is are born to be evil. Others say that magic is a metaphor for different skills people have. In Zoriana, I've never heard anyone talk about magic. It's just a story.

But is it? Lady Tempest seems to think otherwise.

"I'm afraid it does," she says gently, like my head will explode at the news. Maybe it will, if I'm so magical.

I fold my arms, heart banging around like a trapped bird. What I'd give to run away right now. But something in me forces me to stay.

She sighs gently, and kneels like I'm a child. Her elegant white robes swish around her like they're alive.

"I promise I shall explain everything. You have more power than you know, and it needs nurturing."

"I don't understand," I say, "More power? What are you talking about?"

She shakes her head, "I cannot speak here. Please, follow me."

With that, a few warriors step out from behind the marble pillars. Now that I look closer, they're not quite human. They shimmer slightly, just a haze around them. And they don't seem capable of speech. Lady Tempest must see my expression of horror and my fists clench, because she quickly says, "Don't worry, they shan't hurt you. They are just here to escort you to the Hall. Come with me, please."

She says the last part like a command. A tiny part of my brain thinks, *what will she do if I don't?* I don't want to find out.

With that, I follow her out of the courtyard.

5
THE COPPER HEAD SPEAKS

What the hell am I doing? Is all I can think as I scurry after Lady Tempest. Her feet hardly seem to touch the floor as she walks, striding forward so determinedly I can hardly keep up. Surrounding me loosely are more hand-drawn guards, eyes pinned ahead. They're so detailed it's creepy. They look just like…regular people, I guess. But even more unsettling is the spears they're clutching. Definitely wouldn't want to get on the bad side of those things.

That's really the only thing that's kept me from running so far. I know I could make it out of here if I climb up one of the towers. The one covered in engravings would be full of handholds. But taking on five guards at once with not even a weapon? That's pretty much impossible.

You've done it before, my brain whispers urgently, *So why aren't you running now?* I don't really have an answer. All I know is that I want answers. Lady Tempest is keeping everything I need from me. Like, what really is magic? What are the seven kinds? Are there real kids here? What's so special about me? Why am I here? How long has she been following me? How did she know I existed? Where are we going?!

Lady Tempest glances behind like she can hear my thoughts, "Nearly there now. Hurry, we mustn't keep the others waiting!"

And, who, pray tell, are the others?

My question is answered almost right away. We come to a halt at the grand doors to a large glass conservatory. It's shaped in a hexagon, with a turreted glass roof and gold leaf trim on the doors. The glass walls are so clean they sparkle. Somehow, even though it's clear, I can't see inside.

Lady Tempest catches me looking, confused, and she smiles, "It's enchanted. You'll see soon enough."

I nod stiffly. Enchanted? You can do that to buildings? You can do that at all?

Lady Tempest raises her arms and declares, "This is the Hall of The Copper Head. Please, follow me."

"The copper *what?*" I ask, but she doesn't seem to hear me as the doors swing open smoothly.

I lose my breath. Inside it's breathtaking: high, ornate glass ceiling, and rows of seats filled. With kids my age, strangely enough. They're all clad in black and gold uniforms, clean and neat. Upon Lady Tempest's arrival, they rise to their feet in respect.

When their eyes land on me a whisper rings out. They glance at each other and nod in my direction. The feeling of so many eyes boring into me is unsettling.

I notice a boy watching me with narrowed eyes. His hair's brown with an ice blue tip that hangs into his eyes. Probably dyed it. He just radiates money. He's almost glaring at me, like I shouldn't be here.

Yeah, you're not the only one who thinks that, pal, I think. I shift nervously under so many gazes, and almost take a step back when Hiro's voice echoes in my head: *Show them you're not afraid. Give them attitude, because you want them to know that if you die, you'll go down fighting.*

Ok, the last bit doesn't apply to this situation (not yet) but none the less I straighten, tilt my chin up defiantly, and meet their curious and wary expressions with a cool one of my own. I don't smile: it's not like I'm trying to make friends here. I want them to understand not to mess with me.

It works. Their eyes dart away and some of them look a little uncomfortable. The blue-haired boy tilts his head slightly, interested.

Lady Tempest clears her throat, "Students, you may sit."

She glides down the aisle smoothly, and comes to a stop at a table at the top. Sitting on the table, in pride of place, is a human head. Except it's made out of metal.

A bronze sheen glows off its copper face. Its eyes are blank and staring. Its mouth is shut. Its features are plain. It stares straight ahead, straight at me.

It's just a statue, I think. So why are my palms clammy? I feel like I'm about to faint.

Lady Tempest closes her eyes, faces the rows of kids, and raises one hand high to the air, the other on her heart. This must be some kind of ritual, because the students follow suit.

Even the guards do it, but I keep my hands firmly by my sides. I'm out of place here. It'll seem weird if I join in.

Lady Tempest takes a deep breath and opens her eyes, "welcome students. I have summoned you here for a matter of much importance."

The students start muttering. A few glance at me. I can practically hear their thoughts, 'How is *she* important?'

Lady Tempest continues, "Students, for years you have trained here, learned here. You have mastered your skills. Or shall I say, you are mastering them. For there is still so much to learn. So many people to meet. And now it is more important you learn than ever."

Her voice takes on a grave tone, "I sense much danger."

Most of the kids look nervous, shocked, confused, and glance at each other fearfully. Like danger is something that never happens to them. However, there's a group of kids near the back that nod solemnly, like they knew this was coming. I immediately feel respect for them.

Lady Tempest continues, "The end of an age may be near. For now, according to the prophecy, the one it spoke of has risen."

She points at me. The students crane back in their seats and start whispering again.

Prophecy? I think, *What prophecy? How does it include me?!*

Lady Tempest continues, "And as per the Alchemist's instructions, the Copper Head shall now speak the rest of the prophecy that determines the fate of our world."

Great. So now I've got the fate of our world on my shoulders.

All the students look expectantly at the statue. I cringe. It's not going to say anything, then I'll look like an idiot. For a second, nothing happens. The kids start to glance at each again.

But then, the copper head blinks. A gasp fills the Hall. It blinks, slowly, again, then, with the slightest creak, it opens its mouth.

By now I'm rooted to the spot. *What the HECK is going on?* Then the copper head speaks, and its booming voice fills the hall.

I almost would've imagined a metal head would talk in a squeaky, dry voice. Or in a robotic way, like a machine. But no. The head's voice is deep and commanding, and seems to echo off the walls, sweeping through the hall.

"The girl raised in the city of shadow
Shall rise with magic left unknown
Two birds shall sing three times at dawn
From the death of a hero a legend is born"

You could cut the silence with a knife. *The death of a hero?* I think. I don't want anyone to die. Not because of me.

"Five shall face the Wild, seek the descendant of gold
Three castles hold answers, the journey behold
One shall face their worst nightmare twice

A deadly weapon lies in wait beneath fire and ice"

The kids are sizing each other up now. Who are the five? What will happen to them? I see a couple shudder at the mention of their worst nightmare twice. That must suck. But my eyes are fixed on the head, as it continues.

"Two armies will clash in a battle for power
The lost twin shall fall, the other shall cower
The king will not live while the kingdoms unite
The Infinite will rise where the stars meet the night."

Then it's voice fades away. *The Infinite.*

The word rings a bell. Why does that sound familiar? My legs are shaking by this point. The students burst into chatter, anxiously talking. I catch snippets of conversations

"Stars meet the night…that's Astrology, isn't it?"

"What do they mean 'worst nightmare twice'?"

"Is she the Infinite? Is she the one?"

"A deadly weapon…I don't like the sound of that!"

"We're all going to die!"

"Shut up, we're not all going to die!"

"She's dangerous. We have to get rid of her before this can come true!"

Lady Tempest looks lost in thoughts. She sees my expression, blinks, shakes her head, and raises a hand for silence. When that doesn't work, she coughs. The students still don't listen. Tempest throws her arms wide, and a shock wave of air sweeps through the hall with a boom. It almost sends me off my feet. The kids turn to the front, as Lady Tempest clears her throat, looking unsettled, says, "Well, that was—"

She's cut off by a BANG, as the Copper Head explodes.

Debris rains down on the shell-shocked students as they duck for cover. I get a mouthful of soot to the face. Shards of copper land in my hair. I can't feel the pain, though. All I feel is numb, shocked.

Did I just do that?

Lady Tempest's dress is scorched black. Her grey eyes are wide with shock as she scans the room. Her eyes lock onto mine, full of something like fear. I stare back, blood dripping from a shrapnel cut on my cheek down onto my clothes. The kids uncover their heads and sit up, terrified. The silence is broken only by the tinkling of glass. The copper head is nothing more than a pile of smoking rubble on the table.

Slowly all heads turn to me. The guards are gone, vanished like they'd never existed. Fear overtakes me, and I'm aware that I'm trembling slightly.

The silence is too overwhelming. The eyes on me are too much. Fighting the urge to throw up, I do the only thing I'm good at. The only thing I have right now.

I run for my life.

6
NEW ENEMIES

I have no idea where I'm going. All I know is that I have to get away. Away from the stares, away from Tempest's look of utter horror, away from the images of the copper head staring at me whenever I close my eyes. It's too much. I need to get out of here.

I sprint through the courtyard, boots slapping against the clean stones. So perfect. I couldn't be less perfect. I make a beeline for the nearest tower, which is built with swirling walls like it's a huge drill bit.

There's a golden door with an image of a cloud carved into it at the bottom. I yank at the door handle, but it doesn't budge.

"Come on, come on," I urge, jiggling the handle but the door doesn't move. I spin around wildly and scan the courtyard for any towers with unlocked doors. Unless I climb the walls of the courtyard, which are smooth and far too steep, these towers are my way out. Once inside I can find an exit.

My eyes land on a tower wrapped with golden creepers and decorated with images of birds and other animals. It seems to have a flowered arch instead of a door. I sprint for it but hesitate just before the door. What if it's guarded by something, like an invisible shield? Cautiously, I stick a hand out. My fingers find nothing but air. Taking a deep breath, I step through the arch, eyes squeezed shut. No alarms go off. I don't get zapped by lasers. Exhaling in relief, I open my eyes and look around. For a second, I'm speechless.

I'm in a hall with a high ceiling, but there must be floors above. There's a waterfall of golden liquid trickling down. Plants bloom in large pots and colourful creepers climb the walls. The floor is white and clean, like a hospital. There's a huge golden doctor's cross built into it. Sunlight streams in through large windows. Golden stairs spiral up and up, but there's also a large elevator in the corner. Even though it's inside, I can hear birds chirping. It's like the most beautiful vet's office ever.

But there's no time to get distracted. Shaking myself, I sprint up the stairs, trying not to stop and gawp at all the things I see.

A floor like a forest, with real trees and even a babbling brook, sparkling in the sunlight. A floor parked with stretchers and filled with doors reading 'STOREROOM'. A floor that's simply a huge glass tank, filled with bright fish and coral.

Finally I arrive on an empty floor with a circle of lockers around the edge and large pillars. Perfect to hide behind. I crouch down behind one and let my breathing steady. I'm ok. I'm ok.

I'm not really ok. In fact, I'm on the verge of a panic attack, but I swallow the bile that rises and take a deep breath. The air is clean and fresh. A cool breeze that feels natural but is probably air conditioning blows across my scratched face. It's soothing.

My hands are shaking, and covered in little scratches from sharp pieces of the head. I hope no one else got hurt. That would be one heck of a first impression: *Hi, I'm Avery. Sorry I almost killed you. Oh, yeah, I might be responsible for the destruction of the whole world. Nice to meet you!*

I press a hand against my aching temples and close my eyes. Something is tingling in my head, but I can't put a finger on what. The tingling feeling is in my fingers too, and when I pull my hand away, I gasp. The scratches are gone, like they never existed.

Speechless, I hold the healed hand in front of my face and compare it with the other, which is covered in soot and cuts. The skin on my healed hand is practically glowing with health, my nails pearly and clean for what I think is the first time in my life. What just happened?

The healed hand should make me feel better, but instead fear takes over me. What is going on? What did I just do? What is this prophecy? How does it involve me? Am I the hero that should die?

I feel helpless. I know that soon guards will find me, or students, and I'll be carted off to where Tempest will probably call me all kinds of things and demand I be executed. Maybe she'll draw a big axe or something and do it herself.

That's what I would do if I was in her position.

All the adrenaline that fuelled my flight has long since abandoned me, and my body is aching all over. I tuck myself into a ball and try to think things through. Is there a way I can get out of here? Maybe if I try a top floor? Who knows, there might be a skylight of some sort.

Then, when I'm out, I'll climb down…? One wrong move and I could plummet to my death. But if I stay much longer, I'll die anyway.

Then I'll get back to Zoriana. Tempest said we're in the Midlands, so that means it won't be too far. Merchant towns are dotted along this place like hidden jewels. I can always stop for supplies there.

Ok, that's a plan, then, I think. *Now I just need to get out of here without being seen.*

That's easy enough. Surprisingly there's no one around. Surely Tempest would have sent the students back to the towers to look? Or is this where they sleep?

I push myself to my feet, and creep slowly along by the lockers. An archway covered in plants leads down another empty corridor. I hesitate, fingers against the arch, but the murmur of voices far below motivates me. The students will be back any minute.

I tiptoe along the corridor, masking my footsteps and keeping one ear out. Nothing. I can feel a breeze, meaning that there must be a window nearby. Perfect. I break into a run, turning the corner and— slamming straight into a group of people.

I stumble backwards and steady myself against the lockers, as an annoyed voice says, "Watch it!"

Shaking my head, and blinking, my vision focuses to see the blue-haired boy from the hall. He's looking at me strangely.

"Sorry," I mumble and try to push past, keeping my head down so he can't recognise me.

"Excuse me!" Another voice says, this one high and female. A hand grabs my arm and twists it round. I turn to face a beautiful girl with long, flowing golden hair like Rapunzel. Her skin is suntanned and flawless. Her eyes glow golden, and she has long dark false lashes. False nails, too, which are digging into my arm. She's glaring at me.

"Um, hi?" I ask, shaking her off.

"You can't just bash into people, can you?" She snaps. I blink, "Oh, sorry, I was just—"

"It's you!" Cries another girl with dangling golden earrings shaped like stars, and long brown hair, "The girl from the hall!"

The rest of the group, which consists of all girls and the blue-haired boy, start murmuring. I feel myself flush.

The blonde girl's golden eyes flash, "Well, well, well. Look what the cat dragged in. Tempest will be so pleased when we bring you to her!"

"Oh, that's really not kinda necessary—," I begin, but she clicks her fingers, and two of the girls grab my arms.

"Hey," I exclaim, "Let me go!"

"Hmm. No," says the girl, "Let's get you out of my tower, shall we? I hate things that are covered in dirt," she's smiling like a Cheshire Cat.

"That's rich coming from someone with plants on their walls," I retort.

She doesn't even look fazed. Instead she laughs, fake and high pitched. The rest of the group laughs too, except the boy. The girl sneers, "You're funny. That's cute. Still, you're no chosen one, are you?"

"What are you talking about?" I snap.

"You're just not…hero material, are you? Do you always look like that?"

I look down at myself, "Like what?"

"You know. The rat's nest hair. The mud," she shudders, "It's not hygienic, is it?"

I laugh derisively, "Who do you think you are?"

By now the rest of the group have circled me, arms crossed, and are whispering. The blonde girl tosses her hair, "I'm Chloe Moscopello. You, you are an inconvenience, aren't you?"

The others titter. I've never been to high school, but suddenly I feel like this is exactly how popular bullies would act. Anger surges through me. I've had enough of this for one day.

"Ok, look lady," I say, easily shrugging off her minions, "I'm 'so sorry' I crashed into your boyfriend or something, but-"

"Ok, first things first, he's not my *boyfriend!*" Chloe snaps, tossing her hair again.

I mimic her high voice, "Ok, first things first, he's not my *boyfriend.* Are you always this annoying?"

She flushes a little, "You little—"

I step forward, my voice cold, "Do it. Provoke me. I'd love to wipe that arrogant smirk off your face."

She takes a step away. For a second, fear flashes in her face. Then it's replaced by smugness, "You're bluffing. Tempest would have you kicked out forever."

"Fine by me," I shrug, "I don't want this, anyway."

Chloe Moscopello tilts her head, "You've got spirit. And maybe you'd be pretty, if you weren't so," she waved a hand, "Messy. But you'll never be wanted here. We certainly don't want you, do we girls?"

The girls nod and chip in. The boy's face is impassive. My fists are clenched. I can't stand this. The window's just there…

I roll my eyes, "Sure. You done yet?"

Chloe sniffs, "Matter of fact, I'd rather not spend any more time wasting my breath on you."

"Cool," I say flatly, "You know you could have opened with that."

Chloe obviously can't think of anything to say, because she tosses her hair (again) and stalks off, her entourage following her. Only the boy hangs behind.

"Well, what are you doing?" I snap at him.

He meets my eyes with his dark ones, "She's not my girlfriend."

Then he walks off. I blink. Okay? Weird conversation. Never mind. There are more important things right now.

I walk over to the window and judge the distance down. It's reckless, but what Chloe said has me filled with residue anger. The look in her face if she could see me right now.

Then I jump out the window.

Yes, I know what you're thinking. That was a pretty stupid thing to do, wasn't it?

The air whips past me as I fall, but I refuse to scream. Instead, I stretch out a hand for the side of the tower, fingers clawing at the vines wrapping around it. Anything to break my fall.

I manage to hook my fingers around a creeper and hold on. Pain shoots up my arm as it yanks upwards and I'm left hanging off the tower wall. I try not to have a mental image of a very much dead version of me on the stone courtyard floor, so far down it makes me dizzy. I grit my teeth and clench my jaw. I've done this before. It's no different to Zoriana.

I place my legs on large mushrooms growing out of the side

of the tower. Luckily, the spongy fungi hold my weight. Brushing my hair out of my eyes, I look down to see a vague staircase pattern of mushrooms descending to the courtyard below. Perfect. And there, shimmering like the gates to heaven, is the entrance to this place. My way out.

Filled with new determination, I start to climb down, digging my fingernails into rough vines and placing my feet on the mushrooms.

I'm just beginning to think that this is actually pretty easy, when of course, my luck runs out.

The vine I'm clinging onto slowly but surely begins to come away from the tower with a loud ripping sound, like a tearing seam. I don't have time to do much more than start to panic before it comes away completely and I'm left grasping at air.

My feet skid on the mushrooms, and I try and snatch the end of the vine, dangling off the tower. It's swinging wildly in the suddenly agitated winds, and before I can see it coming it hits me hard in the chest. Then I'm falling.

The ground comes rushing up to meet me and I squeeze my eyes tight shut, praying for a quick, painless death. But just before I hit the floor, my fall halts. My body feels weightless. Maybe I've died and gone to heaven? Slowly, I open one eye a crack. I'm levitating only inches from the stones. Flabbergasted, I open both my eyes and crane my head. My arms and legs are splayed, palms facing the ground. Slowly, I push down. It's like pressing on a cushion of air.

I clench my fist and suddenly the air cushion is gone. My right hand side falls to the floor. I cough as the air's knocked out of my lungs. Clenching the other fist, the air releases me and I'm left lying there, holding my painful ribs, the tingling sensation in my fingers back again. I hold them against my ribs, hoping maybe the weird healing thing will kick in, but nothing happens. Maybe it only works when it wants to. Maybe it was a fluke. Maybe it was a hallucination. Maybe it was a thing that happens in the tower?

Or maybe it was just my eyes deceiving me. I'm exhausted. My legs feel like iron as I stand up, as if my brief moment floating makes my body feel heavy on ground. And I feel drained. How I'd love to sleep right now.

But the gates are only metres away. Glancing around, the courtyard seems empty. Taking a risk, I run for the gate.

I'm within centimetres when the guards appear, materialising out of thin air like mirages coming to life. One takes my wrists, forcing me to a jolting stop. The other stands behind me to stop me from running again.

"Let me go," I growl, but they obviously can't understand me. One nods to the other and they sharply turn, taking me with them. I struggle as much as I can, but the guard's fingers are like steel around my wrists.

No, no, no, no, no, I think, twisting in their grip. I look over my shoulder at the gates, my last chance for freedom, so far away.

I'm really in this now.

7
THE ALCHEMIST'S PROPHECY

The guards drag me through the halls, not roughly, but not comfortably. Then again, that's probably because I'm writhing and struggling. If I came quietly like a good little girl, I would make this process easier.

Easier for them, maybe. For me, the person they're dragging to their death? Not so much. I have no idea what Tempest will do when she sees me. Maybe she'll use her insane powers and disintegrate me on sight. Maybe she'll lock me up. Either option doesn't inspire confidence.

But she doesn't do either of those things.

When we arrive at what I presume is her office, on the very top floor of the tallest tower, I'm speechless. The room is circular and has slanting walls curving around to create the cone shape of the tower roof. The ceiling is covered in timber rafters. There's a large glass chandelier with seven candles hanging from the ceiling. Sunlight pours into the room generously from a circular window.

The floorboards are golden and there's a plush wine coloured rug in the middle of the room. A desk with two comfortable chairs faces the window, which offers an incredible view of the glittering towers and rolling green hills surrounding this place. And shelves and shelves of books line the walls, sunlight making their gold embossed titles glow. The whole place feels like the most incredible library ever.

I inhale deeply. It smells of dust and old books. Why does that remind me of home?

There's a flurry of dust motes around my feet as the guards push me forwards. Tempest is sitting at the desk, head bent over an old book. When she hears our footsteps, or at least, mine-the guards walk silently-she looks up and frowns at my entourage, "You two need to learn to knock."

She snaps the book shut, stowing it away before I can glimpse the title, and gives me a comforting smile, "My apologies, Avery. My protectors are so very rude sometimes. Release the poor girl," she orders them.

Obediently, the guards step back and melt away into nothing. I stand, legs shaking, before Tempest.

Give them attitude. I tilt my head and do my best to look confident.

"Would you like to take a seat?" She asks. I nod wordlessly and sit stiffly in the chair, back rigid.

"Not quite as comfortable as clouds, I'm afraid," she sighed, "But they are dreadfully tiring to control. Fickle thing, the weather. With so many Anemology students nowadays, the winds have been more unpredictable than ever."

Anemology? I think, *What's Anemology?*

Tempest looks at me as if expecting an answer, or a smile, or anything. I don't give her it. She's being kind, but maybe that's a trick. Maybe it's like how they fatten the lambs before they slaughter them. She sighs, "I expect you want me to explain. In our world—"

"Wait one second," I interrupt, "Why aren't you just killing me?"

"Killing you?" Tempest looks horrified, "Why would we kill you?"

Wait. She's not going to kill me?

"Because, you know, I could destroy the world and stuff," I say, confused, "And I destroyed what was probably a really valuable object."

"Oh dear me no!" Laughs Tempest, "Of course we wouldn't kill you, Avery! And certainly not for the explosion! The copper head was prophesied to explode after it spoke the second part of the prophecy!"

I must still look unconvinced, because she leans forward and says, "I promise you are safe here. No one would harm you. You are more important to us than you could ever realise."

She sounds really serious, but I can't help wondering if Chloe Moscopello treats everyone here like that, or just the people from weird prophecies. I'm not important to them, that's for sure.

"I don't understand," I say helplessly, "What's Anemology? What does magic involve? Who's the alchemist? What's the Infinite? How does any of this involve ME?"

Tempest looks grave, "I shall explain, as I promised."

"That would be nice," I say, folding my arms and giving her an expectant look.

"Magic through the ages has been seen in many different ways," says Tempest, "To some, it was a great honour. People with magic were healers, rulers, creators. But to some, they were destroyers. People fear what they cannot understand, and magic was an unknown power,"

"Throughout the years, magic was persecuted. Sorcerers were hunted, and killed. Magic was also used for greed and money. Enslaving a sorcerer was guaranteed to bring you riches," Tempest says, and shudders, "Dark times. In such times, there were," she hesitates, "Ways to rid yourself of magic. It was safer for some families, for their children."

I nod to show her I'm keeping up. She continues, "There are seven branches of magic. Anemology, which is the power of controlling wind. Anatomy, which is the power of healing living things. Artistry, which is the ability to bring your artwork to life. Astrology, the ability to control the stars. Archery, the ability to craft weaponry out of thin air, to give those weapons special powers. And Alchemy, the ability to craft potions."

"Hold on," I say, "That's only six. What's the seventh?"

Tempest's face darkens, "You will learn in time."

"Ok," I say slowly, "What does this have to do with me? Are

you saying I have one of those abilities?"

Tempest nods. "Which one?" I press.

"There is no way of knowing until you demonstrate your powers."

I slump, "My 'powers' have a mind of their own, lady."

Tempest chuckles, "Magic tends to be like that. And it can be dangerous. Hence why I started this school, to teach younglings how to control it."

"So what's different about me?"

Tempest smiles, "Patience. Long ago there lived an alchemist. Not a regular alchemist. They called him the most powerful, wise alchemist the world had ever seen. He was a genius inventor. And he had a vision. A prophecy was spoken to him."

"But couldn't he have been lying?" I ask, "This dude could have done it for money, right?"

Tempest shook her head, "The prophecy was spoken by a falling star itself. But it only gave him part of the story. He dedicated the rest of his life to building the copper head, placing the star in the very heart, for the star had told him that the second half of the prophecy would be spoken when the Infinite approached it."

"And that's…me?" I say.

"As it seems, yes," says Tempest. A shadow crosses her face, "Others believed that they might be the Infinite, but none were correct. The Alchemist promised the world of magic that she would arrive at the end of an age. That she would tip the balance of our world forever."

I shiver, "That doesn't sound good."

"The Alchemist died an old, old man," continues Tempest, "And the legend of the prophecy went on. One day, the Copper head vanished. It appeared in the centre of the courtyard. Where it stood, a fountain grew. I found the fountain, and the head, and built the Hall to keep it safe. Then I built Infino, in the hope that one day, I would find the Infinite and train her to use her power for good. For if she used her power for bad..." she trails off, and for a second, I see fear in her eyes, "It would be the end of us all."

"No pressure," I practically squeak, "So, this 'Infinite' what do they do? Do they have, like, infinite power?"

"No one knows," says Tempest, "The prophecy was vague. The powers of the Infinite are yet to be determined. You will determine it."

"Why me?" I ask, "Out of everyone, why me?"

"The universe chose you," says Tempest.

I snort, "Yeah, right. Like the universe can do that."

"Did you ever wonder who your parents were?"

I freeze, "No. they died," I say shortly.

That's not the whole truth and I know it. Tempest looks unconvinced, too, "You'll learn."

"I don't want to learn," I snap, "That's the past."

"And you must confront it, if you will succeed in the future."

"I don't *want to succeed.*" I growl, "Whatever this way is to get rid of your magic, I want to do it. I don't want this!"

"You'd rather be back in Zoriana, where you have to fight every day to survive?"

"So far every second I've been here something bad has happened," I say, my voice rising, "Go figure. If I'm the Infinite, what's to say I won't go crazy and destroy the world or something?"

"Because I see you, Avery."

"Well duh," I roll my eyes, "I'm sitting right in front of you."

Tempest smiles, and shakes her head, "I mean, I really see you."

"You hardly know me," I hiss.

"You remind me of someone I've met before. She's gone now, but you are so alike her in many ways."

"I'm flattered," I say flatly.

Tempest chuckles, "You have her spirit. But be careful. A spirit like that is not easy to be broken, but I don't doubt they'll try."

"So, what am I supposed to do now?" I ask, "Seek this 'descendant of gold'? Who's that?"

"I cannot interfere with the quest any further. Tomorrow,

you shall depart. I will provide resources, of course, and your companions. But," for a second, she looks just a little sad, "You must find your own path."

I don't know what to say to that. Tomorrow? Am I ready to go save the world tomorrow? Let's be honest, it wasn't like I was busy. By now I thought I'd be dead.

And this has all happened so *fast*. Only, what, a couple of hours have passed? It seems like weeks ago that I was standing outside Bilter's with Hiro. Thinking of him makes me feel awful. He probably thinks I'm dead. He must be out of his mind with worry.

Maybe there's a way for me to find him and tell him I'm ok, a way to see him again on this quest. But then there's the nagging question: if he asks me to come home, what would I say? If it's Chloe Moscopello I'm on a quest with, I'd say yes without question.

Tempest stands, "Come now. We'll put you up in Anemology for the night."

I stand too, "You mean the tower? Will there be room for me?"

"It is the biggest branch of magic. The tower adds new floors every time they are needed."

"Sounds like a cool place," I say as she opens the door.

8
THE TOWER OF WIND

Turns out Anemology tower is the one with the swirl shape, like a giant swizzler. Its roof is also swirled, like a shell. The effect's stunning.

As we approach it, the wind becomes louder and rougher. It switches between agitated and calm, like it's got a personality of its own. Tempest seems unaffected, but half my hair's sticking up by the time we reach the door.

Lady Tempest knocks politely, and within a second the door's opened by a short boy with black hair and brown eyes peeping back at us. He reminds me of Jack Frost, if Jack Frost was electrocuted. His dark hair is sticking up straight and there's soot on his face.

"Evening, ma'am," he says when he looks at Tempest, trying to act nonchalant even though the collar of his white shirt is smoking.

Tempest looks amused, "Jamie. Don't tell me you gave yourself electric shock again?"

"Not at all, ma'am," the boy, Jamie, says, shaking his head a little too fast, "Just trying a new style here."

"You look like you just stepped out of a tornado," I comment, which probably isn't helpful of me.

Jamie gives me an offended look, "Got struck by lightning, *actually*—" Tempest raises her eyebrows and he backtracks, "I mean, I didn't summon it. Of course, I know that's against the rules. It was Leo I promise!"

Tempest sighs, "Will you please fetch me Anita?"

"Huh? Oh! Yeah. ANITA?" He yells over his shoulder.

"Coming!" A voice answers, and behind Jamie a girl floats down to the ground, landing neatly and walking towards us.

She's got tumbling black hair, light brown skin, caramel eyes and the brightest smile I've ever seen. The second she looks at me I feel the knot of tension in my stomach unravel. She just radiates cheerfulness. As if on her command, the winds around me calm considerably.

"Hi," she says to me, then looks at Tempest, "You requested me, ma'am?"

"Yes," Tempest says, "May you please take in Avery for the night? She needs a place to stay. Tomorrow she will set off for an important quest."

"Of course, ma'am. We'll look after her," she directs the last part as me, giving me a warm smile.

"I am," continues Tempest, "recruiting the five the prophecy spoke of. Would *you* be so kind as to accompany her on her quest? Feel no pressure, of course. I would completely understand. It is a big task, and dangerous."

Anita hesitates. I would, if I was in her position. Going on a dangerous journey with a stranger who just blew up the world's most famous artefact? Not something I'd jump at the chance to do.

But, surprisingly, she nods, "Of course, ma'am."

"Good," Tempest nods, satisfied, and pushes me forward, "Goodnight, Avery. Sweet dreams."

Jamie shuts the door behind me, and turns to Anita, hands on hips, "What's this quest, then? Why didn't I get invited?"

"Trust you to miss the assembly because you were in detention," scorns Anita, rolling her eyes, but smiling fondly. Then she looks at me, "Come on. I'll show you to your dorm."

She leads me across the marble floor. I look up, but there's no ceiling. Instead, the inside of the tower is a hollow chamber filled with winds, with circular balconies winding round the edge. It goes up as far as the eye can see.

"Usually we take the breeze travel," Anita notes, "But I think stairs are safer here."

She nods to a rickety iron staircase in the corner. It's apparent this tower doesn't get a lot of visitors from people who can't fly.

"Ok," I say, shifting nervously. I'm not particularly good with new people, if you haven't already guessed.

As we start to climb, I blurt out, "Thank you for doing that for me."

"Huh?" Anita looks over her shoulder, eyebrows knitted. "Thank you," I repeat, "not a lot of people would have done that for me. Going on a quest. I think it's really brave."

Anita's eyes crease with a smile, "Oh. No problem!" Her expression turns sympathetic, "I can only imagine how scary it is for you."

"It's terrifying," I admit with a laugh, "And I don't want to let everyone down," I look at my hands, "I don't even know what I can do yet."

"I'm sure it'll be something awesome," reassures Anita firmly. She grins, "The way you stood there when that head was creeping me out? Brilliant. You just looked like 'yeah, talking head, you're not gonna scare me' then it exploded! That was really cool!"

I can't help but crack a smile, "Thanks. So, what do people with Anemology do?"

"Most of the time we fight over who gets to control the weather on a given day," she laughs, "Or we have fun electrocuting each other."

"Isn't Anemology study of winds?" I ask curiously, "Why can you control lightning then?"

"Magic's a vague thing," Anita shrugs, "Some people's

powers are slightly different. Wind has a part to play in every weather situation, so sometimes kids can have those powers as well."

"And you can fly?"

"I can," Anita chuckles, "Jamie… let's just say he tries to. It takes time and practice, and he has the patience for neither."

I smile, "He seems like a good kid. How old is he?"

"Thirteen. A number as unlucky as him, I guess."

"True," I laugh, then another question springs to mind, "Isn't everyone here 14, though?"

"Most people are, including me," Anita says, "The school education for magic kids officially starts at 14 'til 17. That's when people can apply. But sometimes, Tempest will bring them here earlier."

I nod, then nearly jump out of my skin as someone soars past me and vanishes onto a high balcony. Anita smiles, "Don't worry. You'll get used to that. Hey, are you hungry?"

That reminds me. I haven't eaten since yesterday morning, and I've ran about 3 miles in total since then. I'm starving.

"Oh. Yeah, actually," I say.

Anita beams, "Perfect. We'll make you dinner!"

"You really don't have to—" I start, but she shakes her head.

"You've just been handed a huge responsibility. The least I can do is help by giving you food. Besides, Keiko is the best chef in Infino, and that's saying something. Have you checked out the mess hall yet?"

I shake my head.

"It's a must-see. Anyway, come on, I'll show you your room!"

As I follow her up the stairs, I can't help but feel lighter inside. To have her help means so much to me. Even just to have her on my side. It feels like everyone here hates me. But that Anita is still showing me kindness even after I could potentially destroy the world?

We arrive at a balcony so high up I don't even want to think about want would happen if I fell off. Other students, however, have no such qualms. As I watch, Jamie and another boy- maybe his friend Leo, judging by the way the boy's fingertips are crackling with lightning- run past us to the edge and jump off. Seconds later I hear a whoop and they reappear, high-fiving in midair. That looks awesome.

Anita sees my face, "I know. It's fun. The tower is filled with wind, and it catches our fall. We use it to get to the high floors. It's called breeze travel."

"Do you get a lot of broken bones from doing that?"

She chuckles, "Not if we can help it. The Anatomy kids are good at fixing that stuff. Besides, there's so much wind down there even a regular person would be fine. still, it's against the rules to jump off. But, like with all rules—"

"—kids jump off anyway," I finish.

Anita grins, "Pretty much. Here," she leads me to a door with

111 written on it, "This is my dorm. Five people per room. Mine's pretty crazy."

"I think I've had too much crazy for one day," I say, "How crazy are we talking?"

Anita's eyes flash, "You'll see."

She pushes open the door to the most dangerous pillow fight I've ever seen.

Girls my age are whacking each other round the head with cushions, which they pluck from a whirlpool of pillows and cushions that spins overhead. There's the added fact that the room is filled with battling winds, which send girls flying across the room shrieking. Occasionally one will stick out her hand and blow her opponent across the dorm using a gust of air.

Loud dance music is playing from a speaker hanging precariously off the ceiling. The girls seem to be in teams, with two on one of the elegant grey couches, two on the other. The coffee table in between is crammed with cups of steaming hot chocolate and cookies.

My jaw drops at the sight of it all. Anita laughs at my expression. Then she raises a hand and clenches her fists. With a boom, a shock wave of air fills the room. Suddenly I see why Tempest asked her to join the mission out of everyone. She's not just the nicest person I've ever met, she's mega powerful.

That catches the girls' attention. The winds go silent and they look at us as Anita clears her throat, "Guys, this is Avery, uh, last name?"

"I don't have one," I say skittishly.

"Ooh! Can we give her a last name?" One of the girls asks. She's my definition of quirky, with glittering gold eyeshadow sweeping out from her green eyes and shoulder length blonde hair filled with streaks of different colours.

"No, Coco, I don't think that's a good idea," laughs Anita.

"I recognise you," says one of the girls, squinting, "Ugh, Coco, where did you put my glasses?"

"I think I hung those off the telephone wire," Coco peeps, "Sorry."

"You're so annoying!" The other girl says, but she's laughing. Then she turns her attention back to me, "Are you the girl from the hall?"

I shift from foot to foot, "That would be me, yeah."

"Woah, what you did with that Copper Head was amazing!" Coco exclaims.

"Oh. Thanks," I leave out the bit about how it wasn't actually me.

"So I'm gonna get Avery some food, then I think we need to sleep. We're going to be leaving for an important quest tomorrow," Anita says.

"The quest from the prophecy. Jeez, Anita, you got chosen for that?" Says the girl who lost her glasses.

Anita blushes, "Yeah."

"Yay! We're proud of you, babes!" says Coco, punching the air then reaching for a cookie.

The glasses girl is looking at Anita worriedly, "You'll be careful right? It's pretty dangerous in the Wild."

"We'll be fine," Anita reassures, then nods to me, "Come on. I'll get you something from the kitchen."

I give the others a salute, then follow her.

When we're sitting outside on a balcony and I'm (finally!) eating a bowl of lasagne, I ask, "Why doesn't everyone make a bigger deal of the fact you're leaving? Like, it's gonna be dangerous."

Anita smiles, "Everyone's been expecting this for years. Especially our cohort, since it's nearly the end of the age. We all accepted that any one of us could be called on immediately when the Infinite appeared."

I sigh at my lasagne. Anita catches my expression, "What is it?"

"It's just… everyone's so sure I'm the Infinite, and that I'll do great things," I say, "But what if I don't? What if I'm secretly evil and I'm going to go haywire and destroy the world?"

"You won't do that, silly," Anita laughs, "You're great!"

"Thanks," I grin, "It's just…there's a lot of expectations. I get the feeling a lot of people don't like me. And don't want me here."

Anita tilts her head, "you ran into Chloe Moscopello, didn't you?"

I almost drop my lasagne, "Can you read minds? How did you know that?"

"Chloe's well known in our tower for being the biggest diva in the world. She may be popular among the other towers but no one here likes her. And she's probably jealous."

"Of me?" I ask, "Why?"

"Because. You're everything she's not."

I scrunch my nose, "I guess. If it means being less snooty then, I'll take it."

Anita nods, "Also, she's probably kind of scared of you."

"Great," I say sarcastically, "Another person convinced of my evil tyranny. Just what I need."

"No, because you're not from round here," Anita says, "You're from Zoriana. Chloe's from Violana. They're basically all snobs up there. They look down their nose at people from the Midlands towns, like me, but they're intimidated by someone from Zoriana."

"Why would she be intimidated by me?" I ask.

"Because I'm guessing you can punch pretty well. She doesn't want anything ruining her 'perfect manicure'" she imitates Chloe's voice.

I laugh, "I can punch pretty well."

Anita grins, "You ever been in a real fight?"

"That's pretty much all I did," I say.

"What do your parents think about you coming here? They must be worried sick!"

"I don't have parents," I say.

Anita's face falls, "Oh, gosh, sorry that was insensitive of me!"

"No, it's fine," I reassure, "Everyone does the same thing. You're a lot more tactful about it than this guy I met at a store. You should've heard him: Where are your mummy and daddy missy? Well, then you should be in an orphanage, shouldn't you? Well then you should build an orphanage and put yourself in it, shouldn't you?"

Anita laughs, "Sounds like a nasty guy."

"Gave us enough money for food for a week," I shrug, "And he was stupid, so we stole extra and he didn't notice."

"Who's we?" asks Anita.

I almost say, 'my gang' but then I realise how that'll sound. Everyone already thinks I'm evil, or, if not evil, weird at the least. I don't want to give them more ammunition to tease me. The gangs in Zoriana are rough and streetwise, and sometimes plain nasty. Let's just say we don't have a good reputation. Fights with other gangs could end up with either one of us dead.

"My family," I say carefully.

If Anita's got questions, she doesn't ask them, which I

appreciate. I scrape the spoon round my bowl for the dregs of lasagne and look out across starlit Infino. Tomorrow, I might never see it again.

9
THE QUEST

The next morning, I take a long-needed shower. Back in Zoriana, our gang was one of the only ones who had a shower. We stole it out of someone's derelict bathroom. Amazingly it still worked. It was not a pretty sight, with rust and peeling, chipped paint, and only really a dribble came out. Besides with so many of us using it, the last time I showered was…never mind. You don't want to know.

This one confuses me. I always thought showers were simple technology, but this one is high powered, sparkling clean, and has a row of different buttons for different features. Wisely, I don't click any.

After I've showered, I put on the new clothes Tempest set out for me. My aviator's jacket is still there, freshly washed. Tempest must've realised it's from home. Apart from that, there's camouflage cargo pants, and a cream shirt to tuck in. The outfit's completed with a brown leather belt with pockets for different resources. In one is my dagger.

"You got a knife?" Exclaims Coco when I step out from the bathroom.

"Yeah," I say, slightly defensively.

Coco looks excited, "Can I try?"

Absolutely not.

"Uh. No," I say, "I don't think so. Sorry."

Coco looks disappointed, "Aww."

Just then Anita steps out from her room, wearing the same outfit as me aside from the jacket. She's got a black jacket instead with a grey and black camouflage pattern.

A bell rings, reminding us in a tinny voice that all students must report to the Hall. That's us, then.

I take a deep breath, "Let's go."

A few minutes later, we're sitting in the front row of pews with the other people on our quest. Tempest goes on about what an honour this is and how the prophecy chose us and how we all must be careful. I want to get a better look at the people I'm on this thing with. It'll be useless if they're idiots. I crane my head to take a look along our row.

Sitting at the end, arms folded, is a girl with long black hair. Acid green eyes glare from underneath a heavy fridge. She's wearing all black camouflage, with a studded silver belt that I have a feeling she picked out herself. She's wearing dark eyeshadow on her eyes and a silver necklace with a miniature crossbow on it. A real bow and arrow are slung across her back, along with a black quiver filled with silver tipped arrows. She looks like a useful ally, but not someone you'd want as your enemy.

Next to me is a boy with dirty blonde hair and a smattering of freckles. His pale green eyes are rimmed with glasses. He looks sort of nerdy, and nervous. But who knows, maybe potential lies underneath?

And the final person, another boy is…oh. The blue-haired boy. Chloe's minion. Great. I lean back and say to Anita, quietly, "What's he doing here?"

"Who?" She asks. I jerk my head and her eyes widen, "Oh. That's Evan Onceller. He's in artistry."

Artistry is the only branch of magic I can remember, because of the hand drawn guards. That and Anemology (probably because I spent the night at a tower filled with wind).

"Is he any good?" I ask Anita.

She almost laughs, "Evan? He's the best in the business."

"He's also a giant annoyance, from what I've seen," I mutter.

She grins, "You ran into him with Chloe?"

"Yep. And the worst part, he was the one I actually *ran into*. Chloe was defending him because she's, I don't know, his friend?"

Anita shakes her head, "Chloe's totally into him. He's kinda quiet, so I don't even know if he likes her, but she's got a fantasy that one day she'll be Mrs Chloe Onceller."

I dart a glance at Chloe, who's whispering with her friends in one of the pews. When she sees me watching her, she sneers. I roll my eyes and turn back to the front, just as Tempest says, "And now, I few words from our quest leader."

Wait. That's me. The hall goes silent, and all eyes turn to me. *A bit of warning would've been nice, Tempest,* I think through gritted teeth. Tempest beckons me from the front. Anita gives me a helpless look. I stand with a sigh and walk up the steps to the table. The copper head has been cleared, the wood is smooth and flawless. Still, the place where it was radiates magic.

I turn to face the audience and am immediately lost for words. I've never stood up in front of this many people, if you don't count what happened yesterday. At least yesterday I didn't have to say anything. I pick a spot by the entrance and focus on it. In my mind, I conjure up my gang cheering me on. Hiro's smile gives me strength.

"A lot of you won't know me," I say, which is a weird note to start on, but I'm rolling with it.

"I'm not the, um, average student here, I guess. Let's be clear, I didn't ask to be handed a prophecy."

The hall is dead silent. Everyone's watching me. Anita looks worried, like she doesn't know where I'm going with me.

"But sometimes," I continue, voice gaining strength, "This stuff happens. That's life. And mine's an unpredictable one. It always has been. I don't know if I am the one. The Infinite. That doesn't feel like me. But," I look to Tempest, "To have this all thrown at me has changed everything. Maybe for better. Maybe for worse. I don't know yet."

"This quest is going to be dangerous," I say, "I think you all know that. I don't want to be a downer, but some of us might not make it off this alive."

The kids glance at each other, sensing the stakes.

"All I can say, is that we'll try. Say a prayer for us. We're gonna need all the help we can get. But I have no doubt," I look at Anita, "That the people who are coming with me will be the next heroes of the age," I turn back to the audience, "Farewell, cohort 111. Wish us luck."

Everyone rises, as one, and applauds. I suck in a breath and look down. To have them all clapping for me is…so weird. A few of them are even wiping tears. Others are smiling at me, like they have no doubt I'll do great things. Chloe and her friends look bored.

Tempest smiles proudly at me, "A true leader."

I squirm under her gaze. I don't feel like a leader. This whole thing still feels really surreal.

I sit back down, and Anita punches my arm playfully, "Look at you. Didn't know you could talk like that in front of a crowd."

"I was just improvising," I shrug.

"It was still amazing," Anita says, "don't sell yourself short. Also, how in the world did you remember our cohort name?"

"The number on your door," I say, "And it was written on every locker I passed in Anatomy."

"Clever," muses Anita, "You're gonna be great for this."

I laugh shakily, "I don't know about that."

Tempest motions for the questing students to stay behind as the students disperse and the hall empties.

"A good quest needs good team work," Tempest declares, pacing, her white robes billowing, "You have all been chosen for a reason—"

The girl on the end puts her hand up.

"Ma'am, if I may," she says, "Why us? You could've picked any student in the school. And the alchemist never made a prophecy about *who* would go."

The others nod along.

Tempest's eyes crease with a small smile, "You will realise in time."

She says it like it's a satisfactory answer. I'm beginning to think that's kind of what she does, though. Vague, vague, vague. Let them figure the entire thing out for themselves.

"As I was saying," Tempest continues, "You must work well as a team. For that, you must know each other. Evan, Charlie, Skye, Anita, you will all be vaguely familiar with each other, correct?"

Anita nods. The others nod too. The boy, Charlie, darts a glance at Skye, who has a sour expression on her face, goes slightly pink, and looks away. Evan just looks bored. I'm beginning to think he always looks bored.

"But none of you, with the exception of Anita, will know

Avery," Tempest says, and turns to me, "Quest leader, do you wish for a moment to converse with the team in private? Just so you are all more familiar with each other?"

I have no intention with getting any more familiar with Evan, but the other two seem nice enough, though I'm slightly afraid of Skye.

"Uh, yes," I say, then, more confidently, "Yes please, ma'am."

Tempest nods and smiles, "As you wish, commander," then she vanishes in a swirl of light.

Silence follows. Awkward. Anita's the first to speak, "Who else wants to be able to do that?"

"Looks awesome," Charlie agrees.

I take a breath, "Ok, so, um, first things first, I guess. I need to know you guys' last names, anything about you, your magic type, I guess and, uh, any ideas for where we go first?"

Skye looks up, disinterested, "I'm Skye Archer. I'm in Archery, as you can see," she gestures to the arrows, "Oh, also, these are silver, which means they'll kill basically anything that attacks us."

Charlie looks nervous at the thought of that. Everyone looks at him, and he blinks, "Oh, yeah. I'm Charlie Walker, I'm in Alchemy. I can…um, do this, I guess."

He taps the bench next to us and it turns to gold. My brow furrows, "I didn't know Alchemy kids could turn things to gold."

Charlie blushes, "Yeah, well, some of us can. I think that's the reason Tempest put me on this quest. I'm the only one in our cohort that can do that, so, yeah."

"Impressive," I say, giving him a grin. Turning things to gold? That could be useful. Especially when we're paying for things.

Evan looks up, "I'm Evan Onceller, I'm in Artistry. I think we should start at Picasar."

"Wait, one second, what?" I say, frowning at him.

He looks annoyed, "Picasar. It's a little town in the west Wild dessert, known for—"

"I know what it is," I interrupt. He falls silent, looking miffed. The wheels in my head are turning. *Three castles hold answers, the journey behold.*

Three castles will show us the way. There's a castle in Picasar. Most famous in the midlands. Will it show us the way? But to what? That's the question.

"Evan's got a point," muses Anita, "Picasar's known for its castle. The entire town's built around it. It's guarded twenty four seven."

"And the alchemist said we should start in the wild," adds Skye.

I'm still thinking. Not just about Picasar. I think I know where the other two castles are. I might be wrong. I'm sort of hoping I'm wrong.

"Yeah," I say eventually, "Yeah let's start there. Just…never mind."

"What?" asks Skye.

"What are we looking for?" I say, "What's the descendant of gold?"

"You don't know?" Evan looks surprised. Everyone looks at him, confused, "Wait, none of you actually know?"

"Obviously not. Care to tell us?" I say, exasperated.
He scowls, "There are rumours that the Alchemist had a daughter. She lives, well, that's the point. No one knows where she lives. The location of the Alchemist's home has been lost for centuries. They call her the 'descendant of gold' because the alchemist who made the prophecy had the same ability Charlie has."

"Do you think the two are related?" Asks Anita.

Charlie blinks, "Not by blood, I don't think."

"I mean the reason Tempest put you here," clarifies Anita, "did she know he had that ability? Is it because of that ability?"

Charlie frowns, "I-I don't know."

"We should probably set off soon," Skye says, picking up her quiver and glancing at the sun.

"Yeah. We've not got a lot of time," Evan says.

"I wasn't aware we were on a time limit?" I ask innocently.

Evan rolls his eyes, "Added complication about the

Alchemist's home. It's cursed. It changes location every month. Since today is the 26th, that gives us four days before it moves again."

"Then don't the castle maps alter as well?" I point out.

He shakes his head, "I wish. But think about it. The prophecy predicted now, this month, was the time we had to set off for the descendant of gold. And it said the three castles have answers. That means the castles will only give us the answers for this month, because that was what was prophesied."

Skye frowns, "That's sketchy logic."

"We don't really have anything better to work with," points out Evan.

"Ok, then. Let's set off now," I say. Underneath our chairs are backpacks Tempest packed with supplies. I lift mine up with ease (I used to do chin ups off the base door frame, so I'm used to heavy weight) but Skye struggles with her quiver.

"You need help?" I ask.

She glares at me, "No."

"Sorry," I back away.

"Don't worry, Skye's like that with everyone," Anita mutters to me. I nod absent mindedly. Skye Archer is the least of my worries right now.

Soon we're standing just inside the glittering gates of Infino. It's so weird. Just yesterday I would have given anything to escape. Now, I'd rather stay than face what could be out here.

"You alright?" Anita asks me. That one action reminds me that everyone on the team here is on my side. Even Evan. They've chosen to do this.

"Yes," I say determinedly, as the gates swing open.

There's no going back now.

10
NOTHING BUT SHADOWS

I've heard of the Wild desert. Not in context, of course. It wasn't like we sat down and said, 'hey, let's talk about the geography of our world. First topic: deserts!'

But whenever things got bad, when we didn't have enough food and it was below freezing and one of the little ones' coughs were racking and bloody, Hiro would always say, a grim look on his face, "At least we're not in the Wild."

The Wild is the nickname for that desert in particular. I don't know how, but Hiro always had a connection with that place. And he hated it. I couldn't imagine a place worse than Zoriana, but the stories he told me? Of merchants swallowed by sand, monsters attacking helpless children? That scared the heck out of me.

And that desert just so happens to be the one we're heading to now. Yay.

I've never been in the midlands, because…well obviously I couldn't just hop on a train. It's basically just flat planes of countryside interspersed with towns and cities. That's where we walking now. Along a dusty road through a field.

The temperature's average, and the skies are a blank canvas of dull grey. That's a relief. Pouring rain or burning heat would be a disaster.

Anita's by my side, while Evan and Charlie absently talk behind us. Skye walks ahead, glaring the world like she wants to pick a fight. Occasionally I see a rustle in the grass, but I ignore it. Nothing's bothered us yet. That might change when we get to the Wild.

It's not far. I can see the plains on the horizon. It'll take us a few hours at most. And with every step I take, the coil of fear in my gut deepens.

We walk for what feels like years, though it's probably only two or three hours. Anita jogs ahead to attempt conversation with Skye, and I find myself walking next to Evan.

"Call me crazy, but I get the feeling you don't like me much."

I blink out of my thoughts, "Huh?"

Evan rolls his eyes, "I said, call me crazy—"

"I heard you," I interrupt, "What do you mean?"

"Oh," he looks exasperated, "You've got to stop saying 'what' and 'huh' then because it's really confusing."

I tilt my head, "And you wonder why I don't like you much."

Evan gives me a flat look, "You know, if you want to be a responsible quest leader you've got to have *everyone's back*. That's the point."

"I do have everyone's back," I laugh, "I said I don't like you, not I want to let you die. Jeez."

"Is it because of Chloe?"

"No, it's your annoying accent," I say sarcastically. To be honest, his accent is really annoying. It's so *posh*. It's obvious Evan grew up in a rich, snobby household.

He doesn't look amused, "Well, I can't help *that*. I'm just saying if it's because of how she treated you then you shouldn't put that blame on me. You ran into me, if you remember?"

"Yes," I say irritably, "And I never said I'm blaming you for Chloe being an annoying little-oh never mind, you get my point."

"She can be disrespectful," Evan agrees with a shrug.

"She's certainly not to you," I snort.

"What Chloe Moscopello wants with me is none of my concern," he dismisses.

"But I'm sure it gives you an ego boost," I mutter under my breath.

"What?"

"Never mind," I roll my eyes.

Charlie jogs up, "Hey, according to this thing," he's holding an old, faded, tattered map, "There's a service station in half a mile. Just in the border. Is it worth stopping there to eat, before…you know?"

I hear the unspoken words, *we have to go in there.*

I shrug, "I'll ask the others. Skye, Anita?"

Skye turns, "Yeah?"

"You guys want to stop to eat?"

"Thought you'd never ask," sighs Skye.

The service station is run down and looks empty, so we sit outside on the withering grass and eat some of the supplies Tempest packed. I eat a sandwich absently. The others seem nervous to be sitting on the grass, like something will jump out of the marsh and eat them. Anita keeps making little breezes rustle the reeds to distract herself. Charlie jumps every time they rustle. Evan's fiddling with his hair, and Skye's holding an arrow like she'll throw it at anything that attacks us.

Eventually I stand, and they follow suit eagerly. "Ok," I say, "So we're just in the border right now. Everyone get out a weapon, just in case," they don't hesitate to do so.

"And, um," I hesitate, "Try to stay alive I guess."

Not a very encouraging pep talk.

The Wild is like something straight out of a dystopia. Empty and desolate, it stretches before us for miles. It's dotted with jagged rocks looming against the landscape, and crushed metal machines that might once have been ships, but now resemble dead spiders.

A cool breeze sifts through the air, but it's not Anita's doing. The wind here feels different. Sinister, almost. Like cold fingers.

The first mile, we stop at every noise. I keep imagining something watching us from the rocks. At some point, Charlie stumbles, and Skye catches his elbow. We all look down at what he tripped over and there's a unanimous intake of breath. It's a human skull. The bone's bleached white and cracked now, but it's still stomach turning to look at.

"Come on," I say bravely, "Let's keep moving. Charlie, watch where you're going."

Charlie nods hastily, and, going slightly pink, Skye lets go of his arm.

The next mile, the consistency of the sand changes. It's squishier, and easy to sink into. *There could be quicksand nearby.* With that thought in mind, I take us far around that particular area. Yet no danger arises. The only sign of life apart from us is a beetle scuttling along the dunes. The hazy sunlight makes its shell glint turquoise.

By the third mile, we're all tired and aching, not to mention feeling anticlimactic. We've been clutching our weapons tight for almost three hours now. Nothing's attacked us. The whole place is dead silent. It's like the desert is laughing at us.

The air is dry and brittle, and sand keeps blowing into my eyes. I rub them, but my sleeve has sand on too and I'm just making it worse. Cursing under my breath, I squint through the stinging and scan the horizon. Nothing. No town, no monsters, no people. Nothing.

We stop for water, and I swing my bag off my back. There's a bottle tucked neatly into the side pocket. The water feels like crystal slipping down my throat, which is parched and sore. I ration it, of course, because who knows when our next chance for water will be?
As I'm bending to put the bottle back, something moves in my peripheral vision. Immediately I whip upright, hand on my knife.

"What is it?" asks Anita.

"I thought I saw something," I murmur, looking around, but nothing's there.

"Nothing but shadows," Evan says, "It'll be fine," But even he sounds slightly afraid?

I gingerly put my bottle back and pull the bag onto my back, "Let's go—"

A dark blur races out of the shadows so fast I only have time to yell, "Look out!" Before we're surrounded.

More dark shapes follow the leader and form a circle around us. They're wolves, I realise. They're almost the size of me, with rows of vicious, needle sharp teeth and glowing red eyes. Their fur is so dark it blends into the shadows. In fact, the ground around their feet is shadows. Smoky darkness seems to drift around the wolves like it's part of them.

Hand on my knife, I pick up a jagged stone from the floor. The wolves bare their fangs and growl.

The others have their weapons drawn. Anita's got a knife,

Evan's got a sword, Charlie's got a grenade, and Skye's got an arrow at the ready.

The wolves growl to each other like they're deciding who to kill first. One locks eyes with me and I ready myself. Then another pounces at Skye from behind. I hurl the rock and it hits the monster, which howls and dissipates into black mist. Like a barrier has broken, they all attack.

The one in front of me leaps, claws reaching for my face, but I stab my knife into its neck. It turns to dust with a howl. Another runs at me and I throw my knife at it, but it melts into shadow before the weapon can hit, and reappears behind me. I spin around, only too late realising I'm weaponless.

An arrow embeds in its neck and I look at Skye, stunned, as the wolf falls. She gives me a salute, her face hard and determined. Another wolf leaps up behind her, but she spins and slices it with the sharp edge of her bow. Now I see why her power's Archery.

I grab my knife just in time to slash a wolf ahead of me, but it pulls the same trick as its friend. It's like realising fighting a shadow. Then, suddenly the air is filled with dense smoke from Charlie's grenade. I cough and splutter. The wolves growl and roar, discombobulated.

"Run for the rocks!" I yell to the others, who are coughing and blinking. We do, sprinting for the nearest one and scrambling up the side. After climbing brick walls and vines up towers, this is a breeze. I'm first to the top, and pull Anita up just as a wolf snaps at her ankle. Turning around, Evan's climbed up and is kneeling, drawing a net of some sort. Charlie's still scrambling up the steep side. Skye's standing at the bottom, taking the wolves head on. Buying Charlie more time, I realise.

"Stay here," I tell Anita, and run to the side. Charlie's hand is just out of reach. He looks plain terrified. His foot slips off a crevice and a wolf seizes the opportunity, clamping its jaws over his ankle and dragging him down. He cries out.

"Don't panic Charlie!" I call, and aim my knife. His eyes widen, "What are you—?"

I hit the wolf right between the eyes and with a startled yelp, it falls. Charlie attempts to climb back up the rock, and I hear a yell of pain. Skye's clutching her shoulder, bow on the ground. Three wolves are advancing towards her. I slide down the rock and run to help her, but just as I near-BOOM! A sandstorm erupts round the wolves, swirling faster and faster into it swallows them whole. When the sands settle, the wolves are nothing but dust.

I look at Anita, who's hand is outstretched, stunned. She winks. But as fast as wolves are vanishing, more are melting up from the shadows. I turn to Skye, "Get to the rock! Help Charlie!"

But it seems Charlie doesn't need any help. He's nearly at the top, and as I watch, he kicks hard at one of the wolves who leaps up. It falls down with a whine. Another, larger one tries, claws scrabbling at the rock, but Charlie unlatches a grenade and pulls himself over the edge just as the rock and sand beneath is drenched in acid. The wolf howls and disintegrates.

He holds out a hand for Skye to grab, and pulls her over the edge. I'm the only one left down here. Pulling out my knife, I grin at the approaching wolves, materialising from everywhere, "You want some of this?"

I back towards the rock, drawing them in, but the wolves keep on coming. One of Skye's arrows lies abandoned on the ground. Suddenly I have an idea.

"Charlie, toss me an acid grenade!" I yell.

"Avery, they'll cover everything within distance with poison! You'll be killed!" He says, eyes wide with fear.

"Just do it!" I say.

"Here!" I catch the grenade as it falls, but something else falls as well. The net Evan drew. I look up in confusion. He mimes throwing the arrow. Catching on, I grab the net and wrap it around the grenade. Then, I hook that onto the tip of the arrow. Standing up, I see that the wolves are meters away, crowding in front of me. They know I'm easy prey now.

Except they don't realise I've got one last trick up my sleeve. I hurl the arrow and jump backwards, "Hasta la vista!"

The grenade explodes, and the acid drenched net expands, killing every wolf. I squeeze my eyes shut and cross my fingers, but the poison doesn't touch me. With howls and yelps, the wolves dissipate into nothing but darkness.
I let out a breath, adrenaline rushing out of me so fast I almost fall over. The others slide down the rock, looking speechless.

Skye gives me an appraising look, "Good job."

"Could say the same about you," I say. Slowly, we both start to smile.

"Is your shoulder ok?" Anita asks, running up, then looking

to Charlie, "And your ankle?"

"One second," Evan crouches and sketches something against the sand. A bandage. He presses his fingers against the drawing and closes his eyes. It materialises into life.

"Here," he rips it in two and gives one strand to Skye, the other to Charlie, "And I'll draw you a splint for that ankle. It's broken."

I'm sorely regretting not having an Anatomy student on this trip. Just as I'm thinking this, the tingling in my fingers is back. I'm still standing next to Skye, so I reach out my hand, "Do you trust me?"

She tilts her head, "After that? I'm thinking about it. What are you about to do?"

"This," I place my hand on her shoulder.

She jerks, "What the—?"

But then she stops. The wound is closing up. Within seconds, it's gone. The tingling feeling fades away and I pull my hand back, "Better?"

Her eyes are the size of baseballs, "Y-yeah. How did you…?"

"I don't know," I shrug, "It happened while I was in Anatomy tower."

"Anatomy magic," says Evan. He frowns, "That's odd."

Charlie, who's pale, with beads of sweat on his forehead, says, "Um, hey, can someone do that to me, please?"

"Oh! Yeah. Sorry," I kneel down and try again. The tingling feeling faintly returns.

"Come on," I urge it. Charlie's wound begins to heal slowly. Then suddenly it stops. The tingling feeling sputters out

I glare at my hand, "You pick your moments, don't you?"

Charlie looks a fraction better, though his ankle is still scratched, "It's fine. That's a lot better. Thanks."

Evan's watching me curiously. I put my hands on my hips, "Nothing but shadows, huh?"

11
WELCOME TO PICASAR

Evan scowls, "I didn't know they would attack us," he defends.

"Guys, don't," sighs Charlie. He still looks pale, and hurt. I curse myself, "I'm sorry Charlie. I can't fix your ankle. Whatever happened with the healing thing…it keeps going away."

"Yeah, I get it, don't worry," Charlie says, but I still feel like a terrible leader. Me and Skye help him to his feet, "How far can you walk?"

"Probably not all the way to Picasar," he says, gingerly testing his ankle.

"What you did there with the smoke was really cool," Skye tells him. Charlie goes red, "You-you think so?"

"Yeah," Skye says, smiling for possibly only the second time today. Charlie's face brightens. I bite back a smile and look away. I'm beginning to think there's something in the water there.

Anita's standing and squinting into the horizon, hands on hips. I stand next to her, "Hey, you ok?"

"Huh? Oh, I'm fine," she says, still squinting, "Can you see that?"

"See what?" I look where she's looking.

"The dot on the horizon. Could be transport?"

Sure enough, there's black shape on the horizon, silhouetted against the watery grey sky.

"Or something else trying to kill us," I say doubtfully.

"It's our best option," says Evan from behind us. I didn't realise he was hovering. He nods at the blob, "I say, let's go towards it."

So we do. As it turns out, the blob isn't transport, but two merchants pulling a horse drawn cart. They take one look at us, armed and dirty from walking through the desert all day, and immediately try to steer the carriage in the other direction. *Wise move, all things considered,* I think.

"Wait!" I say, putting myself in front. The horses rear back with nervous whinnies.

"Get outta the road, lil girl!" one of the merchants demands.

"We're friendly," I promise, holding up my hands, "We just need transportation."

"That knife don't look very friendly," mutters one. The other narrows his eyes, "Whatcha doin' in the desert then, eh?"

Evan steps forward, "Good afternoon. I'm Evan Onceller. Our being here is of none of your concern."

"What are you doing?" I hiss at him out of the corner of my mouth.

"But we can pay you handsomely for transport," Evan continues.

"Well, goodness, gracious, I don't believe it for a second," one of them says, mimicking Evan's tone. Next to me, he flushes.

"I did warn you the accent was annoying," I mutter.

"Shut up," he says, red in the face. It clashes with his hair.

"You got change?" One of them asks, looking thoughtful.

We all look at Charlie, who blinks, "Do we have what-oh yeah!" He reaches into his pockets and pulls out a drawstring pouch. Tipping it out, gold coins overflow his palm. He holds up the glittering pile nervously, as if it might explode.

The merchant's eyes flash with greed, "Well, well. That's quite a stack you got there, boy."

"I suppose it is," the other one says loftily, still imitating Evan.

Anita has to fight back a laugh. Evan looks like he wants to sink into the ground and disappear. Even Skye's struggling to keep a straight face.

The merchant scratches his stubble, eyes narrowed, "Very well. We'll take y'all to…Picasar, right?"

"Right," we chorus.

"For forty gold coins."

My bargain instincts kick in, and I bite my tongue to stop myself from haggling the price down. The horses look sketchy. And who knows what those merchants could have in ways of weapons. We don't want to get on their bad side.

"Done," I say.

Charlie piles the gold into the man's hand and we all climb onto the back of the cart, which is loaded with sandbags. It sets off, trundling along painfully slowly. But at least we're not walking.

"I didn't know you had that much on you," I say in a low voice to Charlie. His eyes dart to the merchants, but they're sitting in the front, backs turned.

"Yeah," he says, "It, um, kinda happens when I'm nervous."

I nod and lean back into the sandbags. Evan's watching me.

"Well?" he asks.

"Well what?" I say, confused.

"What happened back there?" He said, "The healing?"

"And the fighting," chips in Skye, and she scowls when Evan

looks skeptical, "You think I don't know Archery when I see it?"

I shrug, "If I'm the Infinite, doesn't that mean I technically have every power?"

"Maybe. But powers usually appear a lot earlier," says Anita.

"Unless," Evan trails off, frowning, deep in thought. For a second, his eyes flash with fear. He and Skye exchange a silent look.

"What?" I ask, curiosity burning in me, "Unless what?"

"It's probably nothing," Evan says.

"Right…" I say, frowning. There's something they're not telling me. Charlie leans forward, "Also, um, guys, there's something I forgot to mention to you. The gold I created back there?"

"Yeah?" I ask.

"It's, um, kinda gonna vanish."

"Huh?" I say. Evan shoots me an annoyed look, and I give him a smirk.

"It's gonna vanish, because it's Alchemist gold," Charlie said, "Alchemists…they can't create real gold. Or at least, they can, but it doesn't last. After a while it turns back. They don't know that I'm an Alchemist, so they don't know it's Alchemist gold. But they will soon…"

"So…it's just going to turn back into rocks?" Evan asks.

Charlie nods, "Yeah. Basically."

"How long do we have?" Presses Skye.

Charlie falters, "It's not exact, but," he pulls a crumpled sheet of calculations out of his pocket, "I drew this up last night when I got chosen."

I glance at the sheet over Skye's shoulder. Charlie's handwriting is almost an illegible scrawl, but I make out the words, underlined in red ink *TWO HOURS FROM CONJURED*.

"Well, how long has the gold been out?" I ask.

Charlie looks slightly lost, "I don't know. I just, kinda do it at random moments when I'm scared, so a lot around the wolves time, a bit after, and loads before."

"Which means that some of it will have already turned back," Anita finishes. We all look at each other, panicked.

"At most we have an hour," says Evan, "And they may not notice until the end of the journey. If they do, we run for it, ok?"

"Yes sire," I say, imitating his accent as the merchants did. He goes scarlet, "*Please stop* doing that!"

"Yes sire," chimes Anita.

Evan shoots her an offended look. Anita holds her hands up in surrender and a little burst of wind shoots out of them by accident. One of the merchants looks back, annoyed, "What was that?"

"Nothing," I say, "How long to Picasar?"

"You gotta learn to be patient, lil girl," the other merchant calls over his shoulder, "We'll get there when we get there."

"Which is now," says Evan, nodding ahead.

One of the merchants mutters something rude, but I'm too busy staring. Picasar is…breathtaking. Sandy streets wind together like a maze, and palm trees sway gently in the breeze. Even from here, at the entrance to the town, I can see the magnificent shadow of the castle rising over the rooftops. Stalls pepper the street, selling everything from exquisite jewels to carved wooden trinkets to exotic foods that I can smell from here. Evan and Charlie sit up straighter at the delicious smell of toasting waffles, eyes the size of marbles. Skye rolls her eyes at me and I grin back. *Teenage boys, honestly.*

The air is filled with the voices of vendors shouting prices and the chatter of people. It's mingled with the noises of animals: grunts and squeaks. The stalls are decked out in bright colours and glittering gold, giving me the feeling that I'm inside a kaleidoscope. It's too much to take in, but in a good way.

"This place is not for real," breathes Anita.

"Yeah," agrees Charlie dazedly, "I'm definitely dreaming. Someone hit me."

Skye slaps him round the back of the head and he winces, rubbing it, "Ow! That hurt!" But he's smiling, and…blushing? Yeah, blushing. I'm getting the impression Charlie blushes every time Skye acknowledges his existence.

Skye shrugs, smiling mischievously "You asked for it."

Over their shoulders, Anita makes a finger heart at me and I have to stifle a laugh in my sleeve.

The cart trundles to a stop just in front of a small stall bedecked in extravagant purple and chartreuse. The vendor is a scrawny man with an oily black moustache.

Chained to the stall are three leopards, with beautiful silver marked fur glittering in the sunlight. They're huge, the size of horses, and their golden eyes blink dolefully up at us. They look sad, the way their heads are bowed. The rough chains dig into their fur tightly. One of them has a scar on its paw. I feel a pang of pity, and then a spike of anger. Who does this guy think he is?

Skye's looking across the street, eyes narrowed. Her grip tightens on her bow.

"What is it?" I mutter to her.

"Something's not right here," she murmurs back. I follow her gaze to see three armoured men making eye contact with the merchants. One of them dips his head slightly. A nod.

Instinctively, my fingers stiffen on my dagger. The others haven't seemed to notice anything's up yet.

"Ok, we're going. Pleasure doing business!" I say, voice falsely bright, and grab Evan and Charlie's arms, hoisting them off the cart. I don't look behind me, but I assume Skye's helping Anita get out as well.

We're almost away when the three merchants move. They're faster than I thought. They surround the three of us in a flash, and I take a step back, pulling the boys with me. Evan frowns and pulls something out of his pocket. It's a pen. Not exactly the best weapon. On my other side, Charlie blinks, then hesitantly reaches for a grenade. I shake my head at him, just the tiniest glance.

"Hey guys," I say warily to the merchants, "Let's just, um, talk about this…"

"Not so fast," says a voice behind us. I turn to see the two merchants from the cart, grinning like demons. Anita and Skye are kneeling at their feet, hands chained. More enemies appear from the alleys, forming a loose circle around us. The vendor leans forward, eyes glittering evilly, "Congratulations, Mateo. You've brought me a few new slaves. I have a feeling these ones will do nicely."

12
TRAPS

Oh, great, the helpful little voice in my head whispers sarcastically, Way to go, Avery. You've got your friends surrounded. Again.

That in itself is terrifying, but...friends? I already knew me and Anita were friends, I guess, and now me and Skye are on good terms too. Charlie's...like a little brother, almost. And Evan's just annoying. If there's one person here who isn't my friend, it's him. But it's my duty to protect him, and everyone else here. Which is why I've got to think of a way out of this mess, and right now.

The vendor stalks regally round his stall, giving the nearest leopard a contemptuous kick as he does so, "Right. Let's take a look at them, shall we?"

He walks up to me first, "You, girl. You're the leader here?"

"What's it to you?" I sneer. Unlike the others, I've had plenty of experiences with people like…well, this. The trick is to make them angry.

"Use their own judgment against them," Hiro's voice echoes in my mind, "Make them angry. Make them blinded. Make them do something rash. Then run."

Evan seems to be a pro already: eyes narrowed and cold, face disdainful. I didn't expect this to be hard for him, since he always looks disdainful.

Charlie, on the other hand…not so much. His face practically screams: oh-my-gosh-take-whatever-you-want-just-don't-hurt-me-please!!!

He smirks, "You got attitude. Don't worry, we'll soon whip that out of you."

I'm pretty sure he's serious. I force myself not to shiver, instead to laugh, "You're funny. But…you're sort of pathetic, aren't you? Tell me, Mr Big Guy with The Big Whip, how much do you pay this lot to keep them from siding against you?"

I've hit a nerve. Insulting his leadership. Check. His face is purple with rage, but he forces a cold and furious smile onto his face, "How naive of you. Be careful. I wouldn't play with fire."

"Hmm. I would," I snatch the grenade out of Charlie's hand and drop it. The motion must trigger it, because acrid, stinging smoke explodes outwards. I slam a hand over a shell-shocked Charlie and Evan's eyes, and wisely close my own.

The thugs yell, disoriented and confused. I run, flying across the market as if I've been pushed by a hurricane. At the entrance to an alley, I turn back. Why aren't they following me?

Skye and Anita are struggling in their chains. I curse. I'm so stupid. I should have got them out of there. The thugs are still on the ground, groaning, but the vendor is upright. He locks eyes with me and gives me an evil smile. That's when I realise Evan and Charlie haven't ran. Evan's on the floor, clutching his jaw. Charlie…Charlie's standing there, frozen in confusion.

"Charlie, come on!" I yell. He snaps out of it and starts to run, but the vendor easily grabs his collar and yanks him back. Stronger than he looks.

"Come back for him," he taunts, "Try to free them. I dare you."

Skye lifts her head, and shakes it. She mouthes the words, get to the castle. Prioritise.

Gritting my teeth, I shake my head at her frantically, but the merchants are stirring, getting sluggishly to their feet.

Skye gives me a death glare, and mouthes JUST GO.

As I turn and run, I swear to myself I'm coming back for them.

I lose the thugs quickly, which is shocking, considering they're on home turf and I'm not. But then again, running for my life through labyrinths is an everyday occurrence. Which the last few days have definitely not been. How fast my life has flipped upside down.

Their shouts soon peter out and I slow down, peeking around every corner for signs of trouble. The castle looms, overhead, casting shadows like a sundial across the alleyways. The only way I know how far away I am is by judging the size of the shadows cast. Very practical, I know.

Then there it is, the sandstone walls towering above me. It looks rough, and sturdy. Alright, I think to myself, let's try this again.

I unzip my backpack and pull out gripping tape Tempest packed. Biting pieces off, I stick them carefully to the bottom of my shoes and place strips on my palms as well. Then I start to climb. I must look ridiculous: a teenage girl covered in tape climbing up a castle wall. If guards see me, I'm dead. That's assuming this place is guarded. So far I haven't seen any, but maybe there's some on the roof. Anita said they kept this place protected.

But there's another issue, beside the guards. I don't know what I'm looking for. I assume the map is paper, because a digital map would update every month, wouldn't it? The sun is sinking in the sky already, reminding me I've only got three days left to complete this mission. Find the Alchemist's daughter, find answers.

I'm in desperate need of answers. For example, what are these powers? Am I the infinite? That's the big thing that everyone's just assumed…oh, yeah, she's definitely got infinite power. What if I don't? Am I just a regular Anatomy student? Then what about the flying yesterday? What's this seventh kind of magic? And why did Evan look so scared earlier?

It's weird. I feel like a stranger in my own body. And I have a feeling everything's about to get a lot worse. The castle walls themselves are simmering with magic. My legs burn, reminding me that I'm currently clambering up a vertical wall. I look down: big mistake. Hot tip, you shouldn't look down. Ever. I blanch at how high I've already climbed. But I'm running out of time. Evan, Skye, Anita, Charlie, they'll all be dead soon if I don't hurry.

That thought spurs me on. I pull myself up the castle walls, muscles screaming at me to slow down, but I can't. And I'm not going to. With a final heave, I collapse onto the cool tiles of the roof. Peering upward, I can see a turret stretching into the darkening sky. Even in the sunset light, I can make out the guards manning the turret. In their arms the light glints off silver rifles.

One bullet from those things and I'll be dead. Then my friends will be, too. The thought weighs me down more than I would have expected. Before, in Zoriana, death was a part of life, the inevitable, the common, smothering the city like shadows. In a place like that, near death makes you feel alive. It kept my adrenaline up. There wasn't any time for fear.

Here, it's different. Because I'm not just staying alive for me. I have to save them too. If I die, I've failed them. I can't let that happen. Pushing myself slowly to my feet, I press my back against the slope of the roof and strain my ears for any sign of guards. Hearing nothing but the distant chatter of the market, I slip out from behind the slope and tiptoe along the stone edge rimming the roof, masking my footsteps as best I can.

No signs of danger arise, but I almost walk off the edge and teeter briefly, stumbling back. I let out an involuntary gasp and one of the guard's gazes snaps to my direction. I flatten myself against the sloping tiles and cross my fingers, but with a grunt of dismissal, he looks away.

I scan the turret for a possible entrance way, and my eyes land on the faintest outline of a trapdoor, at the base of the turret. It's dusty and probably loud to open, but maybe if…I have a minor epiphany standing there, pressed against the roof. Opening the backpack, I pull out a bottle of olive oil. Tempest must've thought I need more oil in my diet. But I won't be eating this.

I creep towards the trapdoor, alternately glancing between the watching guards and the stone edge, just so I don't wander off and plummet fifty feet to my death. Crouching down before the trapdoor, I run my fingers along the edges, wiping the dust away. As I thought, it's old and the hinges are rusted and creaky. I unscrew the olive oil and let it pour over the hinges slowly, then I drip some around the edges.

You're probably wondering, why exactly is she painting a trapdoor using olive oil? The answer to that is the fact that I've heard machines run smoother with oil. It acts like…what do they call it? A lubricant? And it loosens hinges like this one.

Well, here goes nothing, I think, tucking the olive oil into my pockets and wiping my hands on my trousers. I hold my breath as I gently ease the trapdoor open. It swings open with hardly a sound. Thank goodness.

I let out the breath I've been holding, then slip through the trapdoor silently and fall into the darkness below. My first instinct is to tuck myself into a ball and brace for landing. It's a short fall, but pain still shoots up my arm, this time coming with a nasty twinge which makes me hope the bone's not snapped. Why do I always have to leave that side unguarded? I uncurl myself and stand up. I'm in a corridor, tiled wooden floorboards beneath my feet, dusty chandeliers above my head. Dusky light pours in through the windows, but it doesn't illuminate everything like normal light. Instead a ray of the fading golden light is directed straight at the doors closest to me. A golden bird is engraved in them.

Is that a weird message, or a coincidence? No time to find out. I pull open the door and step inside. Immediately I catch my breath.
The room is magnificent, with elegant marble pillars supporting a low hanging ceiling. A golden chandelier twisted to look like vines descends from it, casting warm golden light across the room. The floor is so spotless I resist the urge to wipe my feet before I enter.

Shutting the door behind me, I take in the murals across the walls: a dark sky scattered with stars, a fox and a girl sitting, staring at each other, a hurricane sweeping across icy terrain, a warrior, frozen in midair, an arrow strung across their golden bow.

These are murals to represent the different branches of magic. Curious, I turn to the other wall, and stop short. The final wall, the place where the seventh kind should be, is blank. No. Not exactly. Like someone's gone over it. There are still little pieces of colour around the edges. But so much for finding answers.

I turn to the centre, where a wooden table stands proud. And nestled on that table is a scroll. The map.

Gingerly, I reach forward, fingers tingling. I open the scroll, just a little, to see a winding golden line leading across an unfamiliar terrain. It's showing us the way. I rest my fingers on the golden line, breath catching.

Then all of a sudden, I'm somewhere else.

13
THE FIRST MAP

When I open my eyes, I'm standing in a grassy meadow, sunlight pouring onto the blades from a brilliant blue sky. Fluffy white clouds drift lazily over the hills, and a warm breeze sifts through the meadow. Whoever's controlling the wind today obviously thought: you know what, meh. Give them nice weather.

At first I think I'm alone, but then a murmur of voices reaches me, and I step forward, curious. A tall, elegant woman with kind, tired eyes, and long hair loose round her shoulders is speaking in soft tones to something in her arms. It's a baby. No, two babies. One's swaddled in dove grey, the other in sky blue. That matches their eyes. One's eyes are grey, the others, pale blue.

"My darlings," whispers the woman, "Look how beautiful you both are. One day you will bring great things to the world. I'm certain…"

Suddenly, the grass crumbles beneath my feet, and I'm falling. I don't even have time to scream before the vision changes. Now I'm standing in blazing fire up to my knees. I've been here before. I lift my head and there's the girl, red eyes full of fire as she faces off the ghost girl. She clenches her fist and, like a candle, the spirit snuffs out.

Then a voice echoes behind me, racked with pain, "No, please, WAIT!"

The girl turns. Someone else is running towards us. This one has messy brown hair and her face is stained with soot. She's slightly, just slightly familiar. But from where, I have no idea. She sprints through the carnage, part of her dress aflame. Tears are streaming down her face. She pauses in front of the girl, "Please, you have to stop this!"

She sounds desperate, choked. The girl doesn't move. Her voice echoes, hissing, "You can't tell me what to do. You are weak…"

"I know you!" says the girl desperately, "I know what's behind those horrible red eyes! I know you wouldn't do this! Please, just stop—!" she gets cut off as she slowly rises slightly from the floor, voice gone, struggling to breathe. The red-eyed girl has one hand outstretched, energy crackling around it. I hear the chorus of wolves in the distance, and shadows melt into the shapes of the monsters we faced in the desert.

The red eyed girl has no mercy, just anger. She looks the other dead in the eye, and says, "You don't know me. Not anymore."

I realise too late what she's about to do. Even though they can't hear me, I lunge between them, "Stop—!"

The girl in the air gets hit in the chest by the darkness, and goes flying back into the flames. The red eyed girl stands alone, breathing heavily. For a second, she looks almost unsure. Then the cold, furious look returns, and she looks at me. Even though she shouldn't be able to see me. My heart is pounding like I've just run a mile. I stumble back, slightly, petrified. The red eyed girl's face twists into a cruel smile. Another voice, slightly deeper but with the same quality, like metal against stone, echoes above us both, "It's time. You've ran too long, Avery…"

Just as quickly as it came, the vision is gone. Blinding pain shoots through my head and I stumble backwards, terrified. Away from the scroll. Away from the girl, and her glinting red eyes. I double over and wait until the pain clears. Then I lift my head and stifle a scream.

Surrounding me are hooded people in black armour, holding crossbows. The arrow tips look lethally sharp. These are definitely not guards. Like the wolves, darkness seems to radiate from them, coiling around their feet. Masks cover half their faces, but I can see jet black eyes staring at me from underneath their hoods. They're stood, frozen, crossbows raised as of waiting for a command. Then they seem to get one.

My instincts finally kick in and I drop to the floor as a barrage of arrows sails above my head. The shadow warriors reload and aim again, but I throw myself out of the way of the firing line. I slam into the wall, blink the stars out from behind my eyelids and gather my senses. Shadow warriors close in on me and raise their weapons, but this time I'm ready. Whipping out my knife, I slash at one. The blade passes right through their hood and with a screech, they vanish. I turn to the other one, who's blocking the door.

"You might want to move," I tell it, then run it through with my knife and sprint for the door. The whole situation only catches up to me as I'm running down the corridor. What *are* those things? They're not human, that's for sure. More like demons. Without even realising it, I must've slipped the map into my pocket, and now it's tingling through my jacket.

My boots echo loudly, but the shadow warriors move like, well, shadows. They materialise from every dark area I encounter, around every corner I stumble into there's a weapon-wielding enemy. As fast as I can wildly slash my knife, they reappear, cold fury in their black eyes.

My heart is somewhere in my throat and my stomach has taken this moment to drop into my shoes. My brain is screaming at me, while my instincts are trying to keep me alive and I'm wildly formulating a plan.

If you're me, when in doubt, jump out the window, I guess. But only if you're being chased by shadow warriors. Don't repeat the whole Chloe Moscopello thing because, long story short, your parents will hate you. Good thing I have none.

I scan for an open window and make do with a closed one overlooking the alleys. I slam my elbow hard into the glass and it shatters with a loud tinkling. I pull myself through, hands skimming the jagged edges, and let myself free fall.

As I fall, I think to myself, *I've really got to stop doing this haven't I?* Then I summon all my willpower. Now would be a really good time for that Anemology magic to kick in.

Sure enough, the tingling returns and I picture going upwards. But nothing happens. I'm still falling.

COME ON, I think, *UP. GO UP. UP. UP. UP—*

I shoot upwards like I've been launched from a cannon. I scream as I fly through the air, the wind stinging my cheeks. Now that I'm up here, I have no idea what I'm doing, and so my flight path is that of a headless chicken with usable wings. I bounce around, slamming into chimneys and rooftops painfully. My vision is spinning so fast I think I'm about to black out, and I'm being buffeted around like a leaf in a storm.

"CAN YOU PLEASE JUST PUT ME DOWN?" I yell at the sky, and, as if the winds can hear me, it all stops. I hover for a second, getting my bearings, blood dripping from a new cut on my forehead as my heart rate drops. Then I float down to the ground as peacefully as a dandelion seed.

My legs buckle the second they touch the cobblestones, but I push myself to my feet and smear the blood away from my forehead. Patting my jacket to make sure the map is still there, I force myself to keep running, glancing over my shoulder every few seconds, but the shadow warriors are gone. Like they never existed. For a second, I wonder if it was all part of the vision, but lying on the ground in front of me is an arrow, exactly like the ones they used.

Even stranger, attached to the arrow is a tiny note. I pick it up, handling it as if it might burst into spontaneous flames. The note is blank on one side. On the other, it reads, in coal dust letters: *It begins.*

The words send a chill up my spine. I'm about to pocket the note, to show the others, when it crumbles to dust in my hands. Whoever sent that meant the note just for me.

Too bad, I think, *I'm definitely telling the others about this.* I have to. Then I remember that they're about to die.

I'm running again in seconds. Soon the alleys open back up into the market, and I see them, tied, chained, and looking terrified. Charlie looks like a ghost. Anita has her head bowed, but her hands are trembling. Evan has a cut on his jaw and bruise on his forehead. And he's out cold. They hit him.

The thought makes me angry. The merchants are guarding them, scanning the market for any signs of danger. Like me.

I shift closer to the alley wall and think. Skye's words come back to me: '*You think I don't know Archery when I see it?*'

That's a thought. There's an arrow lying abandoned next to Skye. If I can somehow control that arrow, free the leopards…not only does that free the animals, it gives us a distraction. And, actually, a ride.

I focus on the arrow and summon the magic. With a tingling feeling in my temples, the tip shifts. Just an inch. Skye sees me then, and her eyebrows furrow. I keep my gaze focused on the arrow, but with one hand I mime a cutting motion. One of the thugs looks in my direction and I dart behind the wall again.

Carefully, I peek around the wall and summon the feeling again. This time, when I focus on the arrow, it nudges a bit more. Then a bit more. Just a little further…

One of the leopards is watching it curiously. Every time it moves, it shudders, then turns it's large, lamp-like golden eyes to me. As if it knows I'm controlling the arrow.

I can see the movement out of the corner of my eye. Then I'm grabbed by the thugs. I kick one hard, and dodge a blow from another. I punch one hard in the face and, sensing one behind me, spin and give him the same treatment. Their hold on me loosens and I run. But not to the alleys. To my friends.

I swing my arm forward with all the strength I can manage and the arrow does my bidding. It jolts, then rises and whizzes over to the leopard's bonds. The animal gives a yelp of fear, but the arrow slices its binds open with ease.

With a growl of amazement, the leopard steps out of its chains. Then it turns those huge glittering eyes to the street vendor, who's watching, looking slightly afraid. The message in the leopard's golden eyes is clear: *you're in for it now pal.*

Then it pounces. The vendor screams like a little girl and the other merchants rush to assist, completely ignoring me. I run to the other leopards and start sawing at their chains. It's not as efficient, but I've done one quickly, and start on the other. It urges me on, butting me with its head, but friendly enough. There's scars on its paws and forehead, from abuse in the past. Poor thing.

Evan, who's lying next to the leopard, comes round with a groan, and says, "So leopards are more important than saving us, I assume?"

"Nice to see you're awake, sunshine," I retort.

I finish the final leopard but it doesn't run to help its friends. It stays by my side. I move on to Evan, who's drifting off again. The cut on his face is bleeding badly, but there's no time to sort it now. I slap his cheek gently and his eyes flutter.

"Come on, get up," I say. He nods blearily and I cut his binds. The other merchants across the alley are beginning to stir, looking mutinous. I frantically cut Charlie's binds, then Anita's. When I turn to Skye, she's already standing up. Giving me a smug look, she holds up the arrow I left.

"Come on," I say, "Everyone distract the merchants. Evan, you're not going nowhere in that state. Stay sitting."

"Fine by me," he groans.

"I'm going to get us a ride, ok?" I continue. The merchants across the alley start to sprint towards us, cursing at the top of voices.

"Now!" I say to them, and they disperse. Charlie unlatches a grenade and drenches two of the merchants in...ketchup? Yeah, ketchup. I almost laugh. Skye launches an arrow which expands into a net, trapping one. Anita's using winds to knock the merchants over.

I turn to the leopard, who's still by my side, though watching me nervously.

"Ok," I say, "How do you feel about a ride?"

It tilts its head, like it's considering its choices. Then, gently, it lowers itself so that I can scramble on. I don't hesitate. But riding a leopard is definitely not the same as riding a motorbike. The animal beneath me feels alive in a way vehicles can't. It's like a horse (I've never ridden a horse, but if I did, I imagine this is what it would be like). Its fur is coarse but soft, making it easy to stay on its back. When we start moving that might not be the case.

"What the heck are you doing?" asks Evan, who's trying to push himself to his feet.

"You know, the usual. Being awesome. Saving your life. Get on," I say, and hold out a hand. He eyes it like this might be a trick, then grasps it and I pull him on. The leopard shifts slightly under the extra weight and I whisper to it, "You ok down there?"

It purrs, which I take as a good sign. I wheel it around and face the merchants, who are being rapidly outnumbered. Skye's taking them down like dominoes, and Anita...Anita's midair with one of them, clinging onto her foot and swearing. She sees me, gives me her lopsided, cheerful smile, and flicks the thug off. He falls to the ground below.

"Get a leopard," I call to her. Just then Evan shouts, "Duck!" and I flatten myself against the leopard just in time avoid a bullet soaring over our heads. The merchant, looking livid, is blocking our path.

"Draw me a can!" I call to Evan.

"What?" he asks, utterly confused, "Why would you want me to—"

"Just draw me a can!"

"There's nowhere to draw!"

"Just do it!"

"What do want me to do, draw on the leopard?"

It seems, even when he's injured, he's still got an attitude.

"Never mind," I growl. The merchant holds up a gun. I recognise it. A series X pistol, same as the Zoriana guards. Deadly. Fires silver bullets. Better not get hit by that thing. My steed seems to know it too. The leopard shifts nervously. It paws the ground and snarls, raising its hackles.

"It's ok," I mutter to it, then launch myself forward, off its back. I take the merchant by surprise, kicking him hard in the stomach and knocking the gun out of his hand. He doesn't even seem fazed, however. He grabs my neck but I twist out of his grip and knee him in the chest. He laughs, unaffected, and I curse. What's going on?

I bring up my leg again but he's ready. Dodging my blow, he punches me hard in the face. I stumble backward slightly, stars flashing behind my eyes, then aim a punch for his chest. My fist meets metal.

A thought whizzes through my head. Two words. *Bulletproof vest.*

Of course. I can't beat him. He's wearing armour. For a second the merchant lets go of me and I prepare to hit him hard in the face. But I don't notice the glint of metal in his hand. My reflexes aren't quick enough and in a flash, he pins me against the wall with a knife against my neck.

I gasp for air while he presses the blade into my windpipe. Laughing. He's laughing. It's faint, like I'm underwater. For a second, I hear the voice of the girl from my vision, hissing and distorted, *"You are weak…"*

No, I think, *whoever you are, you won't get to me. I'm not weak.* The voice cuts out abruptly, like someone's switched off the mic. Then it's replaced by Evan's voice calling my name as my hearing clears. The world rushes back into focus.

I meet his panicked eyes just as he tosses something to me. My fingers fumble, but catch it. The can. I pray it's open, then lift my hand and dump the contents on the merchant's head. He lets go of me, yelling, and I gasp in air, doubling over. Looking upwards, I blink away the blurry landscape and see him, covered in thick black stuff. Bike oil. A nightmare to clean and doesn't come off. Perfect. Taking advantage of his distraction, I chuck the can at him and run for the leopard. Evan holds out his hand but I shrug it away and jump on. Charlie and Skye are on one leopard. Anita's on the other. Only one merchant remains. The leopards seem keen to attack, but instead I urge mine forwards, and then we're running. We're free.

14
WHERE TO?

People scream and panic as we crash through the market. The leopards are fast: so fast we're almost blurring. I can feel mine's heartbeat going at 1000 beats per minute beneath my fingers as I cling into its silver fur. Glancing over my shoulder, I can see the others right behind us, the leopards' hackles raised like they're looking for a fight. And maybe they are. They're free, after all.

"Ok, um, I don't know if you can understand me," I whisper to the leopard, "But could you get us out of here?"

The leopard seems to get the point, because it takes a sharp left and then we're racing down a back alley. I narrowly avoid getting hit in the head by washing hanging from a string. The leopard is vibrating with energy as we turn corners and sprint deeper into the heart of this place.

All of a sudden the animal beneath me shudders to a stop. We've hit a dead end.

"Are you ok down there?" I ask it. At the speed we're going, I would've dropped dead by now if I was on my feet.

It purrs happily in response. Though its heart rate is still quick, the leopard itself hasn't broken a sweat, and seems perfectly energised.

"Ok, good," I say, tentatively stroking its head, "so, maybe we go the other way now-?"

I don't even get a chance to finish my sentence. The leopard launches itself at the wall and claws into the bricks. Then it bounds up the wall so fast my head gets yanked back and I almost black out. We're on top of the roof in seconds, but the leopard keeps running.

"Ok," I croak out, "That also worked."

The cold air stings my cheeks and I get hit by a wave of déjà vu. We're so high up it makes my head spin. Picasar sprawls beneath us like a labyrinth. The leopard jumps the gaps between rooftops easily, its friends following. Looking back, I see Anita looks like she's just been dragged through a hedge backwards. Charlie looks stunned, Skye's blinking groggily. And Evan…

I look over my shoulder as our pace slows slightly to a fast but not gut-wrenching speed, "Hey, you alright?"

His face is as pale as milk and his eyes are a little unfocused, but he nods, "Mhm hm-WATCH OUT!"

I shriek and cover my head as we nearly slam into a steel chimney. The leopard bounds to the edge and jumps off.

The air rushes past me and the ground shakes under the impact of three huge animals slamming into it. I accidentally bite my tongue and taste blood in my mouth, but I swallow the copper taste down as we swerve along the alley wildly. The entrance to Picasar is just ahead, but the street is blocked by a wooden cart and people doing business. They scream hysterically as we come barrelling through, jumping over the cart and crushing it into splinters.

"Sorry!" I yell over my shoulder at the confused people. The leopard yowls smugly as if to say: *Not sorry. See ya suckers!*

Then we're through the gate and away, into the desert. The leopards seem to be on home turf, because all three steer to the west, towards the sun, which is no more than an orange pinprick of light staining the sky. I shield my eyes against the burning light and look back at the others. Night is fast falling, and behind us Picasar is no more than a silver glow on the horizon. The sky is dark and speckled with stars.

It's cold, too, not freezing, but bracing and chilly. It bites at my cheekbones and whips my hair back from my face. And it's silent out here. The wind is faint, howling forlornly like a wolf crying at the moon. Now that we're away from the danger, the leopards slowly, slowly start to slow down to a gentler pace. The other two draw alongside us and Charlie manages to choke out, "Thanks for getting us out back there, Avery."

"No problem," my voice sounds hoarse from screaming, "I've got your back."

Oh, heck, that reminds me. Evan's injured. It's not like he was the only one who got punched in the face but the difference is that he got knocked out by it. A punch like that could cause serious damage. And he needs medical attention.

I wish Miya was here. But, just maybe I'll see her again soon. That is if the others agree…

"Stop for a second," I tell the leopard. It tilts its head, like: *Uh, you sure about that? It's not a very good idea.*

And it probably isn't. Who knows what could attack us out here at night. But Evan's losing blood and the others are probably hurt too. Aside from the cut on my forehead and a few bruises, I'll be fine.

The leopard growls something to its friends and all three come to a halt.

"Why've we stopped?" Charlie asks nervously, voice hardly more than a fearful squeak. After the wolves, I sense he's not keen to repeat the experience.

"We need to think about our next move," I say, "And I need to check everyone's alright. Skye, Anita, Charlie, are you guys hurt?"

Anita shakes her head and looks at Skye, who also shakes her head, "We're fine."

"Yeah, me too," says Charlie, "But Evan definitely isn't."

"Yeah, I'm definitely not," mutters Evan, voice hoarse. I turn around and wince, "Ouch."

On closer inspection, his jaw may be broken. He's definitely bleeding, and, I didn't see before, but his arm's hanging weirdly. He must have landed on it.

"Ok," I say, "Charlie, you got any med supplies?"

"Uh…"

He fumbles around in his backpack and hands me a pouch. I pull out gauze and bandages, but aside from that there's nothing else useful. I don't know how to set a splint-I doubt the others do either-though Evan mentioned something about that. He's not really in a state to do anything about it right now, however.

"Ok, I really usually leave this up to Miya," I say, ripping the gauze, then stop short. Two thoughts enter my head. One, maybe I could call my…Anatomy magic? Would it work? The Anemology did. And Archery. Second, none of the others have any clue who Miya is, and I'm not keen to tell them I'm in a gang. They're often seen as bad guys.

Who are you kidding, they're gonna find out if this is going to work, I scold myself.

"Who's Miya?" asks Skye.

"Um…" at that moment the tingling comes back and I fight the urge to smile. But if I overthink it, or concentrate too much, it goes away.

"Ok, I've got to talk to you guys about something," I say. The tingling doesn't go away, so I place my hand gently on Evan's face. He flinches, so I quickly reassure him, "I'm using Anatomy."

He relaxes, "Ok… you were saying?"

I take a deep breath and keep my eyes focused on the healing wound as I say, "I know where the next map is. I've got the first one. And…someone's chasing us."

The silence is stunned. Skye's the first to speak, exhaling,

"Ok. Let's start with the chasing us thing. I sort of had a feeling someone was after us, but do you know who?"

"A girl. A woman. I don't know. I've seen her in my visions," I say.

"Now you're talking riddles," says Evan, shaking his head. His jaw and cheek look healed, so I move onto his arm, "Visions? You've been hallucinating and you didn't tell us?"

"Evan," scolds Anita, "They're not hallucinations. It could be Astrology magic at play. Avery, what were these visions like?"

"I've had them twice," I explain, "Once holding the scroll. Once holding this."

Using one hand, I pull out the silver piece and hand it to Charlie, who runs his fingers over the engravings, pushing his glasses up the bridge of his nose, frowning, "Where did you get this?"

"Back in Zoriana," I say, "For context, that's my home. I was," I cough, "I was kinda part of a gang."

Skye blinks, "Wow. That actually explains a lot."

"Why I'm…magical?" I ask, confused.

"No," she clarifies, "Why you're so good at fighting. But the visions…you were in Zoriana when you had the first one?"

So I tell them all about the vault, and my gang, and the visions. Evan's arm heals quickly and he tests it gingerly, but doesn't interrupt. None of them do.

As I talk, we hand around food and water. I realise I haven't eaten in ages, and my throat feels like sandpaper. The water slips down like sweet honey. I tell them about the castle and the missing wall, and the scroll, and the second vision with the two girls. And about the shadow warriors. And the arrow I found with the note.

By the time I'm finished, the tingling in my fingers is stronger than ever, like talking makes it feel more powerful. Or maybe it's the nostalgia.

"Wow," breathes Anita, "That's…wow. So, you think we need to go back to Zoriana for the next map?"

"Yes," I say bravely, then remember something, "Oh, and Charlie, do you want me to heal your leg?"

He looks up eagerly, "Can you?"

I wave my hand, "It's still tingling."

As I heal his leg, Skye muses, "Archery, Anatomy, and now maybe Astrology…maybe you are the infinite."

"You doubted it?" I can't keep the edge of hurt out of my voice.

Skye shakes her head, "Wouldn't you? It's…it's just a lot to take in. But now with all these powers appearing…"

"I hate to be a downer, but not necessarily," chips in Evan, "The visions are too vivid for Astrology. We know you've got powerful Anatomy magic, but Archery? We'd need a bow and arrow."

"It's not just that," I say, slightly defensively, "I've also flown."

Anita claps her hands, excited, "Really? Anemology? Oh my gosh, we can be fly friends!"

I laugh, "That we can. And um, yes, Anemology. That's how I got this," I tap my forehead.

Evan frowns, "That looks painful. What'd you do?"

"Roof tiles are sharp," I say wisely. The corner of his mouth twitches, "Wise words."

"I'm fine. You should heal yourself," urges Charlie.

"If it works," I say doubtfully, "I'll try. Besides, if it doesn't work, Miya can heal me."

"There's that name again. Miya was your med person for the gang?" asks Skye.

"Oh, yeah," I say, realising I never clarified the members of my gang, "Yeah she was."

"So…" says Charlie, "To Zoriana?"

"Road trip!" Choruses Anita.

"We need to take into account this mystery villain," says Evan, "Will she attack us again?"

I swallow, "I'm certain of it."

Charlie gulps, "Shadow warriors. I don't like the sound of that."

"It'll be fine," I reassure, turning back around and facing the east. Placing my tingling fingers against my forehead, I exhale as the pain dissipates. My head clears slightly. I stare at the horizon, trying not to picture the girl's red eyes, "Besides, I know people that can help us."

With that, we gallop into the night.

15
VISITING HOME

By daybreak, my eyelids are drooping slightly, but I force myself to stay awake. I've gone at least three days without sleep before, and that's not changing now. The others are fast asleep behind me. Charlie's glasses are crooked and he's slumped over his leopard. Skye has her arms around his waist as she sleeps. She looks almost peaceful.

I smile at the sight, then turn back to the fast approaching city skyline. Tall, dark skyscrapers pierce a rare blue sky. Skyways and motorways crisscross between the buildings. I can already faintly hear the sirens. Advertisements flash up a kaleidoscope of colours. Zoriana. I'm back.

It's asking for trouble to be out alone. It's asking for trouble to be out in a group. It's *definitely* asking for trouble riding in on huge silver leopards with claws like meat hooks.

But no one bothers us, probably because we've taken a back route, and probably because the leopards are the size of horses. I steer us towards Bilter's, but slow down my leopard, which is panting beneath me.

"You ok?" I whisper to it. It purrs faintly.

"Don't worry," I assure it, stroking its beautiful silver fur, "We're nearly there."

The second the familiar shop comes into view, I pinch Evan and slide off the leopard. His eyes fly open and he flinches, "Excuse me, that hurt considerably!"

"You're fine," I say, tugging him off the leopard, "And try not to talk while you're here, ok? People around here hate posh accents."

"You're just saying that because you hate my accent," he grumbles.

Skye wakes up, blinks at her position nestled next to Charlie, and retracts her arms quickly. I smirk at her as she dismounts the leopard and she glares at me, "Don't even—"

"I won't," I say, holding my hands up.

Anita hops off her leopard, followed by a ruffled looking Charlie, glasses askew. He hurriedly adjusts them and everyone looks at me expectantly.

"Ok, so, here's the deal," I say, "Follow me, let me do the talking, and, if someone attacks you, fight back. Don't yell for help, because aside from the rest of us, no one will come. People here won't lift a finger for each other, ok? Even the nice ones are psychos."

"Does that include you?" asks Evan warily.

"Oh, me?" I ask innocently, "Oh goodness gracious I should hope not!"

Anita high fives me. Evan looks stony. I force myself to stop smiling, "Ok, everyone follow me."

Inside, Bilter's is just as I remember. No one bats an eyelid as we enter. Jingle, the assistant is standing behind the counter. When he sees me, he drops the glass he's cleaning. I saunter over as confidently as I can, and place my knife on the table to show I mean business. Hiro taught me that whenever you're doing one on one, always have your weapon out. Like I said, I've never used my knife on people, but it's a necessary precaution. Behind me the others mingle, standing at least three feet away from us and watching me nervously.

I jerk my head at a booth and they take the hint. Turning back to Jingle, I say, "Any chance Bilter's in?"

"Uh, I don't, I don't think so, m-miss," stammers Jingle, "Y-You be needing him?"

"Yes," I say, "For a message delivery. You do that sometimes, right Jingle?"

Jingle fumbles his glass again, "S-sometimes miss. It's just, um, ain't you p-part of that gang that's in 'ere sometimes? With the tall guy with the g-grey eyes?"

Hiro's…sort of famous for his grey eyes. Heaven knows why, as far as I can tell they're just eyes. It's not like he practices intense eye contact. Sometimes I think Evan does, though. Half the time I swear he knows exactly what I'm thinking.

"Yeah," I reply casually, "Oh, that reminds me. You seen them around?"

"C-can't say I 'ave miss," Jingle says helplessly.

I sigh, "Ok. Ok. Thanks anyway Jingle."

Bilter's not in, Jingle's useless, the gang is plainly not here. We're running out of time. I know the location of base, but going there is a suicide mission. If they don't immediately recognise us, which they won't, they'll attack us on sight. It's our best option now, though. I stand up, ready to tell the others, when the door swings open.

I look up, blinking. It's Hiro.

He looks almost the same as when I last saw him, which was only really a few days ago. But it's clear he hasn't been sleeping. His brown hair's tousled and his famed grey eyes are shadowed and bloodshot. He looks paler, and there's new lines creasing his forehead. Worry lines.

I feel drenched in guilt. He's been worried sick. I should've sent a message.

Then he looks up, and sees me, and his jaw drops. His face lights up, "Avery?"

"Hiro!" I exclaim.

He runs towards me and hugs me tight, a real bear hug. He's shaking slightly with joy. The air is squeezed out of my lungs, but I laugh and hug him back, "Oh gosh I've been worried out of my mind! It's really you, isn't it?"

135

"It's me," I say, "and I can't breathe…"

"Oh. Sorry!" He lets me go and shakes his head, "Where the heck have you been?"

"I'm sorry, I would've written," I say, "If Infino had letters, I promise."

Hiro looks confused, "Infino? What's Infino? And, more importantly, are you alright? Are you hurt? What's happened?"

He touches my forehead gently, "You're injured!"

"Oh!" I didn't realise my scratch might have left a mark, "That's nothing. I healed it."

"You what?"

"Never mind. I can't talk here," I say, looking around.

Hiro seems to get my drift, "Of course, I'll take you back to base! They'll be so happy to see you! But…Avery, what's happened?"

He looks so worried, but also so relieved, like he can't believe I'm alive. I feel another pang of guilt.

"I promise I will absolutely explain everything," I say, "But it's not safe to talk here."

Hiro nods eagerly like he completely understands, "Of course, of course. Anything as long as you're safe!"

I laugh, "You worry too much. I'm fine!"

"I have a right to be worried," he says seriously, raising an eyebrow. I look down, "Yeah. You probably do."

"Anyway, I've, um, also got some people for you to meet. We kinda need your help."

"Are they trustworthy? Did they do this?" He nods to the scratch, looking horrified.

"No! No, of course not! They're my friends!" I reassure him, and take his arm, "Come on."

The others, who have been watching us curiously the whole time, quickly hasten to pretend they weren't looking as we walk over.

"Guys," I prompt, "This is Hiro."

He sticks his hands in his pockets and nods to them casually. Charlie looks slightly awed, like he can't believe I know someone who looks this cool. With his aviator jacket, ripped jeans and tattoo on his neck, I guess his does. Even though his hair looks like a haystack and I know for a fact he did the tattoo himself.

"How do you know Avery?" asks Anita curiously, "Are you two related?"

"I'm technically her brother," Hiro shrugs, "If adoption papers existed here."

Skye gives him a suspicious glance up and down, "You part of this gang?"

"I am the leader of said gang," says Hiro slightly smugly.

"Show off," I nudge him.

"Someday you will be," he reminds me. I feel myself stiffen. Because considering how much has changed, I can't go back to my old life. I can't be the leader of said gang. Because I'm needed elsewhere. As the infinite and all.

Sensing the mood shift, Evan buts in, "I'm Evan Onceller. And this is Charlie Walker."

Charlie gives Hiro a shy wave, "um, hello."

"I'm Skye Archer," says Skye.

"And I'm Anita Zohar," says Anita, "We're Avery's quest team."

"Quest team?" Hiro looks confused, glancing at me. I clear my throat, but Skye rounds on me, "You haven't told him?"

"Told me what?"

"Like I said, not in front of this crowd," I hiss, "Let's just…get back to base, ok? Hiro, can you take us?"

"Have they got weapons?" he asks suspiciously.

"Duh," Skye mutters and I widen my eyes in a 'what are you doing stop being rude!' gesture. She scowls. I'm beginning to think Skye's always like this with new people.

"Yes," I say, confidently, "But I trust them."

"Then I do too," says Hiro, and I'm slightly relieved. At least he's got my back on this.

"Come on, you lot. Let's see if you can keep up," says Hiro, rolling his sleeves up and turning for the door.

The others hesitate, but, seeing the imploring expression on my face, Evan sighs, "Let's go."

"What does he mean 'keep up?'" asks Charlie nervously, "Where are we going?"

"You'll see," I promise.

16
AND THIS IS BASE

By the time we arrive at base, the others are lagging slightly. Evan's arm might be healed but he still has a tough time down the ladder. And Charlie's just generally uncoordinated. The leopards trail along too, even though I expected them to have scarpered by now. The one I rode nuzzles into my hand as we walk. Its fur feels like silk. I'm beginning to be able to tell the difference between all the leopards: the one I rode is slightly larger, with a slightly bigger belly, and a beautiful birth mark between its eyes.

"That thing makes me nervous," states Hiro, looking warily at the leopard.

I snort, "It's harmless," I look down at it and run my fingers through its fur, "I still don't know what to call you."

Even as I say it, an idea springs to mind.

"Nyota," I whisper, and the leopard looks up curiously. It

tilts its head, considering. Then it butts its forehead into my hand and I feel its rough tongue lick my fingers. I smile, "Ok, Nyota it is."

"Nyota?" Hiro frowns, "Cool name. How'd you think of that?"

"I…" I honestly don't know. The word just sprang to mind like it was part of me. I know what it means too. *Star.* But from which language, I have no idea.

I shrug, "Just thought it sounded cool. So, uh, have the others been ok? You know, while I've been missing?"

Hiro's face falls slightly, "The whole gang's in pieces. Parker got in a fight. Jodi's sick. The others have gone hungry the last few nights. We've been searching for you."

"Oh no," my stomach drops, "Oh gosh, I feel so awful. I'm so sorry, Hiro. You guys must have been terrified."

"I won't lie and pretend we weren't, but," Hiro looks at me and smiles, "You're back. You're safe. That's what matters."

I nod and drop my head. I can't believe I'm going to have to abandon the gang again, just after I found them.

Anita runs up, "Someone's following us!"

Hiro freezes. He scans the area, eyes narrowing, "Everyone stop."

The others stop, but I see a flicker of movement in the corner of my eye. The slightest rasp of a breath breaks the silence. I recognise that voice.

A smile slowly creeps to my face, "Parker, we know you're hiding."

"Who's Parker?" Asks Charlie, looking terrified.

"WHERE IN THE GODDAMN WORLD HAVE YOU BEEN AVERY?!" someone barrels into me, almost knocking me over. I look down to see Parker hugging me and shaking me. His expression is one of shock, happiness, disbelief, and anger. I laugh, "Parker! Chill! I'm going to explain everything!"

I wrestle him off me and grab his shoulders, "I'm going to explain everything."

He tilts his head, looking excited. His words tumble out like a waterfall, "It's really you, right? I didn't hit my head?"

"Oh you hit your head," chuckles Hiro, "Those little snakes gotcha bad. But no. She's real."

"I knew you'd come back!" Parker says, punching the air, "Ha! Take that!" He yells at the sky, "She's not dead! Woooohoooooooooooo!"

Skye notches an arrow and I shake my head at her. Scowling petulantly, she puts it away, "Please can I shoot him?"

Parker looks offended, "No you may not! Who even are you, anyway?"

Skye tosses her hair, "That's none of your business, shorty."

I have to restrain Parker, but I can't stop laughing, "Nah uh. Parker, seriously, please chill."

"I have a right to be excited! I still might have a little bit of a concussion anyway," he wobbles slightly, and Hiro steadies him, "Didn't Miya tell you to rest?"

"I was searching," Parker protests, "And I'm fine!"

"You got concussed?" I ask him, shaking my head in disbelief, "What are we going to do with you?"

"Don't patronise me, Miss I'll-go-disappear-with-no-warning-and-scare-everyone-to-death!" Parker sniffs.

"This is all going way too fast," says Anita.

"Copy that," says Evan, "Who are you?"

"'Who are you?' Man, that guy's accent is hilarious!" laughs Parker, doubling over in hysterics.

"So I've been told," sighs Evan, looking annoyed. I grab Parker's arm, "Ok, you need to sit down, and we need to get into base. I can explain there."

"Ok, fine," he sighs, "But I still can't believe you're really back! You hear that?" He yells at the sky again, "She's back!"

"Easy jailbait, I don't think the guy on the fiftieth floor quite heard you," says Hiro, "Now come on. We really need to get in. We're drawing unnecessary attention to ourselves."

"That's my speciality," me and Parker say in unison. He high fives me, "Now that's what I'm talking about. She's back!"

I smile, "I'm back."

Inside, base is just as I remember, except a lot messier. There's a hastily put together hospital bed for Parker, a new steel rafter that looks like it's been made out of a pole, and, surprisingly, a hand drawn picture of me with candles around it. The final image makes my heart ache.

Miya's pacing, dark hair swinging and forehead creased nervously. She looks up when we enter, "Parker! What have I told you? You're supposed to be—"

Her voice catches as she looks at me.

"Oh heck," she says, going white as a sheet, "It can't be…" then she faints.

"Miya? Miya!" Hiro runs to her side, "Well, this is ironic. Parker, get the smelling salts."

Parker, looking worried, runs off and reappears with a bottle of salts, but Miya's already stirring and sitting up, "That was weird. I dreamt that Avery was back."

"I am back," I say, "or at least, I'm visiting. You fainted."

"Oh," her cheeks colour, "Oh! Oh, Avery we've missed you!" She pushes herself shakily to her feet and hugs me. She's laughing and crying.

"It's ok," I tell her, "I'm safe. Nothing bad happened. In fact, something really good happened."

"Ok, now we're in base, you have to tell us everything," says Hiro firmly.

So I do. I tell them all about Tempest, and Infino, and the Copper Head, and being the Infinite, and magic itself. Surprisingly, none of them look shocked when I mention the seven branches.

"We suspected it was real," says Miya.

"Yeah, we sort of had a feeling you were…you know," Parker says.

"You knew I was the Infinite and you didn't tell me?"

"No, of course not," he backtracks, "But you were always doing stuff that was kinda magical. And then the vault—"

"What vault?" Asks Hiro.

Oh. That. So I tell them about the silver vault and my visions, and my mission. I tell them about meeting the others and even meeting Chloe Moscopello.

"Now, that," nods Parker, "Sounds like one brat. Skye or whatever your name is, I give you full permission to shoot her."

"We all do," adds Anita.

"Maybe not Evan," I grin, "Chloe's sweet on him."

Hiro raises one eyebrow, expression unreadable. Miya laughs, "That makes sense. She was being territorial."

Evan looks like he wants to sink into the floor and die.

"Anyway, that still doesn't answer the most important question," says Hiro, "why are you here? You need our help?"

"Oh, I got it," says Parker, "You think the vault is the next castle don't you?"

"Yep," I say, grinning. For all he messes around, Parker's smarter than he looks. Never misses a thing.

Hiro frowns, "Something's still bothering me…you're not staying? You mean after this you've just got to go and save the world again?"

I bite my lip and look down, unable to meet his eyes, "I wish I could stay," I say, "But I'm needed elsewhere. My friends need me," I put an arm around Anita.

Parker fakes a tear, "I've been replaced."

"You? Never," I tell him, ruffling his hair.

He squirms, "Stop."

Skye breaks in, "I hate to interrupt a tender moment, but we need a plan. Right now."

"We'll begin when the sun goes down," says Hiro. I notice he's not meeting my eyes, "It'll be easier at dark. The city's crawling with dodgy people."

"It'll be fine," I assure Charlie, who looks horrified at the thought. I stifle a yawn and Hiro's eyes dart to me, "You need to rest. When was the last time you slept?"

"I'm fine," I protest, "We need to make a plan."

"You need to sleep," he says firmly.

I fold my arms, "Make me."

He shakes his head, sighing, "I can't make you do anything.

But we'll sort the plan, so I'm begging you," he reaches over and tweaks my nose playfully, "To sleep. Ok?"

I roll my eyes, "You haven't done that since I was seven and now you choose to do it?"

"Stop nitpicking."

"I'm not."

"You are."

"Guys!" Miya interrupts, "Hiro's right. We'll plan. Um, Skye, Anita, Charlie, and...Evan? Yeah, can you guys tell me your skills?"

"With pleasure," chirrups Anita, and I push myself to my feet. They'll be fine. I'm annoyed about being treated like a baby, but I know Hiro means well. I can tell it's hit him hard that I can't stay. He's only just found me again. Sure enough, his grey eyes watch me slightly sadly as I climb into the rafters. To my spot at the window. I pick up the drawing, which rests against the window frame. I look so much younger.

I catch my own eyes in the reflection of the window. I've changed so much in the space of days. My hair's straighter, and shinier, probably because I washed it. I tug at a strand of it and hold it up to the light. It glitters slightly. There's a new scratch on my face, just below my left eye. It looks vivid, not painful, but very much *there*. I sigh and lean my forehead against the cool glass.

I've never cared about how I look. There's no reason to, is there? The only thing I cared about was surviving, and that the others in the gang survived too.

And now I'm going to have to put them in danger, if we're to find the vault again. Maybe it moves, like the Alchemist's home. And then there's the fact that we're being chased. I can hear Anita and the others explaining the shadow warriors down below. They sound scared.

Who wouldn't be? I know I'm terrified. One mistake and everyone could be dead. Not to mention there's only two days left. That's hardly enough time to find the alchemists daughter.

One question has been nagging at me. Why do we need her? Does she know something important? Is she in danger? Does she play an important role? Does she own something that we need?

The questions are endless. I still don't understand my vision, the two girls, or any of it. I do know something, however. I think Tempest knew about the villain before we did. So why did she keep it hidden?

Footsteps snap me back to the present. Hiro leans against the rafters, staring at me, "You're supposed to be asleep."

"I'm thinking," I snap. I don't know why I'm annoyed because Hiro hasn't done anything. Except treat me like I'm seven again. But that's…that's just his way, I guess. He's protective of me. Maybe he was silently showing the others that he's got my back, and if they hurt me, he won't stand for it.

Hiro tilts his head, "I remember when you found this place."

"Huh?" I frown at him.

"You were just turned six. You came in one night crying because some idiot had killed a cat in the street. You always had a connection with that cat, before he knifed it. Used to feed it," he smiles at the memory, "You were so proud of yourself. We could've sworn the more time you spent around it, the healthier the cat got."

"Get to the point," I mutter.

"You're annoyed," he states, "I get it. I know this is…scary, right?"

"Good to see you've simplified it."

"Avery," he sighs, "I know you. You close yourself off when you're scared. It's exactly what you did that night. But I'm here to—"

"Shut up and tell me about the cat."

He bites back a smile at my response, seemingly knowing I don't want to talk, "That night it was real cold. You came in and you were covered in snow, and you said, 'Frosty's dead' who knows why you called it Frosty? But anyway, you loved him like a pet. I remember you walked straight over to me and said, 'Frosty's dead' again. Then you burst out crying."

"This story's getting better and better."

He laughs, "I'm getting there, don't worry. I said to you that Frosty was in a better place. And you asked, 'Is that better place heaven?' I said, 'well, maybe. Would you like to find out?' And you nodded and took my hand. You know you were so small back then, your hand was this big," he makes a circle with his finger and thumb, "Your wrists were like matchsticks. Anyway, I led you up through the rafters to this spot. The window was all frosted over. I drew an outline of a cat for you, and told you to look through it at the city. It was a clear night. Lots of stars."

"Hiro, where are you going with this?"

"Give me time!" He laughs, "You looked through it and you said 'I can't see him' and I said 'he'll be there. Up with the stars' and you seemed to think that if you waited there, you'd be able to see him. After a while I headed back down, but you stayed up there all night, staring at the snow and the stars. The look on your face was so peaceful, like being there made you feel closer to home. Back then you were such a troubled kid. Too young."

"We all were," I say quietly.

He smiles sadly at me, "Ever since then you've sat up there almost every night. Looking at the stars. I used to look up and think 'Maybe she's looking for Frosty' but...I think it was something different. I think you were looking for yourself."

I stare at him silently.

"You get it now?"

I nod slowly, "Yeah. I do."

He grins, "Now that I've told you a bedtime story, will you go to sleep?"

"Shut up!" I reach out a leg and nudge him. He laughs, and smiles wider, "Don't worry about the plan, ok? We've got it. Your friends are going to be fine."

He knew what I was thinking. As always.

I drop my head, but what he says next totally surprises me, "I'd go easy on Evan."

"What?" I ask, confused.

Hiro raises an eyebrow, amused, "He's trying. And I suspect he cares more about you than you think he does."

What? Quickly followed by *What the heck is he talking about?*

"What?" I repeat again. Hiro just shakes his head and walks off, laughing. As he does so, he calls over his shoulder, "You should know you need my blessing first as the older brother!"

"Oh my gosh, just shut up!" I call after him, groaning. Because no. Just no. In what world would Evan be attracted to me? He's handsome, if you're into intense eye contact and sarcasm, which I am definitely not. But Hiro's jumping ahead, as always. He doesn't know the first thing about it, let's be honest.

The story with the cat has struck a chord with me. Maybe I have been searching for myself somewhere along the way. I sure as heck haven't found her yet.

Maybe this quest will change that. And even if it doesn't, knowing that Hiro's got my back, and always will, makes me feel stronger.

With that thought in mind, I drift off to sleep.

17
RETURN TO THE VAULT

My dreams pass in a fiery blur of images. I see the red eyed girl glaring at me through the flames, then she's replaced with the grave face of a man, still and unmoving. A trickle of blood runs from a fatal looking gash on his forehead. He fades away and is replaced by a figure in a hood, facing away towards the inferno. The hissing voice, laughing menacingly, returns just as the figure turns towards me. I catch a glimpse of glinting ruby eyes beneath their hood, before the dream cuts out like a movie ending. Then there's nothing but blackness.

"Avery!" someone shakes me awake and my first instinct is that I'm being attacked. Reaching out blindly, I pin the person against the window before I'm even truly awake.

"Avery, it's me," chuckles a voice, and my vision blearily clears to see Parker, grinning cheekily at me.

"Oh," I say, "Oops," I release him and he laughs at my

expression, "You always did have the sharpest reflexes, didn't you?"

"What are you doing here?" I grumble, embarrassed.

"It's time," he says. My stomach drops.

"Have we got a plan?" I ask, sliding down from the rafters to where the others are sitting tersely by the door. It's then that I notice the rest of the gang's not back yet. I thought it was strange enough earlier that base was nearly empty, but this is even weirder.

Hiro sees my face, "Don't worry, the others are fine. Base has been quiet lately, because we've been…well, you know, out searching for you. But we've sent them a message telling them you're ok. They'll be back soon."

I crouch down and examine a worn woolly blanket gingerly, where Jodi always sleeps. Spattering the rim is what looks like blood, "Jodi's sick?"

Miya nods hollowly, "There's nothing we can do. She's started coughing blood."

"Oh, poor thing!" exclaims Anita looking horrified, "That's awful. Is there anything we can do?"

Miya bites her lip, "No…wait," a thought seems to come to her, "Actually, yes. Can you guys take a look at this?"

The others all stand up and come over.

"Which one of you has the drawing magic?" asks Miya.

"That's Artistry," corrects Evan, "And it's me."

"Look at these," she holds up something, and I crane my neck to get a closer look. They're little silver squiggles and rough shapes. The weirdest thing is, they're completely hollow, so they're just little delicate outlines.

Evan frowns and touches one, examining it, "That's Artistry alright."

"How can you tell?" I ask him.

"When a new kid starts to bring drawings to life, they look like this," he says, rather stiffly. He's not meeting my eyes for some reason, "And the texture. It's…like spongy. That's newbie artistry."

"We found some of those around Avery," says Hiro, standing up, "When she was younger. What does that mean?"

Evan falters, and coughs, "Oh, yeah, if Avery's the infinite then, um, she would have those powers, so," he trails off slightly. He's definitely not making eye contact with Hiro either, who's eying him strangely.

What happened there? I think.

Hiro clears his throat, "Ok, so, the plan is this. Evan, Avery and I will find this vault. Parker, Anita, Skye, Charlie, you'll need to be lookouts. In case we get attacked by…what are they? Shadow demons or something?"

"That's basically the gist," I say.

"Yeah, ok, so those things. Miya will stay here and wait for the others. We'll leave in five."

I nod and take in a deep breath. I don't want to have another hallucination. I really don't. But this is important. I stroke the faded, rough edge of Jodi's cold blanket and frown, "Why isn't Jodi here if she's sick?"

"Our attempts weren't working," says Parker quietly and seriously, "So... we had no choice but to try and take her to a hospital. They're out there now, trying to find one for her."

He looks really sad, so I place a hand on his shoulder, "Hey, she'll be ok, alright? I promise? I might…I might be able to heal her. If I get back from this."

"You will," he says firmly.

I smile, "What happened to your concussion, anyway?"

"That's cleared up," chimes in Miya, "I checked him twice."

"Yeah. I'm fine now," says Parker, "So bring the action!"

The look on his face is so determined I laugh.

We set off. It feels so good to have the cold Zoriana breeze on my face. It's summer, maybe mid-July, but the air has a fresh bite. The sun is just going down. It's ironic really, that in a place of shadow and crime and death, we have the best sunsets in the world. The sky is tinted pink and fiery orange, with purple tinging the edges of it like a vignette. The first stars are just appearing, like tiny speckles of pure light.

"So, can Astrology kids control when the stars come out?" I ask Anita, who's walking next to me.

"It depends," she says, "If they're powerful enough."

"Then why do they all appear on time? Wouldn't the kids want to prank and make the skies go haywire?"

"They sign a special treaty," Anita explains, "Because Astrology is the most vague power. It's practically an unknown. To avoid disasters like meteor showers and asteroids that could potentially destroy the world, they take an oath. If they misuse their power…" she frowns, "I don't actually know what happens. But it's really bad. They lose their power forever."

That doesn't sound good. I shiver.

Hiro is talking to Parker, Evan and Charlie up ahead. It's strange seeing them all walk together. I feel like I'm looking at a poster of a boy band or something. Hiro's never really had other friends who are boys, because Parker was always my friend first. I'm not even sure if he's trying to make small talk now, or just telling them the plan.

A little behind us, Skye walks alone, deep in thought, her long black hair blowing in the wind behind her. I nudge Anita and we drop back to match her stride.

"You ok?" I ask her.

Skye nods, "Fine."

I've learnt that usually when people say 'fine' they're not actually fine.

"This place is familiar for you, isn't it?" I ask her. She jolts, casts a wary look over her shoulder, and hisses, "How on earth did you know that?"

I smile, "A few things. You've been unusually quiet since we arrived."

"I'm always quiet," corrects Skye, "I hate talking to people. Silence is the alternative."

"Or talking to animals," Anita suggests, "Like…I don't know, the leopards."

Skye shrugs, "I like those leopards. They're fierce. And fast."

"More like you just liked having your arms around Charlie the whole journey," I tease her, raising an eyebrow.

"Shut up," growls Skye, looking mortified.

"Come on," laughs Anita, "Something's there. It has been ever since you judo flipped him on the first day of school."

"Top ten ways to win over your crush," I muse, "Use martial arts on him the first day you meet him. Then—"

Skye elbows me, "Stop, or I'll impale you. I'm not afraid to do it!" But she's laughing too.

I grin, "Consider me warned. But we're getting off topic."

Skye's face falls and she scowls, "Look, I grew up in midland slums, ok? Zoriana is…" she struggles for a word, "It's the closest thing to my home. And I hate being reminded of that place."

She closes her eyes and shudders, then rolls her shoulders, "Let's just go, ok?"

"Ok," I say simply, nodding, and letting the subject drop. If

Skye doesn't want to talk about it, she doesn't have to. I exchange a guilty glance with Anita as she ploughs ahead. Her stance and clenched fists means it's obvious we've hit a nerve.

Spotting the abandoned subway entrance, I motion to Hiro and dart under the vivid yellow caution tape. The others follow, and I lead the way down into the darkness of the station.

Nothing's changed down here. The shadows are as menacing as ever. The flickering oil lamps cast a little light across cracked tiles. Broken glass scatters the floor, glinting like silver. The walls are dirty and smeared with graffiti, as usual. And the rusted sign for west route is just ahead. I pause underneath it.

"Ok, me, Hiro, and Evan are going to go," I say in a hushed voice, "The rest of you stay here and be silent. If guards find you we're done for, let alone…" I don't finish the sentence, *if anything else finds you.*

Charlie's freckled face is ghost white with fear. Evan looks unreadable as always, Anita's fiddling anxiously with a strand of her hair, Parker keeps looking over his shoulder, and Skye's glaring into the shadows like she knows they're up to something, and she's not going to stand for it.

I look to Hiro, and he looks oddly proud in the half light, "Well, lead the way, Avery."

I draw a deep breath, then turn to go, "Let's go-Evan, what are you doing?"

He's crouching on the floor, drawing something. It looks like a wide circle around the others. As I speak, he looks up, annoyed, "I'm *trying* to draw a forcefield. You know, to protect our friends?"

I raise my eyebrows at his tone, "That's going to work?"

"Not well, but it should hold," he replies, not looking at me as he finishes the circle. Pressing his palm into the ground, the line glows white, and a thin white forcefield springs up, making a large, dimly glowing bubble around the others.

"It's enchanted," he explains, stepping back to observe his handiwork, "They can get out, but no one can get in."

He taps it, and it makes a hollow sound, "Like glass, see?"

"Interesting," says Hiro, tapping it, "That won't hold for long."

"Well, I-I never said it would last," says Evan, a hint of nervousness in his voice, "But it should give them some time."

"Can you guys breathe in there?" I check, stepping forward.

Anita gives me a thumbs up as Parker says, "Yep."

Skye and Charlie nod assuredly at us, and I turn to go, "Ok. Let's go. We don't have a lot of time, so, follow me, ok guys?"

I don't wait for their answer, instead striding forward into the gloom. I push back the boards over the rusted door, and scramble through, the others behind me. Then there it is, glinting in the darkness.

The silver vault.

18
THE SECOND MAP

"We're here," I whisper, my voice hoarse. The vault is as mesmerising as ever, the silver bird winking at us in the glowing light of the vault. Inside my pocket, the map tingles like it knows we're close. The silver piece becomes freezing cold. I slide it out, and move towards the vault, holding forward like a talisman. The whole world goes silent. It's just me.

I carefully slide the silver piece into place, and the vault begins to turn, the circles moving as the bird's eye flashes golden.

"What's happening?" asks Evan, looking terrified. Hiro shakes his head vigorously at him, telling him to stop talking.

Then, all of a sudden, the middle circle swings open with a click. The room beyond is filled with golden sunlight. I take a deep breath, and turn to the others, "Don't come after me."

Then I step through the vault.

The room on the other side is made of wood. Like, entirely wood. The last trees in Zoriana were chopped down years ago, but this is fresh wood, clean and bright. I run a hand along the wall, feeling the smooth surface of it beneath my fingertips. The whole room shimmers with magic. The air hums with it, and every step I take sends a jolt through my body.

The air smells of dirt, and moss. Taking another step forward, I squint through the heavy sunlight, which is pouring in from a circular manhole at the top of the room. The walls are smooth and round, and empty. There's no windows, no doors. But there is a…tree.

It's just sitting there, gnarled roots growing straight out of the wooden floor. Its base is thick with moss. A thin strand of glittering golden ivy twines up the trunk. It seems to be attached to something nestled between the branches. I can't make it out, only a golden glow. Hanging from the branches are glass baubles. There's only seven. One for each kind of magic, I realise, stepping towards the tree for a closer look.

In the closest bauble, there's shifting golden sand. As I watch, it forms the shape of a bow and arrow. Archery. The others also seem to have glittering sand in them, which undulates and forms the symbols of the branches of magic.

That's when I realise the energy in the room is coming from the tree itself. This room *is* magic. I look up and squint through the fresh green leaves at the glow. It must be the scroll. That means there's only one thing for it. I'll have to climb.

I place my feet on the knobbly roots and wrap my arms

around the dry, rough bark. Then I start to climb. The branches are still out of reach, so I'm stuck shifting up the tree slowly using my legs. If Evan was here, he'd be having a field day with this. I can almost hear his annoying voice, mocking me. Shaking the thought out of my mind, I focus on the nearest branch, which seems to taunt me. I carefully stretch out a hand, grasping at nothing, until my fingertips brush the wood, and I grab hold tight.

From here it gets much easier, and I yank myself up, legs kicking for a foothold as my other hand grabs a higher branch, and I pull myself, agonisingly slowly, onto it. From here, the floor looks dizzyingly far away. Is it just me, or has the tree got taller?

The glow is just above me now. Breathing heavily, and trying not to look down, I stand up on the branch, wobbling dangerously as I do so. I have to remind myself to breathe as I take a tiny step towards the glow. Falling from here could break my neck. Slowly I shuffle my feet along, thanking the universe for sturdy boots. There's a tense moment when I catch the edge of my foot on my ankle and nearly fall completely, but I grab hold of a branch and manage to stay steady.

I'm right in front of the glow now, and I'm so relieved I don't think properly about what I do next. It was definitely a bad idea. I grab the scroll, but the second I do, everything goes golden.

There's a forest. The trees are dark and twisted and menacing. They seem to suck the light out of everything around them. A lone figure in a hood stands at the edge of the woods, dark cloak brushing the ground. The shadows seem to draw towards them like they control them.

They don't notice me as I tentatively take a step forward, my voice echoing, "Hello?"

The figure doesn't turn. They laugh. It's like icy fingers down my spine, like metal scraping against stone. It's dark and twisted and hollow.

"So you've arrived," they say, their voice the same hissing and echoing one I've seen in my nightmares, in my visions. It's a woman's voice, but there's an edge of something darker, "Finally. I have waited so long now…"

"What are you talking about?" I demand, "What do you want?"

"What does anyone want?" replies the figure, "To be adored. Respect. Power. And you," they laugh again, cold and empty, "You will help me to get every one of those things."

The shadows take shapes, wolves that circle around me and growl, baring their fangs. I shiver.

"I'll never help you," I say, "Never. Leave me alone!"

The figure laughs again, "Oh, but my dear…this is only the beginning."

She slowly turns towards me. I'm rooted to the spot, I can't seem to scream, to run. Beneath the figure's hood, red eyes flash.

I manage to choke out, "Who-who are you?"

The figure tilts their head, "The question you should be asking is who are you, don't you think?"

"You know nothing about me," I growl.

"I know you as I do myself," says the figure, ruby red eyes glinting maliciously, "We are the same."

"I'm nothing, NOTHING, like you," I spit angrily, fists clenched.

The figure laughs again. It sounds like a cackle, "How young. How naive. Very soon, my dear, you will see that you are just like me. You have more power than you know. And it is dangerous..." She hisses the last words.

"If you think I'm going to ever help you you've got another thing coming," I say coldly, "I'll never be dangerous."

The figure smiles, sharp white teeth glinting, "You still have no idea. Oh, I'm going to enjoy this."

"What are you talking about?" I demand.

The figure's smile widens, "You'll learn. In time. Sweet dreams."

She snaps their fingers, and the wolves pounce, dragging me down into darkness.

My eyes fly open. An arrow flies past my cheek, so close I can feel it graze my skin with a sharp searing pain. It embeds in the tree trunk centimetres from my head. I jolt backwards and nearly fall off the branch as another arrow lands in the bark where my chest was a second earlier. The room seems to have gotten darker. I look down and discover why.

Surrounding the tree are shadow warriors, hoods lowered, sharp teeth bared as they hiss and spit at me. Darkness coils around the base of the tree, the presence of so many seeming to drain the life out of the plant beneath me. The golden glow of the scroll in my hand dies.

I pull out my knife and gently sever the rope attaching it to the heart of the tree. I tuck the scroll into my belt and duck as another arrow skims my head. Then I place the hilt of my knife between my teeth and start to climb again. The only way I can get away from the shadow warriors is up. Towards the manhole. Noticing my intentions, the shadow warriors hiss and screech. One stabs out a hand and shadows begin to seep up the walls, drenching everything around them in darkness. Slowly, tendrils of shadow reach for the manhole.

My heart is racing and my brain is screaming '*Hurry!*'

Yeah, I'm TRYING, I think, *now shut up and let me focus.*

The branches seem to be getting slippier, or maybe that's just my palms sweating. Twice I fumble and nearly fall. Falling from this height is bad enough. Falling from this height into a swarming mass of shadow demons would be disastrous.

The manhole is inches away. The branches around me are creaking and bending ominously, their skinny limbs unable to support me much longer. I slip my knife into my belt, check the scroll is secure, and brace myself. Then I jump. My fingers skim the edge of the manhole and I curl them, but I'm clawing at air. Before I know what's happening, I'm falling down.

I nearly scream, but the sound is knocked out of me as I land in a painful heap among the branches. They snap and send me further down into the tree's tangled arms. My lungs are burning, but I push myself up and spit the leaves out of my mouth. I'm about to claw my way back up the tree when there's a snapping sound. Then a groan. They've cut the tree.

Oh no.

Suddenly the world's tipping sideways and I'm trapped in what feels like a cage of branches as the tree goes down. It crashes through the wooden wall, sending splinters flying.

The crash mingles with my shriek, and the shadow warriors' high-pitched cackles as the tree sprawls across half the subway. I lift my head blearily to see Evan and Hiro, both looking shell-shocked. Scrabbling wildly, I manage to disentangle myself and jump to my feet.

"Where did you learn to climb a tree?" Asks Hiro, eyes wide.

"I don't know! I fell off a tower covered in plants the other day! There's a first time for everything," I say, "Now run!"

They don't need to be told twice.

"Have you got it?" Yells Evan over the hissing of the shadow warriors, which is like a swarm of furious wasps as we run.

"Yes!" I manage to call back.

"What are those things?"

We skid around a corner, narrowly avoiding slamming into the wall. Hiro's pulled ahead by now, and I can see his silhouette in the warm lamplight.

"I don't know," I yell back, "I call them shadow warriors. They could be anything!"

"Well, that's good!" there's sarcasm sharp in his tone. I roll my eyes, "Less talking, more getting out of here, ok?"

We pelt down the platforms, taking sharp turns. I get the sense that we're moving deeper into the maze of tunnels. It's darker here, though. That must mean the shadow warriors are close.

My boots are echoing loudly on the tiles, along with Evan's

panicked breathing. I can hardly see my hand in front of my face, but I can make out the rough outline of a train, sitting inanimately in its station.

"There!" I motion to Evan, who, thankfully, gets the gist. I reach the train first, and use the sharp window ledge as a foothold to boost myself up and onto the roof. I flatten myself against the train, and hold out a hand for Evan. He grabs it and I pull him up.

Breathing as quietly as I can, I watch as Hiro jumps nimbly and climbs onto the roof of the train. He turns his head to look at me, giving me a thumbs up. I've never seen him look more terrified.

The shadow warriors materialise from the gloom, the silver of their weapons glinting and providing a little ghostly light. They walk with menace, every step they take making the room darker. They seem to talk to each other in a hissing language.

I hardly dare to breathe as they gather and converse. One, evidently the leader, holds up a pale hand and they all fall dead silent. The leader hisses something in Shadow-Language or whatever, and the warriors disperse as quickly as they came, melting into the darkness.

"They're hunting us," breathes Evan. He looks so scared. In other circumstances I would laugh, but not now.

"Come on," I say, my voice a tiny rasp, "We need to find the others and get out of here. Evan, can you tell if the shield still holds?"

"I'm an artist, not a telepath."

"Alright," I mutter, "It was a fair question."

He shrugs, "I don't know if it will have held for this long. The only way we can find out is getting there quickly," he looks at me expectantly.

"Don't look at me," I say indignantly, "I'm lost too. Hiro?"

Hiro's squinting at something on the wall, "Yeah, I might know where we are. Evan, give me some light."

Evan seems surprised to be called on by Hiro, and he hastens to do as he says, sketching something on the floor. Placing his hand on it, an oil lamp appears, illuminating the station in a soft warm glow.

Hiro picks it up and turns the light on the wall, "Yep. Let's go."

He sets off running, and we follow as fast as we can. The oil lamp is bumping up and down, so it's next to impossible to keep my eyes on the light.

Eventually we stumble into the right area. There are the others, looking relatively bored as they sit in the still dimly glowing forcefield Evan created.

"What's wrong?" asks Skye, looking at our expressions.

I'm out of breath, but I manage to gasp, "Shadow warriors. They're here."

As if on cue, they begin to materialise out of the darkness only feet away. Their eyes have a triumphant gleam.

"Looks like we have company," says Parker grimly.

19
THE CHASE

"Don't move," I tell the others in the bubble.

"Screw that," Skye says, stepping out, "Don't even try and protect us."

"We're helping you," adds Anita, stepping out as well. Charlie fidgets nervously inside the bubble. Both girls look at him expectantly.

"Oh, alright, then," he says, stepping out reluctantly, then quickly adds, "It's not that I don't want to help Avery, just, um, those things are terrifying."

"Don't I know it," mutters Hiro.

"Is it alright if I skip this fight?" chimes Evan sarcastically.

So apparently those two have become friends in the last twenty seconds. I don't understand teenagers.

"Wimp," snorts Skye, an arrow at the ready.

"Dude, I don't even have a weapon and I'm gonna help," says Parker, who's also stepped out of the forcefield. Apparently deciding it's empty, the bubble fizzles away into nothing.

I draw my knife, the blade shaking slightly in my trembling hand, "Let's kick some shadow ass."

"That's my girl," Parker high fives me, and drops into a fighting stance, fists raised.

"Anita, take the frontline. Use the winds. If you're overwhelmed, get into the air," I say, "Charlie, Evan, Skye, you three are with me. Parker—"

I don't get a chance to finish before he charges the shadow warriors, screaming bloody murder.

"That works," I shrug, then we all attack. Evan's drawn himself a blade, and is surprisingly agile to use it. Skye's taking down demons left right and centre, her bow glinting. She seems to glow-no, she *is* glowing. A faint red light pulses around her. She literally radiates magic and energy. I guess it must be an archery thing.

Charlie's not doing too badly himself, launching grenades into the oncoming tidal wave and dispersing shadow warriors like frightened cats. Every time he throws one of the weapons, it explodes in a blinding flash. The imprints glow behind my eyelids, but for the shadow warriors they do much worse. The demons hiss and screech as if the very light burns their smoky bodies. Some vaporise on impact.

Hiro's using his knife to run a few through. His technique is very street fight centred, so his knife skills are shaky, but he dropkicks one across the platform where it dissipates into dust with an angry shriek.

One comes at me, crossbow aimed for my neck, but I duck to avoid the silver tip and stab my knife into its stomach. Blinking away the black dust as the creature explodes, I quickly slice another, but don't notice the clink of an arrow behind me.

"Look out!" A force slams into me before the arrow can hit, and for a second I think someone's tackled me to the ground. Instead, Anita has a hand outstretched, the wind she used to blow me backwards still circulating around it. I give her a smile of thanks, before rolling over to avoid getting impaled in the head by an angry demon.

But for every monster we disarm and vaporise, more are coming, melting out of the shadows easily. They seem to draw closer towards us, forcing us backwards into a tight circle. I bump into Evan and he gives me a glance which is hard to figure out. It's not angry, though I did just startle him, more helpless, and slightly afraid. He gives me a surprising quick half smile of encouragement before turning to face his attacker (a demon aiming its talons for his face).

Charlie unlatches another grenade and pats his pockets, looking frantic.

"I'm out of ammo!" He yells.

"What do we do?" asks Parker.

"There's only one thing for it," I say, "Charlie, clear us a path. Then everyone run!"

"Where to?" asks Evan.

"I know a place," replies Hiro, eyes on the shadow warriors.

That seems to settle it. I brace myself as Charlie throws the grenade. It flies in slow motion. It's hardly hit the ground when a blinding white flash goes off, almost knocking me off my feet. When I open my eyes, the way is clear.

"Come on!" I say to the others, and we run. Anita's limping, a stark red gash on her leg. Parker's arm is hanging at a weird angle. Skye has a claw mark on her face, splitting her eyebrow right in half.

We pelt up the subway steps, boots clanging on the tiles. Hiro takes a sharp right down a side alley, and we follow. Surprisingly, Evan nearly matches my pace as we run. His jacket is spattered with blood from a cut on his shoulder. My own arm stings, and as I glance at it, I notice a gash where one of the demons got me.

I wish I could heal everyone right now, but we've got bigger problems. The hissing and screeching behind us tells me that our pursuers are not far behind. And these ones are a lot more dangerous than guards.

Hiro jumps a low wall and hurls himself through an open window hastily. I do the same, the air rushing past me as I somersault through. Evan hesitates but does his best, clearing the window with a loud grunt. Parker follows with ease. Skye gives Charlie a hand up, and Anita floats right through. I slam the window shut, though it won't do us much good.

"Follow me!" says Hiro urgently, and he pulls a trapdoor open in the floor. I take a deep breath, and motion the others.

They drop through, except Evan, who hesitates.

"It's not a big drop," I snap, "Go!"

He glances at me, "You're coming, right?"

"I'm right behind you. Just go!"

He drops through the trapdoor and I follow. Seems I was right, the drop isn't far at all. This time, I manage to shelter my arm. *Finally,* I think, *so I can fight shadow demons to save the world but every time I do this I sprain my arm? Lame.*

I push myself to my feet and follow the others down a short corridor into the most beautiful garage I've ever seen. Windows are hung with drapes and dream catchers. Beaded tassels hang from the ceiling, along with glinting shards of glass catching the light in other colours. The walls are bare, but covered in swaths of colourful fabric.

"What is this place?" I can't help but gawp.

"Used to be a craft store. Closed down long ago, and we moved the bikes here," says Hiro.

"The…bikes?"

Long ago, when I was six or something similar, and relatively new to the gang, Hiro told me we had motorbikes, ones that we kept specially hidden for important reasons.

Said bikes are right in front of us.

I've seen motorbikes before, but these ones are something else. Every inch of them is polished and shines with oil work. They look elegant, not too bulky, but big enough to be stable.

Skye jumps on one with no qualms and starts tapping buttons.

"Careful—" begins Hiro, bristling, but she's already turned the engine on and revs the accelerator to prove a point. She raises her eyebrows at Hiro, "You were saying? I've been on these things before."

I count the bikes. There's three. But there's seven of us.

"Pair up," I say, "Anita-?"

"I can fly," she assured me, "Don't worry about me."

"Ok," I say, and swing my legs onto one of the bikes. As the engine roars to life, it lets out a guttural sound, like the bike is growling. The way it's vibrating beneath me isn't dissimilar to the leopards. *Ok,* I think, *so just convince yourself it's the same thing. It'll be easy.*

Evan perches behind me and goes to put his arms around my waist to hold on, but hesitates.

"Don't be chivalrous," I say, rolling my eyes, "Just do it."

Once we're all secure, I nod to Hiro, and the garage doors open on command. Beyond stretches a narrow slope, leading to what I can assume is a skyway. We're really doing this. Well, there's definitely no way to go back now.

I rev my engine and we shoot forward like a cannonball. The wind whips past me, the rush of air cool and fast. The wheels of the bike are nothing but a blur. My whole body seems to be vibrating with the vehicle.

Then we shoot off the end of a ramp and suddenly we're in the air. It's all my strength to hold on the handlebars and not scream as we land with a shrill whistle from the bike. I push the accelerator down hard and we race forward.

Zoriana, no matter how ugly and crime-infested, is a city. And henceforth, it has roads. It has traffic. It has overpasses and skyways. And those skyways have boundaries. We completely ignore them.

I'm swerving the bike around cars as nimbly as I can, all the while hearing a cacophony of shrieks and screams from behind. There's a menacing hissing as well, which tells us we're now being followed by a swarm of angry shadow warriors. This day just keeps getting back and better.

Provided, it's not day right now. The sky is inky black and cloudless, revealing tiny stars winking like diamonds. I can hardly see them through the hazy orange lights on the road. Car headlights glow like fiery eyes in the darkness, and I have to squint to see the junctions.

"Take a left!" says Evan into my ear.

"Why?" I ask.

My question is answered by a screeching demon attacking us from the right. I swerve, and Evan stabs it with his knife. I take a left.

"You drive, I'll fight!" he says.

"A, you don't tell me what to do," I say back, "B, that should really be the other way around."

"I'm not a complete fool," he says. I can't see, but I bet he's rolling his eyes in the dark, "I just saved your skin, didn't I?"

"We're not going over details now!" I snap, "Just keep your eyes on the road."

My point is kind of ruined when I nearly hit a car five metres in front of us.

"You were saying?" Asks Evan.

"Shut up."

"With pleasure."

And so we speed on in silence, the wind and shouting loud in my ears. Hearing a cry, I look up to see Anita struggling as three shadow warriors claw at her. She kicks one away, stabs another and clocks the third one around the head with the hilt of her knife. Then she keeps flying. She must be going at an insane speed, because she's keeping up with us perfectly. I lean to avoid another shadow warrior, which flies out of the darkness at us so fast I almost can't comprehend. Its claws skim my face, but Evan runs it through, and it dissipates.

I choke on the shadow dust, but focus on the road as we reach another junction. This is where things begin to go wrong. Well, more wrong than they already are.

Three shadow warriors come at me from the front. There's the familiar click of a grenade, then one soars past me into the darkness. Right at them. To my horror, it misses. And it hits the junction.

With an ear splitting boom, the rock and concrete holding up the skyway crumbles, leaving a gaping chasm, which were currently speeding towards. Oh heck no.

"I can't slow down in time!" I say to Evan, "We'll be thrown off the edge!"

"There's nothing to draw on either!" He says, looking terrified.

"There's one thing for it," I say, "we'll have to make the leap."

"No," says Evan, eyes on the chasm, shaking his head, "No, no, no, no. We can't do that. We'll never make it."

"Anita!" I call at her. She dissolves a shadow warrior with a flick of her knife, while flying backwards (which is pretty impressive) and looks down at us, "Yeah?"

"I need you to blow us all over the edge!" I say, "Can you do that?"

She looks at the abyss and pales, "Uh. Definitely not while flying."

Another demon comes at her as if to prove a point, and she slices it, but wobbles.

"Ok," I say, desperately thinking, "Can you land?"

"Land? Oh, yes!" she says, and soars ahead, so fast she's like a shooting star. Across the chasm I spot a street lamp, tilting dangerously, but steady enough. Anita perches on it and gives me a thumbs up.

With hisses, two shadow warriors go after her, but I yell at them, "Hey! Over here! You want the scroll, don't you?"

That gets them interested. They attack us as the gap speeds towards us, yawning like the gateway to darkness. Evan slices them, crying out as one rakes it's claws down his back. I wince at the sight, but turn my eyes back to the chasm. We have to be focused. Time seems to speed up. Evan whips his head around and his dark eyes widen when he sees the gap.

"We're not seriously doing this are we?" he asks, horrified.

"Trust me!" I reply, and with that, we go off the edge.

20
THE SKY OF STARDUST

The air rushes past me. Time slows to a crawl. The only thing I can hear is my own heartbeat. My whole life seems to flash before my eyes. We're soaring through the air, holding on for dear life as the bike flies. The edge still seems so far away, but it's rushing to meet us. We're going to make it, we're going to-

The edge of the bike misses the ledge and for a second we're falling. For a second I think we're dead. Then there's a whoosh, and a jolt, and we shoot upwards and forwards, like we've been catapulted into the sky. We soar over the ledge in a huge arc, and the bike's wheels touch down with ease. The impact sends a huge tingle through my body and the air is knocked out of my lungs. I nearly black out. Somehow I manage to stay conscious, and crane my head to look behind us. The others touch down with bumps, and across the chasm, the shadow warriors hiss and vanish.

I frown. It's not like them to give up. Which means that they received an order to go away. Whoever this villain is, they're playing with us. And I'm sure they're the same figure I've seen in my visions. I think of the last one and I shudder. The way they spoke, like they knew me and they knew I didn't have the courage. It seemed to suck the determination out of me. And that dark forest. Why does that seem familiar?

Evan has his eyes squeezed tight shut and he's breathing heavily. I turn around to look at him, "Hey, you ok?"

He slowly opens one eye a crack, then the other, "We're not dead."

"Why do you sound so surprised?" I ask, and laugh. Slowly, he smiles too. Soon we're both laughing hysterically, because we've done it, we're really alive. Anita touches down next to us with a smug smile, "Did you miss me?"

I throw my arms around her, "Thank you! Thank you thank you thank you! Anita, you saved us!"

"It was nothing," she says, blushing.

"ARE YOU KIDDING ME? IT WAS AWESOME!" says Parker, jumping off his bike and jumping up and down. Anita laughs sheepishly, "Thanks."

Skye hops off her bike and gives Charlie a hand, "Well, we can't hang around here for long. Where to, Avery?"

I falter, "I don't know. I honestly thought we'd be dead by now one way or the other. I don't know where the third map is."

"Three castles…" Evan muses, "Three castles…"

His words draw me back to the prophecy. Three castles, and we've found two, albeit one was more of a hidden room. I never thought Zoriana was famous for a castle, but Hiro told me a story about a castle once, and it stuck with me. I guess it paid off as well. Maybe I've got to trust my instincts. But one line of the prophecy is nagging at me. *From the death of a hero, a legend is born.* Which hero? I don't want any of my friends to die. We've come so far together. And I grew up with Hiro and Parker. I can't imagine a world without them.

"Avery?" Charlie's voice brings me back to the present.

"Yeah?" I say, snapping out of it.

"We might know where the final castle is," says Evan, "But we need to get going. There's two days left before the Alchemist's home moves."

"Don't remind me," I mutter, rubbing my head. This is a lot. We've got little to nothing in way of time, and we're all injured. But at least that I can fix.

I place my hand on Evan's back, "Don't move. I'm about to heal you."

He nods wordlessly, but Hiro stirs, "Wait, what? You can heal people?"

"I'm practicing," I say, letting the tingling feeling flow.

Hiro shakes his head, stunned, "Wow. I can't- how- never mind."

He gives me a strangely proud look as I heal the others.

"You forgot yourself again," Evan says, nodding to my own

gashes on my arm and face.

"Oh, yeah," I heal them quickly. It seems to work differently when I'm healing myself. It's faster, and works more effectively, but it's gone quick afterwards. The tingling feeling just...vanishes.

"Right," I say, flexing my hand, "We need to get off this skyway. Hiro, can you take us to the edge of the city?"

He hesitates, "At dark? We wouldn't get five inches."

"Come on, we've just vaporised smoky shadow monsters while on motorbikes, and you *don't think we can walk to the edge of a city?*" Skye sounds incredulous.

"Not this city," Hiro's face darkens, "I've lost too many friends in these streets. I'm not losing Avery."

He says it so firmly that Skye folds her arms, but does nothing. Anita pipes up, "Um, guys? I might know a way? It would take all of my strength, but, um...we could fly."

She winces, as if we're all going to laugh and or dismiss her. The idea is sort of crazy, but hey, the last few days have been insane.

"Ok," I say, "Can you teach me?"

She blinks, "Teach you-oh! You want to use Anemology? Have-have you done that before?"

"Twice," I say, "Not well. But, if it keeps you from draining yourself, let's do it."

And so that is how we end up standing at the edge of the

skyway, while police sirens get louder, holding hands. Anita's on one of my sides, Parker on the other. *This is never going to work,* a voice says in my head, but I push it down. *I can do this.*

"Everyone breathe," says Anita, "The more air inside you the lighter you are."

"That's not scientifically accurate, but ok," peeps Charlie. Parker's vibrating nervously. I nudge him, "You got this, alright?"

He gives me a weak smile. I can't blame him for being scared. We're about to jump off a skyway 100 feet into the air. I would be terrified. But for some reason I'm not. Maybe my body's just decided '*Yep, that's enough of being scared for one day*' And after facing demons and the figure in my vision, I'm ok with that.

How we do it I have no idea. Anita yells "JUMP" and we all leap off the edge. Instantly the tingling feeling overwhelms me, and I try and channel it, imagining the air lifting me up. As if on cue, we stop falling. Then we shoot upwards. Parker screams, but I close my eyes and imagine going higher. Above the clouds.

Obeying my command, the air pushes us up like a geyser, and we burst through the layers of clouds into a star washed world. They twinkle like someone's thrown a pot of glitter over the inky blue sky. In the east, the sun is almost beginning to rise, the edge of the sky tainted golden. The world stops, just for a minute. Everything is silent. I look to Anita, who gives me a mischievous smile. Then the winds take us, and we dive. My feet skim the clouds as we race along like comets, the air rushing past us. I feel like if I reached out I could touch the constellations.

It feels magic. There's no other words. The others look like they're dreaming. We swerve around skyscrapers, the golden light glinting off their windows. The clouds are a ghostly white floor beneath us. I can't help myself, I let out a yell of happiness.

My laugh carries on the wind, any words I could say gone. It's so beautiful, for a second I think we've found the gateway to heaven. I look up at the galaxies above, and, for the first time since I was six, I wonder if Frosty might be up there, frolicking in the nebulas. The thought makes me smile.

My whole body feels weightless as we soar among the skyscrapers. I've never felt this close to the sky.

As all amazing things do, the moment can't last. Hiro yells something across to Anita, and points down. She nods and gently, we steer downwards, vanishing beneath the clouds. When they open up, Zoriana glitters like a jewel beneath us, the skyscrapers reaching up to greet us. We soar between them, making for the edge of the city, where an old flickering sign saying 'the city of dreams' still glows half-heartedly, broken wires buzzing. Slowly, my feet touch the ground, and I nearly collapse. Charlie looks like a ghost, "I'm never doing that again."

"Me neither," Skye agrees, but I can't stop smiling. I just *flew. Like actually flew.*

Hiro clears his throat, looking at the ground, "So, I-I guess this is it."

My smile fades, "Oh. Yeah."

"Can we come with them?" Parker begs Hiro. He shakes his head forlornly, "It's too dangerous. We've helped them all we can. Besides," he smiles sadly at me, "Avery needs to make her own path."

Suddenly I want to cry. These guys are my family. How can I just ride away? Hiro sees my face, and gives me a tiny smile, "It's ok. We'll be ok."

"And Jodi?" I ask, "I could get to her hospital. I could-I could try and heal—"

Hiro cuts me off sadly, "We don't know where she is. She's in the hands of God now," he looks to the sky and seems to make a silent prayer.

My voice won't work properly. My eyes feel wet. I blink back tears and hug Hiro tight, "You'll be ok, right? All of you?"

"Yeah," he sounds confident, "Yeah. We will."

"But what about you?" cries Parker, looking at me, "Avery, you're going to have to go and face those things again! And…" he trails off, looking helpless.

I shrug, "I'll take it as it comes." I fist bump Parker, "Stay safe, ok? No more fighting!"

He laughs halfheartedly, "You sound like Miya."

"Well, we can never thank you enough for everything you've done for us," Anita says into the silence. Hiro nods. I squeeze Parker's hand, "You flew, dude. That's a story you can tell for years."

He shakes his head, eyes looking bright, "I'll never forget it."

I step back, towards the others. Even Hiro looks like he's

fighting back a tear.

"Thank you," I tell them both, "For everything. Tell the others I hope they prosper."

Hiro's mouth twitches, "We will."

I turn away, but I just can't bring myself to go. I run back to Hiro and throw my arms around him, burying my head in his shoulder. Surprised, he hugs me back.

"You're going to be ok. I promise," he whispers into my ear.

"Please stay safe," I tell him, "look after the others."

Hiro nods, "And if you ever need me, just say. I'll be there. Even when you're across the world. Will you save it for me?"

"I'll try," I whisper. He lets me go, "Good luck. I know you'll make it."

I nod, letting a tear trickle down my face, "Goodbye."

"Bye," Parker says mournfully. I give him a final quick hug and go back to the others. As if on cue, the leopards patter out from the shadows. Nyota buts into my hand, purring comfortingly. I get on her back, and silently the others follow suit, Evan climbing on behind me.

I expect Hiro to wave. Or just to walk away. Instead, he salutes.

As we ride away into the night, I look back, at my home, Zoriana, nothing more than a shadow on the horizon.

21
THE WILD AGAIN

"Are you ok?" asks Evan stiffly as we ride. The sun is slowly coming up over the desert, creeping across the sky at an agonisingly slow pace. I wish it would hurry up. The dark makes me nervous. It's not that I'm afraid of the dark. But I've been taught to be wary of it since I was small.

Evan's simple question makes me hesitate. Maybe it's the fact that he asked it. I mean, this is Evan Onceller. I can't call us friends. Not when we're at each other's throats a lot of the time. Almost everything he says has to be sarcastic.

But this is the first time he's asked me if I'm ok. That's…nice of him? I guess. I've checked in with everyone, including Evan, loads to make sure we're all running smoothly. I never thought he was the kind of guy to actually care about people. Or maybe he's just trying to fill the silence.

"Avery?" he sounds slightly confused, "Are you awake?"

"Yes, I'm awake," I sigh, rolling my eyes, "And I'm fine. I'm fine," I'm not sure whether I'm convincing me or him.

"Ok," he says, then, hesitantly, as if he doesn't want me to punch him for this, "I think it was, um, difficult for you to leave your brother and stuff."

I nod, "They'll be fine. I'll be fine."

"I'm not saying they're in danger or anything," he quickly adds, "Just, seemed like a tender moment? I don't know."

I chuckle, "You're bad at this. I've known those two since I was six. Hiro is basically my brother. So yeah, saying goodbye was hard. But it's fine. I'm fine."

That's the third time I've said that. I don't think Evan believes me. I'm still facing forward, so I don't have to look at him, see him looking pitying. I don't need his pity.

"So," I say, "Any idea of where we should be going?"

Evan nods, "Yes, actually. We should be heading East, over there." he points to a spot on the horizon.

"I didn't know you had perfect nautical bearings in the desert," I say sarcastically.

"Ha ha. Not funny. I don't."

"Then how do you know where we're going?"

"I've been going to Adriana since I was nearly 3! I'm pretty sure I know where I'm going."

"Adriana?"

I've heard of Adriana. It's one of the three capitals. Zoriana is one, Adriana is another, and Violana. I've never been to either of the latter. I've heard stories about both. Whenever I asked Hiro, he said, "Zoriana's for crooks, Violana's for snobs, and Adriana is for our useless council."

I've never cared for politics, so to this day I don't know what he means. Violana is the richest state, Zoriana, the poorest, and Adriana manages them both. Aside from that, the outside world has always been somewhat of a mystery.

"Ok, I hate that I have to ask this, but how does the government work here?" I ask, gritting my teeth.

Evan sounds surprised, "You don't know?"

"I grew up learning to dropkick people, not about politics."

"Ok, wow, um…"

I roll my eyes at his tone, "Will you tell me about it or not?"

"Ok, fine," he says, "Adriana is home to a lot of economical buildings. For a city, it's a weird one, because no one lives there. They commute there for work. The Adriana Capital Hall is the biggest castle in the world. Home to the President. The Council of Ministers holds meetings there, where it decides what's best for the cities. A lot of the council, and other working class people there come from Violana, which is a mainly suburban residential area. Not a lot of commercial shops. But it's nice. It's where I live."

"Explains a lot," I mutter under my breath.

"Zoriana is a blank slate for me," continues Evan,

"Obviously not for you, but Adriana mostly casts a blind eye on the crime rise there. My parents always dismissed it. No offence, by the way."

"No, it's fine, I love being dismissed," I say sarcastically,

"Um, I can't tell whether you're being sarcastic or not. Anyway, you know how students are admitted to the school, right?"

"Nope."

"Wow. Ok, well, basically Tempest goes around recruiting really special students. And the rest of us have to apply. If we're magic, she'll let us in, but we still have to apply to be noticed."

"Did you apply, or were you recruited?"

"I was," he coughs awkwardly, "I was a special case."

I raise my eyebrow, but he doesn't explain.

"Anyway," he hurries on, "As I'm sure you know, magic is seen very differently across the states. In Violana, it's something to be proud of. A higher social status."

"Oh, I'm sorry, do you want me to bow?"

"Ha ha. Again, not funny. But I've always been curious about Zoriana. How's magic seen there?"

"Most people don't think it exists," I shrug, "Maybe some dare to hope, but dreamers don't last long where I'm from. It's a dangerous place."

"Sounds like a bad place to grow up. I'm sorry."

"Don't be sorry. I don't want you to be sorry. It wasn't an awful place, anyway," I say defensively, "I had the gang. They were my family. Still are."

"Are you an orphan?"

"What kind of a question is that? Yes, I'm an orphan. Or you would have met my parents by now, wouldn't you?"

"I didn't need to," I can hear the smirk in his voice, "Your brother was quite clear."

"On what?" I ask, narrowing my eyes.

"You know, not to lay a finger on you or he'll hunt me down and murder me?"

"Oh my gosh," I groan and slap a hand against my forehead. So Hiro did talk to Evan about…ugh. That's humiliating.

"I love the guy, but sometimes he's a huge pain in the ass," I say, "Is that why you were sucking up to him so much? Because you were afraid he'd dropkick you like he did that shadow warrior?"

Evan laughs, not his sarcastic one, but a real one. It might be the first time I've heard him laugh, "Point taken. I'd better get off this leopard."

"Yes, you'd better."

We ride on in silence, but it almost feels as if an invisible barrier has broken between us. The tension is lighter. I glance across at the other two leopards, keeping pace easily, with my friends snoring on their silver backs.

The silence is broken by a long rumble coming from Nyota. That's when I realise she hasn't been fed for days. In all the commotion, I completely forgot.

"I'm such an idiot," I mutter.

"What?" Evan asks, confused.

"We forgot to feed the leopards," I say, "Nyota's about to drop. We need to find something for them to eat."

As if the stars are smiling on us, at that moment Nyota's ears prick and she pulls to the left. The other leopards seem to follow her lead.

I squint, and my eyes just about make out the carcass of a huge…boar? I can't tell. Whatever it is, it looks edible. (Not for humans of course. For leopards.)

"Bingo," I smile.

A few minutes later, I'm leaning against a rock happily tucking into some kind of sandwich, while the others attempt to roast sausages over a measly fire. The leopards scrounge through the carcass nearby, occasionally pawing and nudging each other as if to say: 'nope, get out the way. My food!'

"You should go to sleep," says Evan from his position next to me. I roll my eyes, "I'm not tired," but I can't stop myself yawning as I do so.

"I'm serious. We've all slept so far on the journey except you," he says, raising an eyebrow, "I bet you can't keep yourself awake for the next five minutes."

"Go away, please."

"Ok," he leaves with a shrug, "Just try and get some rest?"

"You're not my brother."

"No, but I don't want you to collapse while we're talking to the president. It's not a good impression, is it?"

I nod and let my head loll. I'm tired to try and figure out what he means right now. Instead, I simply let my eyes close.

Sleep hits me like a bullet, and I'm pulled into dreams. They're halting, like my mind can't decide what nightmare to show me tonight. Yay.

I'm running from a forest fire, the trees crashing down around me as the ground goes up in sizzling flames. The image glitches, and suddenly I'm hanging off the frozen ledge of a mountain, sweat pouring down my face, blood pouring from a wound in my side. I'm holding someone's hand, grasping their fragile, cold fingers with all my might. I look down and it's Anita, eyes closed, lips tinged blue, looking dead. I hardly have time to process any of it before the image changes again.

This time I'm in a cosy hut, no danger in sight. An old man rocks a baby in a worn old copper chair. Contraptions and mechanics hang from the ceiling and climb the walls, while the tables in the room are clustered with glass tubes and vials. A warm fire crackles, and the drapes are shut. But as I watch, the fire goes out with a gust of black smoke, and the screeching wind pulls the drapes open and shatters the glass, letting in a freezing blast of cold air. The room darkens.

The man stands up, eyes wild and frightened, clutching the baby. Suddenly there's a flash of lightning and there stands the shadowy figure, darkness curling around her feet as she fingers a sharp obsidian dagger.

The man backs away into a corner, looking terrified.

"It's good to be back," hisses the figure, cackling. The baby starts to cry, and the man hushes it gently, giving the figure a wide eyed, scared glance.

"Oh, don't tell me you don't recognise me?" asks the figure innocently, "No? Maybe this will jog your memory."
She holds out what looks like a gold necklace, engraved with symbols I can't make out. The man goes pale.

"What do you want?" he demands, voice strangely calm.

"You know full well what I want," hisses the figure, red eyes flashing, "Where is it?"

"It's gone," says the man, more confidently, "Leave. Now. Az—"

There's another flash of lightning as the figure hisses, "Don't say it. That is no longer my name. I am Nerezza, now and forever. The darkest shadows will fear me!"

So she does have a name, I think. Nerezza.

She snaps her fingers, and on command, the wolves materialise, growling and snarling. The man clutches the baby tighter, "The head is not here, Nerezza. Leave."

She laughs, "Why? Are you afraid of my pets? Oh, they mean no harm. Give me the head and they will not touch you."

"Never," spits the man, "Leave us alone."

"Oh, dear," purrs Nerezza, "I so hoped we'd reach an agreement. But it seems not. Well, it was your choice…"

She reaches out a hand and suddenly the baby glows with black light.

A thin golden strand starts to drain out of her, into the woman's outstretched hand.

"No," says the man, shaking, horrified, "NO, YOU CAN'T! Stop, please. Don't hurt her!"

My heart is beating fast in fear, terror, horror.
It's a dream, so neither of them can hear me, but I shout, "Stop! What are you doing? Don't hurt her——"

But no matter what I yell, what the man does to shield the child, the golden light keeps draining until there's none left. Nerezza seems to grow taller, the air darker. She exhales.

"It feels good, with more power," laughs the figure, "She would've been a strong one."

"You monster," says the man, hugging the baby tight and sobbing as he cowers against the wall, "I'll never give you the head. Never!"

Nerezza tilts her head, "What a shame. I suppose I'll have to kill you then."

She hurls her knife, and it hits the man in the chest. He falls as blood begins to pour. The wolves lap it up like fresh milk. My legs are about to buckle. What's going on? I need to wake up. I need to wake up right now.

Nerezza steps over him. The man utters a final breath, "You'll never win. The Infinite is coming. And it's not you…"

Then his eyes go glassy and he falls still. Nerezza's expression is empty, but her eyes are full of anger.

"Stupid fool," she mutters, dark cloak spinning as she turns for the door. At the doorway she turns back, "Leave the child to die."

The wolves obey her, slinking out of the door one by one, until it shuts behind them. The fire is empty. Shattered glass scatters the floor. And, in the arms of their dead father, the baby starts to cry.

I wake up screaming. In my mind I can still see it happening, and it's so horrible and terrifying I can hardly breathe.

"Woah, woah, Avery! You're ok! You're ok, calm down!"

I'm on the leopard. Evan's behind me, gently rubbing my shoulders. I'm freezing cold, but the gesture warms me.

"It's just a dream," he whispers, "You're ok. You're ok."

I gather my bearings. We're racing towards another skyline, this one chrome white. Slowly, ever so slowly my heart slows. I push the dream out of my mind, though the images still linger. I'm safe. Nerezza is not here. We can stop her. I'm safe.

I'm safe.

Slowly I steady my breathing. The cold air feels like pure gold. Evan's eyeing me warily, like I might start screaming again. But I don't.

I shake off his hands. My voice sounds raspy, "It was a nightmare. I can't," my voice catches, "I can't talk about it. I'm fine now."

I have to be focused on the quest now. I push the last dregs of the horrifying dream out of my mind, and face the skyline. Adriana.

We're here.

22
THE FINAL CITY

The second we cross over the border, I feel like I've crossed an invisible line. And I know, instantly, that I do not belong here.

For a start, everything is pure chrome white. The buildings, the sidewalks, the roads, everything is made out of what looks like white marble. It's so clean. Not a speck of dirt in sight. For a second I wonder why. Then I see a skinny girl in a plain dress scrubbing at a small smudge of dirt on a set of sparkling white steps. Ah. So they have servants.

I feel a spark of anger. Whoever this president is, I already hate him. Maybe they're paid, but who would enlist children to scrub their oh-so-special city of marble?

I look down. The leopards are leaving dusty footprints as we prowl the main roads. I hate to add to the servants' jobs. I make a mental note to try and clean up before we leave. We're heading for the towering white castle overlooking the city. That castle is another reason I instantly hate this place.

It's huge. Tiers upon tiers of white columns, friezes, busts, inscriptions, and glossy turrets reaching for the sky. Flags fly at the top, a glorious rich red. They're probably the only colourful thing in this city. The few people we pass look tired and drab, their faces wan, their clothes dull and monochrome.

Aside from the servants, which I feel a surge of injustice for every time I look at them, the streets are silent. I guess it's too early for anyone to commute yet. What Evan said about this place must be true, though, because the only buildings I see are office buildings. No apartments. A city for workaholics.

It couldn't be more different to Zoriana. That's probably another reason I hate it. Zoriana may be gloomy and full of shadows, but everything is double-sided. There are enemies. There are allies. I've grown accustomed to the chaos. Here, everything is too controlled, too ordered, too perfect.

The leopards don't seem to like it much either. Nyota's hackles raise and her fur begins to prickle slightly. I smooth it gently, "Hey, girl, it's ok."

She doesn't seem very reassured, however. The white castle approaches, and with every step I take, the feeling of discomfort grows.

The tips of the gate are razor sharp and deadly, to ward off intruders. Nyota snarls and comes to a stop. Just then a young man appears from the castle itself, jogging down the path and coming to a halt at the mechanisms for the gate. He eyes us suspiciously.

"You're not council members!" he says, as if that's not already obvious.

"We come in peace," I say.

He glances disbelievingly at my stained clothes, the snarling leopard, and my different-colour eyes. It shouldn't be a factor, but like I said, most people are thrown off when they meet my gaze. He works his jaw, "Children are not allowed on sight. I'm under strict orders from the president himself. I'm sorry."

He doesn't sound very sorry at all.

I try again, "We have an audience with the president. He expects our arrival."

The man raises an eyebrow, "And I'm the queen of fairies. Scruffy children like you are not wanted here. Go home and stop ruining our marble work."

I grit my teeth, "You—"

Evan stops me. He hops down from the leopard and approaches the man, smoothing his hair as he does. I give him a *what are you doing please STOP* look, which he ignores.

"Michelson?" he asks, surprise in his voice. If he's been trying to tone down the accent recently, he's hyping it up now, "Old friend! Surely you remember your protégée, my dear brother?"

The man, who seems to be called Michelson, gasps, "Oh, Evan Onceller? Skies above, it is you. Oh, joy!"

He grasps Evan's hand through the bars and shakes it

thoroughly, "A pleasure to see you again, my dear boy. A pleasure. How are your parents? Are they well?"

"They're quite well, thank you," Evan assures him, "As is good old Tyler. He's settled quite nicely!"

"Oh, I'm glad! So what brings you here?"

This is by far the strangest encounter I've ever seen. Not only does Evan sound different, he holds himself different. As if trying to assert a higher power, a place in society. It's hard to believe, when he's covered in sand, dirt, and oil like me, but he radiates confidence.

The very idea of Evan being 'an important figure in society' makes me intimidated, though I'd never say that to him. To me he's just Evan, annoying as heck and sarcastic with an attitude and kindness that he only uses very rarely. But Violana folk? They make me nervous, because inside, I feel like they're staring me down and calculating my worth. Like I'm just another jewel to be sold, something to be owned.

And no matter his flaws, Evan Onceller is not like *that*.

"So you see," Evan is saying now to Michelson, "It's quite urgent. Really very important. School business, as you know. Quests and all the like."

Surprisingly, Michelson is nodding along very sincerely, "Oh, I do agree. My apologies for not letting your, ah, acquaintances through earlier," he gives me a look like he wants me to sink into a pile of dirt. I return the gesture.

"Well, come on through then!" says Michelson, clapping his hands. The gates swing open with hardly a squeak, and he beckons us. I glance at the others warily.

Skye looks like she wants to strangle this guy. Charlie looks like he agrees with Skye. Anita is staring through narrowed eyes at the castle. Evan seems to be the only one cool with this.

As we start to plod along the path to the castle, I say over my shoulder, "I didn't think you were the charming type?"

He rolls his eyes, "It's a charade. I hate that guy."

"And good riddance," I say, "Still, keep up the act, because chances are the president will be a lot worse."

"I didn't know you had a brother," says Charlie curiously to Evan, leaning over.

Evan shrugs, looking uncomfortable, "Tyler. He's around 10 years older than me, so we don't talk a lot."

"He works here? Would he help us?" asks Anita.

Evan shakes his head, "He was an apprentice here. He's left for other work now. Any help from him?" he wrinkles his nose, "Probably not. My only memory of him is being rolled down the stairs in a washing up tub with no clothes on."

"Too much information," says Skye, looking disgusted, "Can we please move on?"

I can't agree more.

The long path up to the castle steps is also white marble. I'm beginning to see just how impractical this place is. Charlie looks skittish too, for some reason, muttering under his breath as he eyes the ground like it might explode.

I don't know much chemistry, but Charlie's the smartest guy I know. Science is his home turf. If something's wrong with the surface we're treading on, he'd know. Judging by his expression, he's not particularly fond of being here. The thought makes me nervous.

The leopards bound up the white steps easily, and we reach the huge double doors. Words are engraved on the sleek white surface, but I can't make them out. They look like they're in another language.

Michelson turns to us, looking disdainful, "The animals will have to stay outside, I'm afraid. Please step down off your...steeds."

He says the word *steeds* like he means *pests*. Begrudgingly, I step off Nyota, who pads away and curls up at the top of the steps like a huge silver guard dog. Tucking her head between her feet, she begins to vibrate slowly. The other leopards exchange low, guttural growls, and circle her. But they're not doing it threateningly. They're doing it as an act of protection. Slowly, they lie down and create a circle around her.

I exchange a confused glance with Anita. What are they doing? Could this be because Nyota might be the alpha?

Michelson clears his throat, "Well, come on then. No dilly-dallying."

Inside, the castle seems even bigger than the outside. And again, I instantly despise it all. There are huge pillars of marble, an intricately carved floor, huge glass windows stretching tall. There are curved white staircases, regal plants blooming in white marble pots, and a high glass dome ceiling hung with a crystal chandelier.

And in the middle of it, a man stands, all dressed in white. As he turns towards us, I have no doubt this is the president. His face is stern and authoritative. His smile is poster boy white. He holds himself regally, as if he's the king and this is his domain.

Like this entire city, I hate him already.

"Welcome," he cries, smiling at us, but I can see his eyes doing calculations, asking questions. Are we a threat? What do we want?

"Please," he says graciously, "Join us for dinner."

23
FINE DINING...?

"This is so not gonna go well," I mutter to Skye the second we sit down at the long mahogany table. There are six places set out, with crisp white napkins, glittering silver cutlery, and tall glasses of what I hope is water, but I still don't touch.

The president's coat swishes as he sits in a throne at the head, and I'm reminded of a cat, lounging like it owns the place. His smile is Cheshire wide.

"So, what brings you here, students of Infino?" he asks. I put my hands on the table and push myself to my feet, "Sir, if I may, I'd like to skip the small talk."

He looks surprised at my firm and rough tone, but the expression quickly turns to amusement, "Well, go on, my dear. Enlighten me."

"We're tracking down the Alchemist's daughter," I begin, but instantly I know I've made a mistake. The president's face darkens. Evan winces. I want to throw my plate at him.

"That fool?" asks the president. His smile seems patronising, "He has been dead for decades."

I resist the urge to say *'yeah, I know. I freaking saw it happen!'* Instead, I continue, "Despite that, we search for his brethren. She may be important to the prophecy."

The president pauses. Then, more surprisingly, he laughs, "The prophecy? My goodness, you believe that tosh!"

I frown, "With all due respect sir, I've nearly died about three million times already on this mission, fighting for said 'tosh'."

The president wipes his watering eyes, "My apologies. It's just…surely, you all don't believe that!"

"The copper head spoke, as it was prophesied," Skye stands up, "We've undertaken this quest to find and seek help from the alchemist's daughter, not to be stopped here!"

Evan shoots her a warning glance. The president, however, just raises an eyebrow, "You must be Skye Archer. Tempest's leading warrior. What a spirit. But, my dear, I don't see how I am stopping you. In fact, I want to help you."

I exchange a confused glance with Skye. This guy has really fickle moods.

"So, how can I assist such a fine quest team?" asks the president, seriously enough, but the sparkle in his eyes suggests otherwise. He's humouring us.

This is where Evan interjects, "We seek a final map, sir. One that we believe may be here?"

"A final map? My good boy there's one right behind you!" the president cries. Evan spins, nearly falling over. Sure enough, in pride of place on the wall is a scroll, framed in a regal wooden border. It matches the others I've seen exactly.

"Great! So can we have it?" asks Anita eagerly. Evan winces again. The president falters. A serious pause sets in.

"Let us dine," the president says, as food enters, "We shall talk more after dinner. For now, my dear," he focuses his gaze on me, "Tell me more about you. I've never seen you before. Are you Violanian?"

"No sir," I say, stiffly, "I grew up somewhere else."

Food arrives: plates of tiny potatoes (which I don't touch) tiny mushrooms (which I definitely do not touch) tiny cucumber and elegant crest rolls (you're getting the point) and other 'delicacies'.

The president watches me as he serves himself a platter, "Are you Midlands?"

I hesitate, "I didn't learn Geography growing up, sir. I don't think so?"

I'm keen not to let him know I grew up in Zoriana. Usually mentioning it gives you a one way ticket to jail. Unfortunately, the president is smarter than he looks.

"Ah. No education. A Zoriana child," he says, eyes glittering, "Very interesting. Is that why you believe yourself to be the one of the prophecy? Because you were raised in 'a city of shadow?'"

The way he says it makes me want to sink into the floor. Up 'til now, everyone has been so certain that I'm the one. But this guy? Just because he's rich and powerful, suddenly he thinks I'm nothing. Classic. And no education? Excuse me? Hiro taught me everything he knew, and the guy was no dunce. So what if I didn't learn *Geography?*

Anger bubbles up in me, with another strange tingling feeling. I don't want to start a hurricane in the middle of a dining room, so I hold my tongue and nod.

"And what is your, ah, talent, do they say?" asks the president, eyebrow raised still.

"I," I falter, "I'm—"

Evan cuts me off, "So far we still are yet to discover that, sir. Rest assured, Avery is an asset."

If there's one person who can make me feel like dirt, a shiny piece of jewellery to be sold, and compliment me all in one sentence, it's Evan. I glare at him.

The president laughs, "An asset, oh my! And my dear, might you show us these 'talents'?"

The air quotation marks make me lose it. The tingling feeling seems to flow out of my fingers, and I look down to see golden strands of light coming from my fingertips. I look to the others, confused, but they've pushed their chairs as far back as they can. Even the president looks slightly afraid. The room seems to get…darker?

"Cut it out," I mutter to myself. Nothing happens. I clench my fists, but the strands of light leak through.

"Cut it out!" I try again, louder, and the light vanishes. The room returns to normal. The others still look wary. I'm no longer being stared at like an asset by the president. More like a villain.

"Who are you?" He says finally.

"I'm Avery," I say, "Student at Infino. Here for the final scroll. Please, sir."

The silence is like glass. The president leans forward, all playfulness gone, "Let me get this straight. A child of Zoriana, who may or may not have the," he shudders, "Cursed *seventh magic,* comes to me with a quest team of teenagers, hoping to get their hands on a priceless artefact for free, just so they can go running off to find a meddling crackpot's daughter who hasn't been seen in decades? You know what you are asking me to do?"

"Yes sir," I say firmly, though inside I'm panicking. *Cursed seventh magic?* Was that what Tempest talked about? The worst thing about those horrible strands of light…I've seen them before. In my nightmare.

"We may seem like those who should be behind bars," I say, "Or at least I do. Evan's a powder puff. But we have good hearts, and we mean to use them. This quest is important!"

"And why should I believe that?" asks the president. The words I've wanted to say since I sat down finally come up, "Sir, have you heard of Nerezza?"

My friends freeze. Evan's dark eyes find mine, and I see the message in them: *'what happened in that nightmare?'*

The president hesitates. Just a second. That gives me all the information I need, "No. I have no idea what you're talking about."

"Well, she's evil," I say, "At least that's what I've seen. She killed the alchemist. And she's coming for me."

The president stands, "You lie."

"It's no lie," pipes up Charlie. We all look at him in surprise, "I'm an Alchemist. We learnt of the Alchemist's death. No one could prove it was murder, but for a while...there were rumours of a shadow lady, manipulating darkness, trying to change the future. That...I think that is Nerezza."

"And she's rising, possibly again," I say, "Cursed seventh magic or no, I'm in danger by this. So are my quest team. We need to find the alchemist's daughter, for clarity, if not anything. For answers. To assess the danger. But, if I'm right," I take a deep breath, "She's out for blood."

"Why should I believe you?" sneers the president, "Over years of safety and security?"

"You shouldn't," I say, "Unless you want your kingdom to survive, that is."

The president works his jaw, seemingly thinking. He glances to Evan, "You, Evan Onceller, correct? Tell the girl she's wrong. You've seen my empire with your own eyes! Your father has stood by me as an advisor for years! If you side with me now, I can make you just as important!"

Evan looks stunned. For a second, I think he'll do as the president says. A flicker of confused emotions cross his face: surprise, longing, then anger, and confusion. And the shadow of a memory, just for a second.

He looks to me, "I'm on her side."

I resist a smile, but hopefully the look in my eyes makes it clear I'm grateful. I turn to the president, "Sir, you have his word. This glorious empire of yours will fall if you don't help us. So give us the scroll."

I'm playing with fire and I know it. The president looks conflicted. He growls, "That scroll is going nowhere."

"Then we'll take it by force," Skye says roughly.

"No we won't," I cut in, "We'll bargain."

Skye gives me an annoyed look, "Fine. We'll bargain."

"You have nothing to offer," laughs the president.

"You're talking to the best thief in East Zoriana," I reply.

His eyes sparkle, "Do you want to give yourself a jail sentence, girl?"

"This may be a bad time," chirrups Charlie, "But, um, sir, Avery's got a point. We have things to offer—"

"Your alchemist gold does not fool me," says the president coldly. Charlie frowns, "Well, then listen to us."

He stands up, and I'm amazed at how confident he suddenly is, "Avery is right. If Nerezza comes anywhere near this place, you're doomed. It's built on a volcano!"

"Unimportant, boy!" exclaims the president angrily.

"Very important," counters Charlie, "This palace acts like a cork, holding in years of built up tension inside the dome. The slightest tremor and," he gestures, "It'll blow this place sky high."

"Your choice," I say, "Protect your kingdom, your palace, your honour, and help us. Or, let Nerezza wipe it out."

The president tilts his head. For a second my heart leaps. Maybe he really will help us? But his smile turns fake, then cold. He slowly shakes his head, "Oh, but I have other plans for you. Avery from Zoriana, for years of thievery, trespassing of my palace—"

"Trespassing? Your assistant let us in!"

"-Rude behaviour to your president, attempted thievery of a precious artefact, and other grievous offences-

"What?"

"-you and your quest team are sentenced to a life sentence," says the president, "Guards!"

Armed guards rush into the room. I default into a defensive stance, fists up.

"I wouldn't try fighting," says the president, looking almost bored now, "It's pointless. Enjoy jail!"

Left to my own devices, I'm not sure what I would have done first: backhand the guards, grab the scroll, or punch the president in his smug face. Instead, I'm grabbed roughly and handcuffed before I can utter a word. Skye draws an arrow, but the guard snatches her bow and crushes it in one fist. Skye jolts back as if she's been stabbed, letting out a cry like

211

a wounded puppy.

The others are chained, and one by one, we're dragged away. My brain is frantically searching for answers. My eyes land on a pure golden bird, trapped in a cage in pride of place above the throne. I feel just like that bird.

"You have to listen!" I beg the president, but he ignores me. The bird, previously silent, meets my eyes with its penetrating ones and lets out a high shriek like it agrees with me.

Then I'm plunged into darkness.

24
TRAPPED

We're led, single file, through a narrow tunnel that seems to spiral down underground. It's warmer down here, and the air has a distinct scent of sulphur. Water trickles through cracks in the low ceiling and drips around us, echoing along with the guards' heavy footsteps.

There's a bag over my head, but it does little to cover my view. It's so dark in the tunnel that it really makes no difference. The only way I can tell I'm even in a tunnel is the acoustics. You can't grow up running through tunnels in Zoriana and not know one when you hear one.

I can hear Charlie's heavy breathing ahead of me. Behind me, Evan is silent as a statue. I wish I could see him, or better, hear his thoughts. Maybe he'd have a plan?

Because believe it or not, I currently do not. As far as I can tell, we're being led to the dungeons where they might…what? Torture us? Hang us? Chain us? I have no idea. And frankly, I'm not looking forward to any of those options.

I can hear little whooshes of wind sweeping through the tunnels, but it's obvious that so far down, Anita can't gather enough wind for anything to happen.

I curse myself. If I'd had quicker instincts, been ready, none of this would have happened. Maybe I can still wriggle out of this? I mean, I specialise in escaping guards. But never have I actually been caught and chained. That's new.

The handcuffs are digging into my wrists. Maybe they're specially made, but they seem to tighten the more I move.

The tunnel slants steeply and I nearly trip over my own feet. Stumbling, I manage to steady myself as one of the guards grunts something to the other. The tunnel opens up into a dingy round room, the walls...I can't make out the walls. Luckily, at that moment, the bag is pulled off my head, and I can see again.

Well, 'see again' is a strong word. It's so dark in here that I have to squint to see anything at all. The walls are harsh black stone, with bars built in. A circle of cells. In the centre of the room is a carved stone pillar. Engraved on the pillar are symbols and...a bird?

Maybe the same one I saw in the throne room, I think, *but why would that be important?*

Before I can ponder it any further, I'm thrown roughly into a cell along with Skye and Anita. The door clangs behind us.

I turn to face the others. Skye's flexing her free hands, somehow having already unlocked the padlocks. She turns to us with a businesslike expression on her face, "Right. We're going to get out of here. Anita, give me your hands."

And something hits me. While the others haven't been acting particularly different around me (at least, none of them are cowering away from me) Skye…doesn't want to touch my hands. Because of the light strands. Because I might have the cursed seventh magic.

And if I'm right, the cursed seventh magic is *really bad*. I hope my team knows that I would never do it on purpose. As long as I'm alive, I will never be like Nerezza. No, they're probably worried I'd do it by accident. After all, I hardly have control of my normal powers, let alone this one.

I stare down at my own hands with a sigh. Skye finishes unlocking Anita and approaches me, hairpin clasped in her hand. I don't exactly meet her eyes, "Yeah, you can, um, you can just give that me and I'll do it if you want. You know, after the throne room."

I can't see her expression, but Skye seems to tilt her head, "No, I'm doing it, believe me."

She grasps my hands and starts to unlock the handcuffs. Seeming to notice my embarrassment and shame, Anita gently put her arms around me.

"What is this?" I laugh.

"This is known as a comforting hug," Anita says, parroting posh Michelson, "For those who need it."

I smile, "Thanks."

After a pause, Skye says, "You know, what happened in the

throne room wasn't your fault. And we don't think it's your fault either."

"I mean, it would make sense," Anita says, "If you were the Infinite, that you'd have that one as well."

"Yeah," I nod, "It's just-I don't actually know what it does. I have a vague idea and if I'm right, it could be really bad, but, I still don't know."

Anita nods, "No one has the full picture on it. But whatever it is, we'll deal, ok? We're your friends."

"She's right," Skye says unexpectedly, twisting the hairpin and unlocking my handcuffs with a click, "And, I-I don't have a lot of friends so, you guys are, I don't know, kinda important to me."

Their words warm me, even though it's freezing in here.

"Eh hem," a voice says from to the side of us, "If you three are quite finished having a tender moment, could we get some help in here?"

"You don't know how to pick locks?" Anita laughs.

"Oh I'm sorry, I didn't bring a box of hairpins and the instruction almanac did I?" It's obviously Evan, then.

"I don't think an almanac for picking locks exists," I say, laughing, "Be cool if it did."

"Yeah, step one," Anita says, "Teach the useless people in the cell next door."

"Thank you for that," Evan's voice grumbles.

"You're totally welcome," I say sarcastically, pinpointing the sound of his voice. Built at around eye level is a hole in the wall, just a couple of bricks. There are bars over it, but through them I can see Evan giving me his trademark annoyed look.

"Found them," I call to Anita and Skye.

"Where's Charlie?" Skye asks Evan.

"Currently sitting on the floor constructing a grenade. He's right here, obviously."

Charlie's face pokes through, "Hiya guys."

"Right, give me your hands," Skye says, and Charlie extends his through the bars as best he can. Skye starts to unlock them, but as their fingers touch I notice they both look at each other, meeting the other one's gaze then blushing slightly and glancing down.

I exchange a glance with Evan. His eye brows are raised. I give him a look like: *don't tell me you seriously didn't see this coming with them?*

He shrugs, like: *bigger things to worry about.*

He'd be right, of course. I cough, "Right, if you two are quite done having a teenage romance moment, we'll be trying to get out of here."

"Was that an attempt at mimicry?" Evan calls after me.

"Wouldn't dream of it," I roll my eyes. There's the clink of handcuffs rolling to the floor, but I don't focus on that.

Instead, I inspect the bars, looking for weak spots. If I can find a weakness, and could...punch it? That would work if they were made of bamboo or something lightweight. Not iron, which these obviously are.

I could take a leaf out of Hiro's book and dropkick them, but I think that would leave me with a very sore foot and in no condition to walk. What's clear is that we need to get out of here soon. We have a day and a half to find the Alchemist's daughter. And what if she lives in the north mountains or something? That'll take us weeks to get there.

No, we need to find a way out of this cell now. Hearing footsteps, I take a cautious step back from the bars, but it's just a pair of servants shuffling in, heads bowed. A boy and a girl. Both have red hair. The boy slides bowls of gruel through the bars, the girl starts to wash the grime off the pillar. It must be important then, if they're pampering it in the middle of a prison.

But after a few seconds of this tedious labour, both servants stop. The girl gives the boy a curt nod, then moves swiftly across the room to the door. Peering out of it, she pulls out a set of keys and locks it from the inside. I watch curiously, but try to stay hidden. The others are whispering plans behind me, but the servants don't seem to pay any attention to that.

Instead, the boy stands, turns, and looks straight at me. I jolt back, but he doesn't look threatening. As far as I can see, he has no weapon. Instead, he gives me a lopsided grin.

The girl joins him, and he points straight at me. It seems the darkness wasn't enough to hide me. I narrow my eyes and step back as the two hurry towards me.

"Hey," the girl whispers, her voice urgent, "Are you all alright in there?"

"Who's this?" Skye approaches the bars warily, "Who are you and what do you want?"

"I'm Callum, this is Cecile. We're here to get you out," says the boy, taking the keys from the girl, Cecile. He rattles through the set, muttering under his breath, "Which one? Oh, geez, I'm never felt more jealous of Ceci's photographic memory. The copper? Ah, no, it was definitely silver. That's too big…"

"Why are you helping us?" I ask Cecile, who's watching Callum with amusement. She looks at me with her sharp eyes, like a wolf.

She smiles. In comparison to her brother, the smile looks slightly strange on her regal face. She reminds me of a porcelain doll. Callum, on the other hand, looks about as real as you could get, crimson hair tousled.

"We're helping you because the president's a real—" Callum begins, but Cecile cuts him off, "Because the president is blind to the truth. We heard the entire conversation. We believe you about Nerezza."

"Yeah, that lady means serious shady business," Callum says, "Rumours on the servitude grapevine say she's been doing something important. Out in the North. Whatever it is, it could completely change everything. Not for the better, that's for sure."

Cecile snatches the keys off Callum, "You're wasting time. It's the small copper one. How many of you are in there?"

"Three," I say, "But our friends Evan and Charlie are next door."

"Hi," I can hear Evan through the wall, "Are we missing the party?"

Cecile looks at me, "Is he always like that?"

"You have no idea," I groan. Cecile locates the key and slides it into the lock. The door opens with a creak. Anita appears, bouncing on the balls of her feet, "Ok, what now?"

"We need to get that map," me and Skye say at the same time.

"Oh don't worry about us," comes Evan's sarcastic voice again, "We'll just wait until you're all done."

Callum laughs, "I like this guy. Ok," he grabs the key of Cecile and unlocks their cell, "Now you guys are out. I'll take some of you up to surface. Ceci will take some to get the map and get out."

"Charlie, Skye, Anita, go with Cecile," I say, "Me and Evan will get out and get the leopards. Unless they've been locked up?" I look to the two servants.

"Um, you mean like a load of huge leopards in prison? I'm pretty sure I would've seen them," says Callum, "Or heard them. Or whatever. You ok with this, sis?" He looks to Cecile.

She nods determinedly, "Right, you three, come with me. Oh, and I think these belong to you." she hands Skye her bow and arrows, somehow mended, then the rest of us our daggers.

There's faint voices outside, and Cecile straightens, "Ok, we've really got to go."

"Meet us at the back entrance," Callum instructs. I frown,

"Won't that be guarded?"

He grins like a devil, "Not the way we're going."

25
ESCAPE

For such a nice palace, the prison quarters, in my opinion, need serious renovating. On the other hand, growing up in a shabby one floor apartment with like twenty other people, what do I know about decor?

Callum leads us through twisting and winding tunnels, each one dark with rough walls and the ever constant sound of dripping water from pipes above. We press ourselves against the wall at every corner, but no guards emerge. My hands are tingling again, like they want me to do something, only I have no clue what. And since I'm not keen on a repeat of the throne room…it's better to not think about it.

The fact that Anita and Skye don't judge me for what happened…is really *nice* of them. No matter how courageous in battle, I'd only want to go on a dangerous quest with people I could call friends.

Skye came around slowly, but I think we're ok now. We've

definitely got each other's backs. I think Charlie doesn't mind my company either. Anita's always been there for me. And Evan…again the loose thread.

I don't know what he thinks. It's impossible to tell with anyone, but especially with him. I remember him saying 'I'm on her side' in the throne room. That was after the magic incident. But was he lying for the sake of the team? I wouldn't be surprised.

I also remember Tempest saying that magic was thought of differently in some places. Violana seems to have accepted Evan well enough, but he's artistry. Ah, the joys of having a nice, normal power, instead of this infinite stuff that I've got to deal with.

Dealing with it…isn't the right word. I shouldn't be dealing with it. It's not strong, it's not brave, it doesn't make the good qualities of a leader to just…deal with it. I should own it, use it, master it, and protect my team with it. It's what Hiro would want me to do.

"Alrighty," Callum says cheerfully, "Letting you both know that there's guards around the corner looking for you. I'll distract them with a bit of sweet talk, you two stay here and don't make a sound, ok?"

"Ok," I nod. I don't trust Callum to open a cardboard box, let alone cover for us, but maybe he's a better liar than I thought. He certainly has that streetwise, humorous attitude I see in Parker.

He bounces off down the tunnel, up towards the guards, "Hey, guys, what can I do for you…?"

His voice fades away as he subtly walks the guards in the

other direction. I crane my neck to look. Just then Evan taps my hand and whispers urgently, "Avery!"

"What?" I turn around fast. He points to something on the wall. I squint. The same bird symbol. Maybe it's a national crest.

"I don't get your point," I say to Evan.

He rolls his eyes, "Same bird we saw in the throne room. Maybe it's important?"

"Maybe," I say, "But the important thing right now is getting out of here."

"Of course it is," he sighs, but he sounds sort of annoyed.

I frown, "You got a problem with that?"

He pinches the bridge of his nose like I'm frustrating him, "Are we going to talk about the throne room? At all?"

I could play dumb. 'What in particular might you be referencing?' Tease him. Etc. But he's right (Ugh). We need to talk about it.

"Not right now," I say, glancing down the tunnel again. Callum's still gone. As long as he's not with us, we're in more danger. The president might not be so lenient this time. Our heads on spikes would make quite a mess outside, however.

"Why not?"

"Because it's a really bad time, obviously!"

He frowns, "Ok, look, that came out wrong. I'm not here to

judge you about it—"

"That's a first," I mutter.

"I'm here to check you're ok? Did it hurt?"

Ok. That's a first.

"What are you, a doctor?"

"Someone has to be the responsible one, don't they?"

"You've spent half the trip unconscious," I remind him.

"It wasn't half the trip!" He protests, "It was like twenty minutes in Picasar!"

"Yeah right," I laugh and look back down the hallway. Two shadows appear at the other end and I clamp my hand over Evan's mouth as he starts to say something, "Shut up."

The guards peer down the hallway. Then start walking towards us. Oh no. I press myself as far into the wall as I can and try to blend in, but they get five paces and then, with a nonchalant grunt from one, they turn around and go the other way. I let out a tiny sigh of relief. We're safe. That was close.

I release Evan, who frowns, "Your hands are freezing."

I blink, "Why is that important?"

"Are you in shock?"

"That's enough, Dr Onceller!"

At that moment Callum appears, looking worried and breathless.

"They're c-coming!" he stutters, "We-go-that way-f-follow me!"

We jump to our feet and sprint down the hallway. Again, I can hear guards' shouting following us, but this time there's something else. Rough, loud barks. They've brought hunting dogs.

Callum takes a right, then a left, then a right, until we hit a dead end.

"Now what?" I ask him.

He sweeps away the black curtain to reveal that it is not a dead end at all. My eyes widen. Instead there's a wide silver ladder leading to a manhole entrance. I'm getting flashbacks of the subway with Parker. The day that everything changed.

Callum pulls us forward, "The ladder won't hold, so try not to put weight on it. Instead, try and walk yourself up using these," he holds out a long rope with loops for the three of us. I've never used one in my entire life, but I somehow stumble into the loop and tighten it, until it fits snugly around my waist. Callum does the same, and Evan, who's sketching something on the ground.

"What are you doing? We have to go!" I say to him. The guards and dogs barrel around the corner and my heart stutters.

The dogs are definitely not the scrappy brutes I've seen in Zoriana. These are sleek dogs, half the size of me with faces like wolves. Their fangs are razor sharp. Their eyes glow hungrily. Evan's still sketching.

"Come on!" I say, more urgently.

"One second!"

"What in the world are you doing?"

"This." He steps back as a stone wall materialises. The dogs slam into with the force of trucks. It trembles.

"That won't last," Evan swallows, "Let's go."

Callum's already halfway up the wall. I place my feet either side of the rope and attempt to pull myself along. My palms burn. My muscles strain.

But slowly, slowly we're making progress. Behind us, the wall trembles. A couple of bricks fall. There's a gunshot on the other side. It pierces a hole in the stone and lands an inch from my head.

The top is almost in reach. Callum looks urgent, terrified. Just then the wall behind me caves in, as Evan slips. I catch his hand before he can fall, because the weight of his rope and body on my arm would send us both tumbling down. It's taking all the strength I have to hold him up.

"Hold on!" I say. He nods, terrified. His legs are kicking at the air, trying to find a grip. I know the feeling.

The dogs leap, jaws gnashing at the air. One of them snags Evan's leg and he lets out a cry of pain, eyes squeezed shut. The dogs pull away, fangs dripping with his blood.

"Callum, you need to pull us up!" I say. I'm in no shape to

227

try, neither is Evan. He nods, looking terrified. Slowly, we shift upwards. I grit my teeth and attempt to move my legs. Hoisting Evan up is a strain, but I ignore the pain and push upwards as much as I can. The rope digs into my palm.

My boot slips and hit one of the iron rungs. It echoes with a clang, and pain shoots through my foot. Just like Zoriana, I'm left hanging, one hand on the wall, both legs dangling. *Why does this happen to me so much?* think.

The dogs' eyes are glowing, hungry for blood. They're not leaping now. They know we're about to fall and become their dinner. Callum's holding on with all his might, but if he lets go, we're dead.
The guards are watching, amused. One laughs. I grit my teeth. I can get us out of this. If it'll listen.

I imagine the familiar tingling, but this time, for Anemology. Will it work? The tingling, sure enough, flows through my veins. I try and picture wind pushing us up. Instead, I'm hit with a strong burst coming sideways. I smack into the hard stone wall.

There's a metallic taste of blood in my mouth. I must've bit my tongue. My forehead is throbbing, my painful foot seems to explode, and the tingling is gone.

Where are the others? Are they hurt? I've never needed them more.

The rope in front of me makes a ripping noise. Oh great. Like this situation couldn't get worse. The strands slowly snap, one by one, until we're dangling by a thread. The throbbing in my head begins to make my vision blur. I can hear Callum shouting, panicked, but it sounds like I'm underwater. Evan says something indiscernible, as my hand slowly slips. I grasp it, trying to make the images stay in focus, but my palms are slick with sweat, and stinging.

Nerezza's laugh echoes in my ears.

The rope breaks and we fall backwards, screaming.

Then, all of a sudden, we're floating upwards, out into the sunlight. Are we dead? Are we going to heaven?

But no, around us is Adriana. Our friends are crouched over the manhole and Anita has her hands outstretched. Slowly, we float down to the ground. My vision swims, but I force myself to stay conscious.

"You saved us," I croak.

Anita tackles me in a hug, "You're alive! Yay!"

Skye laughs, "Give her breathing space. You ok down there?" she smiles, looking worried.

"Just a bit dizzy," I say, trying to stand up. The world looks like a funfair ride and I sway. Surprisingly, Evan catches me, "Woah, careful. You hit your head?"

I don't have time to answer before my vision goes dark.

26
JOURNEY

"Is she ok?"

"How am I supposed to know? She's unconscious!"

"No fever from what I can tell. Where did she hit her head?"

"A stone wall."

"Oh heck, that's not good."

"Is she concussed?"

"She's waking up, guys! Everyone shut up!"

The babble of voices wakes me up fully. I blink in the bright sunlight of Adriana. The white is slightly blinding. My vision's cleared, so I can see my friends, kneeling over me, staring down at where I'm lying. I sit up, palms hurting, but otherwise feeling ok.

"You're awake!" Anita cries, looking relieved. Even Skye looks happy. Cecile gently takes my chin and tilts it up, "Look at the sun for me, ok?"

I do as she says, though it hurts my eyes.

"No concussion," Cecile declares, "She's alright."

"Yay!" Anita gives me another hug. Skye squeezes my arm. Charlie, looking hesitant, pats me on the back.

"What happened?" My voice sounds slightly raspy.

"You passed out," Callum says, "Scared the life out of us."

"How long was I unconscious?" I ask, gingerly feeling my head. It throbs a little, but I feel much better. Maybe fainting does that.

"Only around ten minutes," Anita reassures, "And look who showed up!"

There's a mewling sound and Nyota appears, nuzzling her head into my lap.

"Hey, girl," I say, stroking her, "You alright?"

Nyota lets out a forlorn yowl like: *only if you are.*

"I'm fine," I tell her, "It's ok."

She gives my hand a lick, her whiskers tickling. I laugh and scratch behind her ear.

"And, even better news," Charlie says, "We got the map!"

"Really?" I lean forward eagerly, "Where?"

He hands me it. The scroll tingles in my hands, but this time, luckily I don't get a weird hallucination.

Gently, I pull the other two out of my jacket. Miraculously, they seemed undamaged. I lay them out of the floor. The others crowd in, eager to see what will happen.

And what will happen? Will I hallucinate again? Have another vision? I don't even know what happens to me when I have one: do I faint? Do I fall asleep?

"Just warning you all," I say, keeping my voice light, "I might, um, faint again. Or collapse. Or whatever. When I touch these things…that's when I usually have one of the visions."

"Don't worry," Anita says, "We caught you last time. We'll catch you again. Besides, it'll be fine."

I wish I could believe her. Carefully, I unroll the other scrolls. They seem to be…maps. I can see jagged terrain, clusters of buildings for the three capitals, and a long, pulsing golden thread of light, leading across all three. My eyes follow it, from the starting point to…where is that? The place is dark, shrouded with trees. Just looking at it gives me a jolt, like I know it from somewhere, but I have no clue what.

"What's that forest?" I murmur, carefully touching the thread of light. Luckily, I don't zone out.

Evan frowns at it, "I've never seen that place before. Charlie?"

Charlie frowns, adjusting his glasses, "There are stories.

Legends, rumours. But I've never seen it on a map."

"Maybe the president doesn't want anyone to find that place," I say.

"That's near Darkswift," Cecile says, unexpectedly, pointing at a point in the forest, where the golden light thins slightly, as if something's interfering with its magic.

We all blink at her. She frowns, "None of you have heard of Darkswift?"

"Not in the slightest," I say.

"It's like a ghost town," Cecile said, "It's bad luck to go anywhere near there."

"And just our luck, we have to walk straight through it," says Evan flatly.

Callum glances at his sister, looking frightened, "I'm pretty sure we're both in favour of not going with these guys, right? Anywhere near Darkswift and," he shudders, "I might wet myself."

"What's wrong with it? Is it haunted?" I ask.

Cecile frowns, "Not exactly. You'll see when you get there."

"Something's bothering me," Evan says.

"Something's always bothering you," Skye replies.

"No, seriously," he says, rolling his eyes.

"Shoot, then," I say, frowning at him.

"What's Nerezza's plan? What happens if she gets what she wants? What does she want?"

I shrug, "Evan, I...I honestly don't know. She said something to me in one of the dreams, like: *'What does anyone want? Money, power, adoration. And you will help me get all three.'*"

Anita shivers, "That is spooky. Money and adoration I get. Power, sort of. What kind of power is she talking about?"

"There's only one kind of power, isn't there?" I reply, "Power over others."

"And that's bad enough," Charlie says, "But Anita's got a point. Power...like infinite magic?"

"We all know the stakes of the prophecy," Evan whispers, "That kind of power in the wrong hands? Not good. Not good at all."

I think of the stakes. He's right. The prophecy never actually said whether we'd survive. *Five shall face the wild, seek the descendant of gold.*

But it never said we'd succeed. And one of us facing their worst nightmare twice? A deadly weapon? Two armies? A king falling? What does any of that mean?

"Well, there's only one way to find out," I say grimly, "Buckle up. Let's find this Alchemist's daughter."

Soon we're racing across the terrain. The maps are hard to read and keep trying to blow away, but somehow we stay on track. The golden light pulses, as if it has a heartbeat.

I've never been in this part of the desert. Jagged rocks loom up from the ground like broken teeth. We're skirting around the edges of the north mountains, so there's a cool wind blowing.

My head still aches, and my foot still throbs. I tried to heal myself and the others back in Violana, but it didn't work. Maybe the maps are interfering with my magic. Or maybe the closer we get to this haunted town the more unpredictable my powers become.

I banish the thought. I've got enough to worry about without my own infinite powers going loco.

Nyota and the other leopards stand out a mile, which makes me uncomfortable. Their grey fur catches the hazy sunlight and sparkles like molten silver. The whole desert stretches in drab colours of beige and dark grey. Three huge leopards with riders probably isn't helping us blend in.

The air feels static. I feel like I should be holding my breath, so as not to disturb anything. I'm not the only one who's tense. Skye's fingers are tight on her arrows. Charlie keeps glancing at her. Anita's creating little bursts of wind, and Evan's fiddling with his pen. I've not noticed before, but he seems to carry it everywhere. I guess you would, if you could make the things you draw real.

I look back at him, "Can you use Artistry with just your hands?"

He blinks, "What?"

"I said, can you use Artistry with just your hands," I can't help smirking as I remember our first conversations, which went a lot like this.

"I know what you said," he says, exasperated, "And yeah, I probably could. I choose not to a lot."

I give him a questioning look, so he continues, "A pen gives me more control. I'm clumsier with just my fingers."

"Never pegged you as the clumsy type."

"Never pegged you as the type who was interested in my powers."

His statement leaves me feeling defensive, "What's that supposed to mean? That I don't worship you like Chloe Moscopello?"

"No," his brow furrows, "Are you still mad about that?"

"No. She got to me. I'm over it," I snap, "Just don't want you to think I'm an ignorant leader."

"I never said you were ignorant," he points out, "Just that you don't really ask about my powers."

"Is that a problem?"

"No, I-Ah, never mind."

He pushes his hair out of his eyes and looks over his shoulder, "I can't even see Violana anymore. Where are we?"

I glance at the map, "Somewhere near the north mountains."

Evan glances at the mountains, "We're that far up?"

"I guess so," I say, "I didn't learn geography, remember?"

"Yeah, well, that's not your fault, is it? You can't help where you grew up."

"For the record, Zoriana isn't a bad place," I say, "I liked it. I had a family. Most kids didn't get that."

"When did your parents die?"

"When I was really young. Five, younger, maybe. Hiro found me when I was six," I say, "I don't remember much before."

"Oh. I'm sorry."

He sounds genuinely sincere. I wonder if this is always how interactions between us will go. We'll be snapping at each other and then suddenly we'll actually get along. Weird.

"I can't believe Cecile and Callum actually helped us," Evan muses.

"Why? Because they're servants?"

"No," he sounds annoyed now, "Just because I had servants as a kid doesn't mean I think any less of them."

"You had servants as a kid?" To be honest, I probably should've realised that.

"Is that a problem?"

"Was that an attempt at mimicry?"

"Ha, ha," he says sarcastically, "But I'm serious. Does it bother you that I had servants?"

"Only because in a different world," I hesitate, "Well, I could've been one of those servants. If Hiro hadn't found me."

Evan gives me an unreadable glance, "Oh. Yeah," he looks a bit sheepish, "I guess, but…we don't live in that world. And- OH MY GOODNESS WHAT IS THAT?"

I turn, and nearly fall backwards off Nyota.

27
HEADS OR TAILS?

The first thing I think goes something like this: arghahahahagahgghhhhhhhhh!!!

Standing in front of us is the biggest scorpion I've seen in my life. It's taller than me, with a thick obsidian shell and spiked black barbs on its legs. Its pincers are like meat hooks. Its eyes are small and clouded and rheumy. Its mouth is crowded with razor sharp fangs. And its tail is sharp as a spear end, with barbed black spikes and a point like a dagger. Green substance oozes from the end. Possibly venomous, then.

Nyota howls in fear and backs off, but the scorpion swings its long tail and nearly hits me across the head.

I jump off her back and draw my dagger. The scorpion has its attention focused entirely on us at this point. I can only hope the others have gotten away.

A silver tipped arrow embeds in a tiny chink in the scorpion's armour and it hisses and shrieks. The sound reminds me of nails across a chalk board and I wince. It turns to where Skye, Anita, and Charlie are standing in a defensive position. Behind them the leopards have scarpered in fear. Evan jumps off Nyota and she quickly follows suit, giving me a mournful look that says: *'We'll come back for you'* before she vanishes in a blur. I give Evan a nod and turn back to face the threat.

The scorpion is advancing on Anita, Charlie, and Skye, seemingly unhurt by the arrow. Its pincers click ominously. I do the stupidest thing possibly, which is charge.

Before it can register what's happening, I slide underneath it and slit its stomach with my dagger. The sharpened point hardly makes a dent. Instead, the scorpion shrieks and stabs at me with its legs. I roll out of the way and try to keep a hold on my dagger as it deflects another arrow from Skye.

Charlie launches a grenade at the monster, which bounces off its hard shell and nearly blows Evan to pieces. He dodges, "Thanks Charlie!"

"Sorry!" he calls back sheepishly, before the scorpion throws itself at him with the force of a moving truck, hissing in anger. Acid green venom spews from its tail.

"Split up!" I say, "Spread out! Give it more to fight at once!"

The others obey my command. Charlie unlatches a grenade and drops it on the ground where he's standing, then throws himself sideways as the scorpion barrels right into the weapon's range. The bomb explodes, but it only mildly wounds the scorpion, who looks at its charred, smoking claw, bemused, and then at a petrified Charlie.

Furious, it scuttles after him, but Anita sends a gust of wind like a shield, and the monster is slammed backwards. Screeching in anger, it rolls over and whips its tail. Anita's hit hard in the chest and goes flying backwards, crumpling against a rock. My heart drops.

"Anita!" I cry, horrified. The scorpion turns to the sound of my voice. I glower, "You want a piece? Come on, you oversized spider!"

The scorpion roars and attacks, but a net explodes over it from an arrow. It growls and hisses and struggles, ripping the strong golden material like it's paper. Evan aims a throwing knife for its eye, but it misses and deflects off the scorpion's amour. One flick of its tail and Evan's sent flying backwards, clutching his stomach. Unlike Anita, at least he's moving.

"We have to find a chink in its armour!" yells Skye.

"The stomach!" I say. Skye somersaults upwards, pushing herself forward until she's directly on top of the scorpion. She plunges an arrow hard into one of the chinks in its back and it shrieks, throwing her off. She goes flying and smacks hard into a towering rock.

I run at the scorpion again, but it lunges with its pincers. One slices right across my arm, ripping my jacket and leaving a splatter of blood across the sand. Another grenade is unlatched with a click.

"Avery, get back!" Charlie calls, and I do, leaping backwards as a grenade flies towards the scorpion, aiming for its fleshy, exposed stomach. The scorpion flicks the grenade so fast I only have time to start to speak, "Charlie watch o—" before it implodes and sends him flying back into a smoking crater.

It's only me now. Evan's fallen sword is on the ground. I pick it up and wield it, tucking my dagger away. A sword will do me better.

The blood loss is making me dizzy and the stench of the scorpion makes my head swim. The thought of the others' immobile bodies spurs me on. I can't let them die. I will not let them die.

"Avery," a weak voice coughs, hardly audible. Evan, still holding his stomach, a bloodied scrape across his forehead, is sketching something in the sand. His pen is gone, but he's using one fingertip to draw something. He looks up and catches my eye, "Make it-c-come here. Right here," he taps the drawing.

The thought of leading the monster to where Evan's already nearly dead makes me sickened, but I don't have time to ponder the request before the scorpion lashes again. I block the strike, my blade trembling under the pressure of the scorpion's pincers.

I slowly walk backwards. This is the strangest face off I've ever done: me, scraped and bruised with a nearly bust ankle, stumbling backwards towards my half dead comrade. The scorpion, powerful, terrifying, a hungry look in its eye. Impossible to beat. Unless we can get a knife into its stomach.

And suddenly Evan's plan makes more sense.

I take a deep breath. The sharp, venomous point of the scorpion's tail comes whipping round, and I duck, then deflect one of its pincers with my sword. Irritated, the scorpion lunges in an attempt to snap my head off. I dodge the strike and move further backwards. The scorpion doesn't seem to notice nor care about Evan, who's lying there, playing dead. It's worryingly realistic. One of his hands is just lying on the drawing.

I step back over the drawing, but the scorpion doesn't follow. Maybe it can sense the danger. I bare my teeth at it, "Come on then. Fight me."

It hisses, and lunges. Evan's eyes flash open and he yanks his hand up. I close my eyes and brace myself for the pain. But there's nothing. A millimetre away from my face, the scorpion stops, frozen. It looks down in mild surprise at the sharp sword impaling its stomach, right through its gut. Then it lets out a high squeal and collapses, dead.

I sink to my knees in the sand. Evan's hand falls limp and he coughs, clutching his stomach. Ignoring the pain in my arm, I kneel over him, "Oh heck."

"Is it bad?" He rasps.

Yeah, it's pretty bad. His forehead is covered in blood.

I don't answer, instead asking, "Are you winded?"

"Nothing's broken," he answers, "But yeah, I still can't breathe properly."

"Don't move," I instruct, taking a deep breath and placing a hand on his forehead. I place the other one on his stomach, and try to focus. For a second, the only sound is the wind through the desert. I feel nothing but Evan's sporadic pulse. Then the tingling sensation returns, stronger than ever, as if it knows my friends need me.

The cut on Evan's forehead vanishes, and his breathing becomes regular quickly. His heart rate returns to normal, and he sits up, "Wow, that was fast. How did you do that?"

"I don't know, but I'm not going to jinx it," I say. A shape appears out of the smoking craters of grenades and there's Charlie, limping and pale but otherwise ok.

"Are you hurt?" I rush over.

He shakes his head, "Barely. I think I may have sprained an ankle, but otherwise I'm fine. Where's Skye and Anita?"

His eyes land on Skye, who's lying immobile against the rock. His face whitens, "Skye!"

He runs over and I follow, crouching down and feeling her pulse. Strong. None of her limbs look broken. Thank goodness. Charlie whispers her name while I focus on the tingling. Miraculously, Skye sits up, colour returning to her face, "Ouch. I think I've broken a rib. Did we kill it?"

"Yeah. It's ok. Are you alright?" Charlie asks, "Are you hurt? How many ribs? Any concussion?"

"You worry too much," Skye says, rolling her eyes.

Evan arrives, carrying a limp Anita. I beckon him over while Charlie feels Skye's temperature. One hand on Skye's ribs, I place the other on Anita's shoulder, where one of the barbs got her. Her jacket is spattered with blood.

Slowly, I close my eyes. The tingling feels like a river. The others fall respectfully silent, save for Skye's exhale of relief as her ribs mend. I can feel Anita stirring beneath my hand and I focus more of the energy into her, like tilting a weighing scale. I've never tried to control my Anatomy magic like that before. Yet, somehow, it works. Anita sits up, and I open my eyes to see her beaming, "Wow. What a fight. How long was I out?"

I give her a hug, blinking back relieved tears, "You're awake now. Do you feel ok?"

Anita nods confidently, "Perfect, thanks to your awesome Anatomy stuff!"

I laugh, "I try. Charlie, give me your ankle."

He shakes his head, "You're still bleeding, Avery. You should go first."

I blink, "I'm fine."

"No, you're not," Evan says, "Charlie's right. Heal yourself."

"Charlie can't walk anywhere until I heal him," I snap.

"You did just fight a giant scorpion with a sprained ankle," Charlie reminds me.

I put my hand on his ankle and close my eyes so I don't see the others' expressions. The tingling makes fast work, and I take my hand away, "Ok. That should work."

"Heal yourself," Anita urges.

"But what about the leopards?"

Skye folds her arms, "Heal yourself, or I punch you."

I do as she commands. I can't help a smile at their concern for me. It's endearing. I've never felt so…needed. Appreciated. Asset or not.

The leopards arrive on their own, no longer skittish now the scorpion is dead. Eager not to linger, we ride away from that particular area as quickly as we can.

Soon a vast green forest stretches before us. The air seems to drop five degrees. Nyota's hackles raise, and I smooth them down gently, "Easy, easy. Nothing in there is going to hurt us."

We both know that may not be true.

The second we enter the trees I feel like I've crossed a border. The air thrums with energy. Through the evergreens, dappled sunlight casts patches of warm golden light across the ground. I slow Nyota down to a light trot, in case anything springs out at us. Then there's the strangest sound. There's a giggle.

I sit up straight, "Did you guys hear that?"

"Hear what?" Anita asks, confused.

I shake my head, "Never min-there it was again!" as another clear, high chuckle echoes.

Evan leans away from me, looking wary, "What are you hearing?"

"Laughter," I say. Just then there comes another laugh, this one warm and deep. A murmur of voices seem to whisper on the wind. The sounds are clear and strong and definitely not my imagination. Why can't the others hear them?

Nyota jolts backward as a beam of golden light appears on the ground in front of us, leading through the trees.

"Tell me you all see that," I say, staring at it. It looks almost like the one on the map, but different. More direct. More powerful. Like pure concentrated sunlight. I pull out the scrolls. The thread of light is faint here, like the map's power can't connect properly.

"See what? Avery… are you ok?" Charlie asks. Skye shushes him, "Wait."

"I know where this leads," I murmur. There's a strange warm, tugging feeling in my gut.

Evan meets my eyes, "So where does it lead?"

I look back down at the line, which pulses impatiently. The giggle echoes again, followed by the sound of clapping and whistling, voices and laughter. Like a forgotten place.

"This," I whisper, "This is the path to Darkswift."

28
DARKSWIFT

Callum wasn't kidding when he said this place is creepy. I feel like I've walked into a ghost town.

The ground is grey, uneven and charred. The buildings are crumbling ruins: walls caved in, wooden frames shattered, roofs collapsed and shattered tiles everywhere. The lone walls that are standing are choked with creepers or half burnt to cinders. I trace my fingers along one, and they come away coated with a film of soot.

Porcelain statues lie, cracked and grimy, against the ground, staring at us with mournful expressions and blank, unseeing eyes. Blackened trees loom over the village, spindly frames leering down at us. A frayed rope swing hangs from one.

My palms feel clammy, and the chilling wind seems to creep into my very core. Ahead of us, an old dried up fountain still stands, dusty and empty. The inscriptions on its towering tiers are illegible scrawls by now.

Few houses are still remaining, but it seems one or two survived. Their windows are broken or shattered completely, and ivy has clung to them so thickly I can't tell where the vines end and the stone walls begin. Empty doorframes and windows gape back at me like hollow eyes.

Not a sound carries on the wind, as if even the slightest noise has decided to stay far away from this place. The golden light that led us here has faded into a burnt streak. Even magic itself fears this town.

Yet there's an unmistakable cold presence, like something's watching us. Sometimes I swear I can see figures move in the trees.

We've reached what I think was maybe the town square. Once, long ago. I can picture it in my mind: bustling, colourful, the scent of freshly baked bread mingling with the smell of blossoming roses, and the joyous chatter and laughter ever present.

Now? It's desolate. The roses are long since dead and rotting. Maybe once a bakery, the shop is boarded and blackened. The sign still swings in the cold breeze.

And in the very centre of it all, there's a tree. Not charred and cindered like the ones bordering the forest, but old, and bare. As if the summer itself can't touch it.

Hanging from its branches are old glass baubles and trinkets, sparkling gold. I can see yellowing notes, colourful ribbons, necklaces and padlocks adorning its branches. The dead grass we're standing upon feels like sacred ground. If I listen very carefully, I can almost hear the voices of the people who hung these things.

And the most unsettling thing of all. I feel a strange sense of belonging. Like a missing piece. This town means something. I know it.

"We shouldn't be here," Evan whispers, voice hoarse. He looks terrified. They all do.

I shiver in the bracing cold, "You're right. Let's go. Whatever led us here is gone," I nod to the ground. The others turn to go back to where we left the leopards at the forest edge, but I feel frozen in place.

Evan looks over his shoulder, brow furrowing, "Hey? Are you coming?"

I nod, "Uh, yeah. Just…one sec. Go on ahead."

He shakes his head, "No. If you're staying, I'm staying. Being here alone is a death sentence."

He stands next to me but doesn't say anything else. I take the silence as a chance to think. Closing my eyes, I can still hear faint voices and laughter. It all sounds so…happy. What could've happened?

As if answering my question, the voices quieten. Faint shouts, yells, panicked shouting and helpless screams replace them. I take a step backwards as an image hits me with shocking vividness. Fire. A terrible fire. Maybe a tragic accident. Or maybe…

Maybe something else.

My eyes fly open, "I think we have to leave," I say quickly, my voice trembling.

Evan nods, relieved, "I couldn't agree more."

We turn and catch up with the others, who are lingering at the edge of the village.

Skye's eyes are unfocused as she says, "What happened to this place?"

I don't have an answer to that. All I know is that, once a bustling centre of life, this place is...dead.

Nyota yowls behind us. I spin around, dagger raised, expecting an attack, but she's curled up and twitching in discomfort. The other leopards form a protective ring around her, and as I run forward to help, one snaps at me. I take a step back, shocked.

They've never snapped at us before. But now they're all snarling and growling, eyes flashing dangerously. What's going on? Has Nerezza somehow turned them against us?

I hold up my hands to reveal I'm weaponless, "Hey. Hey now..." I use my softest voice, making my tone gentle as I can, "It's just us. See?"

I hold out my hand to the nearest one. It doesn't move. Its golden eyes bore into me with startling fierceness.

"Nyota?" I try, "Can you hear me? Are you alright?"

She yowls in response, but doesn't move. *Because she can't,* I realise. She's hurt. Somehow. But there's no blood, no visible wound.

Then, as quickly as it all started, it all stops. Nyota lifts her trembling head and gives me a mournful look. The leopards visibly relax. With a slightly begrudgingly look in its eye, the one in front of me moves.

I rush to Nyota's side and feel along her ribs for broken bones. She mewls softly, weakly.

"Hey, girl," I say soothingly, "You're ok. You're alright. Talk to me, ok? Are you injured? Where does it hurt?"

I can sense the others giving each other looks behind me. They probably think I've gone crazy, talking to an animal like it can understand.

The look in Nyota's eyes makes it clear she understands, but she can't speak back. Not in a language I'll understand. I feel a surge of frustration. We need her. I need her to be ok. I want her to be ok. So what's going on?

Then something even stranger happens. Nyota rises shakily and tilts her head at me.

The other leopards follow suit, approaching the others and offering their sides.

"Ok, what is happening?" Anita asks, confused, "Last I checked, these guys liked us. Then they suddenly hated us, now they want us to ride them? Is this a trap? Did Nerezza pull some voodoo magic?"

"I don't think so," I say slowly, "If she did, they would have killed us already. Right?"

"We're discussing our hypothetical deaths now," Evan says sarcastically, "This trip just keeps getting better and better!"

The sense that something's watching me creeps up my spine like cold fingers and I cast a wary look at Darkswift, "I think the most important thing is getting away from here. I don't like it."

"Sing it sister," Charlie mutters, "You're not the only one."

I feel the urge to high five him, but Nyota butts my hand and I turn to her, "Can you do this?"

If she understands, she doesn't show it. But she nudges me with her side as if to say: *'just get on, ok?'*

I don't know what happened earlier, or why she was in pain. But if I can't find the problem, I can't heal her. Maybe after this we can find some kind of vet? But right now we need to get to the Alchemist's daughter. We're fast running out of time.

I feel awful, even as I opt to ride on a different leopard with Anita so Nyota doesn't have weight on her. Are we any better than her captors if we're putting her through another journey?

I wish I could know what was wrong. But it all happened so suddenly… everything on this trip has happened suddenly.

No more surprises, I think to myself, *I need to be smarter. I will be smarter. Nothing will take us by surprise again: not on my watch.*

It's almost funny how wrong I am.

We've hardly gone two paces when there's a crack. A net springs up out of nowhere, trapping us and knocking the air out of my lungs as we're thrown into a tangle. Someone kicks me in the mouth by accident, hard enough that I can taste blood. I thrash wildly, trying to get my hand to my dagger, but my vision's clouding over with…smoke?

Then the world crumples to blackness.

29
HIDDEN IN THE FOREST

I'm awake before I open my eyes, and the first thing I register is pain. It's not awful, agonising, but it's fierce and burning and makes my head swim. If my eyes were open, my vision would be blurry.

I'm hanging upside down. Of that, I'm sure about. I can smell woodsmoke, and oil, and wet undergrowth. My hair is in my face, so as I open one eye a crack, my vision is half obscured. I twist my neck to get a better look around.

We're in a small, cosy room, with wooden floors and a low ceiling. A fire crackles in the hearth I'm facing. *So at least we haven't been kidnapped by cannibals,* I muse, *they would've hung us over the fire and cooked us alive.*

Yeah, blood going to my head is definitely making me woozy.

The ropes around me are taut and strong. There's nothing I can do to break out of these binds. I tilt my head again, trying to get a better view of where I am. Out of the corner of my eye I can see Skye hanging to my left, still unconscious. I try turning the other way.

I somehow spin around to face a window. The windowsill is cluttered with copper wires and machines. The glass is patched with thin strands of glue. Like it shattered.

And suddenly an image springs to mind. My nightmare, the alchemists home. The shattered window as Nerezza stepped in, darkness coiling around her...

I blink. I can't get lost in that dream again. It was bad enough living it the first time. But there's no doubt that we've found ourselves in the Alchemist's home.

The room is dimly lit, candles flickering faintly and casting shadows across the walls. An old armchair sits in the middle of the room. And as my eyes continue to adjust, I notice three dark shapes slumped on the floor. The leopards.

The armchair is empty, but laid carefully on it are our weapons. So whoever has taken us has disarmed us, but they're not trying to kill us? This is getting weirder and weirder.

My eyes sweep across the room, and I take in as much as I can. There's a lot to look at.

Machines, pipes, glass chemistry sets, and other gadgets clutter the tables and shelves. In pride of place over the fire is a picture of a smiling man, dark eyes crinkled with joy as he beams down at the room. Over the fire is a pot with smoke drifting from it.

A worn rug lies on the floor, which is scuffed and littered

with mud, presumably from the small pile of uprooted plants sitting by the hearth.

I can't make out the far side of the room, but it looks like there might be a staircase if I squint.

The silence is broken only by the crackling of the fire and the soft whirs and beeps of the machines. We appear to be hanging from hooks off the ceiling. I crane my head to try and see the rope tethering me. Maybe I can reach it?

My hands are bound at my sides so tightly I can hardly feel my fingers. I dig my nails into the rough rope, trying to claw my way free. It has no effect.

I take a deep breath. I can do this. I can get us out of here.

My hand starts tingling on cue, like my magic couldn't agree more.

I focus on the tingling, imagining…what exactly? That one of the daggers will soar over here and cut my binds? That's a risky game, especially as I'm not keen to get cut in half. Still, it's worth a try.

I lock eyes with the handle of one, picturing it in my mind's eye. I imagine it flying towards me, stopping at the safe distance, then cutting swiftly through my binds.

It jolts forward, but the tingling vanishes as quickly as it came. The knife spins through the air and hits a glass bulb with a shattering sound. Footsteps race across the floor upstairs, and a shadow appears at the foot of the staircase. I can just about see two green eyes staring back at me.

Then the Alchemist's daughter steps into the light.

In oil stained trousers and a shirt with suspenders, she could've stepped right out of a workshop. A tool belt is slung around her waist and packed with gadgets. Her dark hair is tousled and tied in a plait over one shoulder. Her eyes are startling emerald green. Her light brown skin is splattered with machine oil and smeared with soot. She's wearing a pair of aviator goggles pushed up onto the top of her head. Her shoes are tall combat boots, two sizes too large but they don't impede her movement at all. She moves like a cat: quick, agile, and regally. There's a curious look in her eyes.

She walks right up to me and for a second I'm worried she's going to backhand me across the face. Instead, she brushes past me and crouches by the broken light bulb. Then she chuckles. Her voice is raspy from smoke, but warm, "Impressive. Luckily you haven't cut off the circuitry there."

She comes back and look me in the eye, "What's your name?"

"Avery," I stammer, then force the nervous edge out of my voice, "Um, would you mind letting us down here?"

"Avery...you got a last name?"

"No," I say, slightly defensively, "Now would you let us down?"

She holds up her hands in surrender, "Ok, one second. I have to make sure you're not going to blow up the place, don't I?"

I level her with the best glare I can, "We've been sent from Infino. We're here for answers. We're not going to blow you up. Can you let me down now?"

She smirks, "Infino, eh? Explains a lot." She taps something behind my back, and there's a click. My ropes fall and I tuck myself into a ball to avoid breaking my neck, though the fall is short. I push myself to my feet to face the Alchemist's daughter.

"Well, Avery of Infino, what brings you here?" she asks, "Please don't tell me you're a tourist, the last bunch nearly killed Bonnie."

"Who's Bonnie?"

She gestures to a mechanical cat, watching us from the shadows. I jump. Because despite the fact it's clearly made out of copper wires and gears, it *moves*. Like a real cat. Gently, it hops down from the stairwell and meanders over, curling around its owner's legs and giving me a suspicious look with its yellow eyes.

The Alchemist's daughter chuckles at my expression, "Oh, she's not that advanced. Not compared to Dad's old head," she gestures to the picture, "Or so they say. I've never seen it myself."

"Wait, you mean the copper head?" I ask.

"Mm hm. Good craftsmanship too. It's a shame I've only got Dad's old blueprints. Oh, I'm sorry, I should explain, shouldn't I?" she adds, seeing my confused look, "I'm Jasmine Sterling. My father was, yes, *the* Alchemist."

"And he made the copper head," I finish, "That's the reason we're here. And you've got…the blueprints?"

"Yep. Been working on them for years. When he died Dad left me a load of old projects and prototypes. Kept me busy, I guess."

That's when it clicks. The nightmare all fits. The Alchemist was the one who was killed. Which means that the baby in his arms...was Jasmine.

"How are you alive?" I ask, gawping, "You-I saw you, you were tiny! And she-Nerezza she left you to-to die! How did you-?"

Jasmine raises an eyebrow, "Have you seen this place? It's stocked with enough automatons for me to have a houseful of servants. Frankly there's not enough room for them all. I dis-activated a lot of them when I was ten. I guess you could say that's when my rebellious era started."

"So your dad programmed them to look after you?"

"Yep," she says lightly, "Gotta say, they did a pretty good job," she laughs, "And since then it's just been me."

"Oh," there's a sinking feeling in my gut, "I'm sorry."

"Hey, I'm fine," she shrugs, "Nobody bothers me here. The location of this place changes. Extra security. Besides, there's traps, as I'm sure you know."

I glance back at the others, who are still hanging up, "I do. Can you let them down?"

Jasmine surveys them, "Are they with you?"

"Yes, they're my friends. My quest team, from Infino," I say.

"Oh, I almost forgot," Jasmine snaps her fingers, "Infino! Did it happen? Did the copper head speak? That's why you're here, isn't it?"

"Yeah, sort of," I say, "We got told in a prophecy—"

"—To find the descendant of gold, of course!" Jasmine laughs, "Oh, gosh, where to begin? I suppose I'd better explain. Let's wake your friends up first."

"What do you mean?" I ask, confused.

The binds on the others click and the ropes unfold around them.

Evan groans as he hits the floor, "Ouch…," his eyes open slowly. When he sees Jasmine he rockets to his feet, "Who are you?"

"Jasmine Sterling," she says cheerfully, "At your service."

"The Alchemist's daughter," I tell Evan, who still looks shocked and bleary from being unconscious, "She's going to give us answers."

The others slowly come round, and after a lot of mumbling and groaning, they're all on their feet. Jasmine gives us all the once over, "Wow. Those jackets have seen better days haven't they?"

She nods to our outfits. I glance down at my jacket, which is ripped, bloodstained, and frankly not in good condition

"You could say that," Anita says, amused, "So…what's the story? Can you help us?"

"Ah," Jasmine's face falls, "That's the hitch, I'm afraid. You've come all this way, but," she winces.

"What?" I demand, panic rising.

Jasmine gives me a sad look, "It's not me."

30
QUESTIONS AND ANSWERS

"What do you mean it's not you?" Charlie asks, baffled, "You're the only descendant of the Alchemist. The descendant of gold!"

"Not quite," says Jasmine, frowning, "I guess I should explain."

She sits down on the chair and gestures for us all to take seats. I lean against the workbench, arms folded, "We're listening."

Jasmine takes a deep breath, "My father was working on the Copper Head long before I was born. One night, he finished it. He had no idea that it would speak a prophecy, but it did. And I'm sure you've all heard that part."

We all nod. Jasmine continues, "Anyway, word spread fast. At the time, Darkswift was still alive and bustling. All across the cities, people heard of the prophecy. Not everyone liked it," she winces, "Some liked it too much. One of these people was Nerezza. She had a name before, but no one knows her as it now."

"What was her name?" I ask.

Jasmine shrugs, "I don't know. Anyway, she tried to shape the prophecy. Take the power for herself, she wanted to be the infinite. She went on a rampage. Dark times," she shudders, "Then she came to my father. He'd hidden the head, but she demanded he give it to her. When he didn't, she killed him, and left me. As I told Avery, I was raised by the automatons he programmed for emergencies."

She nods to the room, "They taught me everything about the magic of Alchemy, but I wasn't magical. Nerezza's fault, but that's another story. Instead, I took to inventing."

Bonnie the clockwork cat appears and bounds over to Jasmine. The others all visibly recoil in shock.

"Is that your cat?" Charlie blinks.

Jasmine looks amused, "She's easily offended, so I'd watch where you tread there."

"She's...very unique," Anita says diplomatically, "You were saying?"

Then Evan frowns, "Wait, if your father hid the head, why didn't you ever try and find it?"

"I did," Jasmine corrects, "One day I found it. Then I had a surprise visitor. Your Lady Tempest herself came to me in grave sincerity, and asked to take the head into her care. To protect it from Nerezza. She'd vanished for now, but everyone still knew she existed. Tempest said as long as the head was here I would never be safe. So," she shrugs, "I gave her it, and she built Infino."

Tempest told me something different. I frown. Now I don't know who to believe: Jasmine, or the headmistress of magic school? Either way, why would she lie?

"But none of this links in to why I'm not the descendant of gold," Jasmine says, with a sigh, "In exchange for the head, Tempest gave me two things. The first was Bonnie," she holds out her hand, and Bonnie the cat scampers forward to nuzzle her, "She was an old prototype for a clockwork robot I had lying around. Tempest breathed new life into her. Literally."

"And that's why she's so…realistic," Evan realises.

"Yep. That and my genius abilities," Jasmine grins, "But the second thing Tempest gave me," she pulls something out of her tool belt and hold its out, "Was this."

I take it gently. It doesn't look like much, just a gold medallion, with a bird carved into it. Wait. Not just a bird. The bird. The one in the throne room, on the pillar, on the vault. There's a connection…

The pieces in my head are slowly falling into place, but I'm still missing a few.

Jasmine continues, "It wasn't really a gift, she said. More of a favour. She needed me to guard this with my life. She never said why, but I thought it may have something to do with Nerezza. She also promised me it would guarantee me answers. If I could figure out how it worked."

She sighs, "That was easier said than done. Like my father dedicating his life to the copper head, I dedicated my remaining years to solving it. It still doesn't work," she slumps, "But apparently they call it a *Visio Discus*. That means disc of visions. I only ever saw one thing."

"What did you see?" I ask, turning the medallion over in my fingers. The light catches in it and dances around in what could be shapes, if they focused.

"A bird," Jasmine says, "The same one that is the symbol of our world. The three cities. If you know your history, which I'm assuming most of you do, you'll know there was a war for this. The cities united under its powers. And yes, the bird had powers. There's only one, always been only one. And it's kept safe in Adriana."

"The bird in the cage," I realise. The cogs in my head go faster.

"Anyway, in the vision I saw it rising up from a pool of gold. And then, for a split second, these words rang out."

She grabs something off the side, "I recorded them while I could," on closer inspection, the thing is a camera like contraption with multiple lenses and covered in dials and knobs. She presses a button and a booming voice rings out, "*Progenium auro.*"

I recognise the voice. The one from the copper head.

"The bird is called a goldwing, because of its feathers," Jasmine explains, "And those words mean—"

"Descendant of gold," I breathe.

The pieces fall into place. Jasmine was never the descendant of gold. The bird was. Suddenly the prophecy becomes clear.

We've been looking at it *all wrong.*

Three castles hold answers, the journey behold. The castles led us to Jasmine, who had answers. Not to mention the bird on the vault, the bird on the pillar, the bird on the wall. Every castle had that symbol. A clue. And we walked right past them.

"That means," Evan looks stunned, "We've been wrong this whole time. The goldwing, the original goldwing in Adriana. That's the key. But…why do we need it?"

As if it's been called upon, suddenly the disc in my hands glows. It starts to vibrate dramatically in my hands, and I nearly drop it. The light swirls and forms into an image.

Evan sucks in a sharp breath, shocked. The others freeze. Jasmine's by my side in a flash, carefully prying the disc out of my fingers. The second it's in her hands, however, the light goes out, like a candle being blown out. Jasmine curses.

"Let me hold it," I say firmly, holding out my hand. Jasmine glances warily at me, "This could be bigger than you would imagine. Are you sure?"

"Whatever's there, we need to see it," I say. I'm confident of that. Something tells me that disc has answers. The answers Jasmine can't give us.

She hands the disc back to me. Somehow I stop my hand from shaking and curl my fingers around it. At first, nothing happens. I tilt the disc left and right, watching as the light catches on its smooth surface and the glinting engraving of the bird. Then suddenly the image glows to life, so real it's like I'm being sucked into another vision.

It's a library. Books cram the dusty, crooked shelves, leather spines warm and cracked. The floor is cold white marble, but faded, like it's years old. Birds twitter outside, and warm sunlight pours through one circular window, spotlighting our view. A man stands at the shelves, muttering under his breath as he examines the books.

Jasmine's green eyes widen, "That's my father."

The Alchemist pushes his glasses up his nose and frowns, squinting at the leather books. Now that I think about it, he looks almost exactly like Jasmine, with green eyes and wild dark hair like a mad scientist. His clothes are covered in soot.

"Aha!" with a triumphant smile, he plucks a book off the shelf and flips it open. Our view tilts, so we're looking down at the page through the Alchemist's eyes. The yellow page is crammed with thick, dark handwriting, but three words stand out.

Lamina Auro Umbrei

Blade of gold and shadows.

Somehow, I know what they mean. Just like I knew *Nyota* meant star. I glance over at the leopards, struggling to take my eyes off the picture, but they're sound asleep and look peaceful. I return my gaze to the image as it changes.

This time it's a forest at twilight. The pale moon filters through the trees, which stand like sentinels, tall and dark and spindly. A hooded figure paces in a moonlit clearing, the moons rays tinting the grass silver.

Twigs snap and the figures head snaps up. Their eyes are shocking blue.

"Do you have it?" They ask breathlessly. That voice is familiar. From where? They seem to be talking to thin air. Just then, a second cloaked figure materialises. Out of thin air. *Teleported?* I wonder. Or perhaps just invisible, watching and waiting.

There's a tense pause, then the second figure chuckles, the whites of their eyes showing as they stare openly at the cloaked figure.

"My my, you've grown," they almost purr. Their voice is high and warm. Female, "And your presence is strong."

"I know that," snaps the first figure, "My powers have tripled since last we met. It will make it all the more easy to destroy you."

The last sentence sounds like a warning. Strands of golden light dance around the first figure's fingers. The same thing that happened to me in the throne room. My stomach tightens. But this person seems to be perfectly in control of what they're doing. Their blue eyes are fixed on the second figure.

Surprisingly, the second figure laughs, "Oh dear. You always did have a dark sense of humour, didn't you, pet?" She smiles, showing gleaming white teeth, so sharp they're almost fangs, "But I'm afraid you wouldn't stand a chance. Still, there's no point with empty threats tonight, is there?" She waves a hand casually and the golden threads vanish. The first figure snarls.

The second figure steps forward, and, almost out of instinct, the first figure steps backwards. The second figure smiles again, but it dies quickly, "You're afraid. And rightly so. But for your journey to succeed, you will need to be only afraid of one thing."

"What's that?" snaps the first figure.

"Yourself," the second figure's eyes glint, "Now, I have little time, so listen carefully."

They pull out a long, sharp blade, "This is the vessel. Seek the place where the sun never rises. There you will find the first ingredient. And I'm sure you know the rest," with a wink, they turn to go.

"Wait," says the first figure. Their eyes are cold and penetrating. The second figure turns, "Yes?"

This time the first figure doesn't step back, "If you are lying to me, I will hunt you down and kill you myself, then scatter your ashes so fine that no sorcerer in the world could ever bring you back. Understand?"

As she speaks, shadows coil around her legs. Suddenly I recognise the voice. My heart drops.

The second figure appraises the first, "I was right. You were always stronger. Use your strength. Darkness obeys only the strongest. And do not fail."

With that, they vanish.

And the vision goes dark.

31
ON THE CLOCK

So much for having questions answered.

Jasmine stands shakily, quickly looking away from the disc as if it's on fire. She starts to pace, boots clicking against the floor as does so, dragging a hand through her dark hair and muttering. We all watch her silently.

Eventually she lets out a long sigh, and turns to us.

"*Lamina Auro Umbrei,*" she whispers, "The blade of gold and shadows. I still have that book."

She spins and rummages through the piles of stray gears and old gadgets until she pulls it out. She flips through, panicked, until she finds the page. Her expression goes from triumphant to terrified in the space of two seconds.

"Here," she says quietly, giving the book to me. Her green eyes are wide with fear. I take the book gingerly and hold the

271

page lightly, as if it might crumble beneath my fingers.

The page is worn and yellowing, with the same dark handwriting I saw in the vision. And there are the words.

Lamina Auro Umbrei.

I read on, "The blade of gold and shadows has been the most terrifying of folklore since the very dawn of beginning. Its power surpasses the greatest of sorcerers, with the ability to kill stars themselves," I swallow. *If that's what it could do to a star, what could it do to me?* Forcing a tremble out of my voice, I keep reading, "The vessel itself is easy to obtain. But the blade can only be controlled by a master of its equal. One of shadows, and gold."

I reach the end of the page and flip it, then see what Jasmine looked so terrified at. Where the writing should be, the page is charred beyond repair. Crimson words stand out. *It begins.*

Reading them makes my head swim. The note with the arrow in Picasar said the exact same thing. I have no doubt it's Nerezza.

The pieces are falling together faster and faster. I feel like I'm clutching at straws.

Silently, I show the others the page. Skye growls, her hands tightening around her arrow. Anita's eyes widen. Charlie practically squeaks. Evan locks eyes with me, "She's after us."

"She's after me," I correct. My voice hardens, "And that's what she'll get."

Somehow, the pieces click.

Gold and shadows. For Nerezza to control the blade, she'd need to have power over gold. The *bird*. And…become shadows? How is that possible? I frown, "I've got it."

The others seem to know what I mean, understanding dawning on their faces.

"Nerezza has the blade," Anita breathes.

"She needs two things," I say, "Control over shadows, and control over gold."

"So she's after the goldwing," Skye says, stunned. I nod grimly.

The bird is the final step.

"Well, what are we waiting for?" Charlie says, standing up. We all blink in surprise. His green eyes are steely as he says, "We can't let her get there first, can we? We know what she'll do if she gets her hands on it! That'll be us dead! Our families too! Our kingdoms destroyed, our school dust, and the only person who can possibly stop her is Avery," he points at me, "I'm an alchemist. Gold is our domain. If Nerezza takes control of it she takes control of us. And she could take more than that," his voice drops to a whisper, "She could take our magic."

The silence is as fragile as glass.

"So are we doing this?" Charlie demands.

I observe the set of his jaw, the determined look in his eyes. His fists are clenched. In his tattered jacket, grenades slung across his belt, he couldn't look more different from the nervous boy I set off on this quest with. He looks like he belongs on a battlefield, not in a classroom.

I'm not the only one who's staring. Skye's looking unblinkingly at Charlie, a faint smile on her face.

There comes slow clapping from the other side of the room and we all turn in unison. Jasmine is leaning against the table, holding what looks like a golden compass. She gestures to Charlie with it, "He's right. You're still on the clock. If Nerezza gets her hands on that bird… how do I put this lightly?" she taps her chin, "We're all doomed."

I push myself to my feet, a new determination surging through me. We're running out of time, "Then let's go. Jasmine, we'll need supplies. What've you got?"

"This," she says, tossing me the compass.

I frown, "A compass?"

"A finder," she corrects, "My own invention, of course. Can track anything. You want to find that bird? That'll do it," she nods at the compass in my hand.

Evan stands up, "What about the leopards? Are they ok?"

Jasmine chuckles, "Well, mostly. Your girl here isn't quite a hundred percent, but that's to be expected at this stage of the pregnancy."

I freeze. For a second a pin could drop.

Nyota's pregnant.

Of *course*. How did we not see this? Evan looks just as surprised as me. I feel a twist of guilt: we've ran her across the desert while she's pregnant?

"She's what?" asks Evan, a stunned, wide-eyed, confused look in his eyes, "She's…pregnant?!"

"You didn't know?" Jasmine frowns, "You guys actually didn't know?"

We all shake our heads. Jasmine whistles, "Well, I'll be damned. Anyway, she won't be able to move again for a while, she's pretty tired and—"

As usual, we can't get through the whole conversation without something going wrong. Because at that precise moment, Nyota's water breaks.

She yowls, the other leopards jolt to their feet with similar howls, and we all take a step back as what I can only presume is fluid seeps across the floor. Jasmine curses under her breath and vanishes up the stairs.

"Where are you-?" I begin.

"To get med equipment," she calls back, "Help her!"

I rush to Nyota's side and kneel down, praying the leopards don't bite my head off for this. She lets out a soft whine and looks at me with her lamp like golden eyes. Gently, I place a shaking finger on her forehead and stroke the crease between her eyes, murmuring nonsense as I do. The others are kneeling around me in a loose circle, but their rushed conversations and panicked voices go straight through my head.

Nyota groans, and almost as if it's been triggered, the golden disc suddenly comes to life. Lifting slightly off the ground, it vibrates with sudden, constrained energy. The air hums with it.

Then a rasping voice echoes, "You're too late…"
And in a bright flash, the disc explodes.

My head is shouting alerts at me. I'm here with a leopard giving birth, Nerezza's voice echoing in my ears and with probably minutes before we're out of time. I exchange a glance with Anita, who looks desperate, "Can you get the others out of here?"

She blinks, "Via wind travel…I think so. If there's not a border on magic here, then yes."

"Good," I turn to Charlie, "I'm putting you in charge. Go with them."

"What about you?" he asks.

"I have to help Nyota," I say, glancing down at her. She's whimpering softly, and panting, her warm breath caressing my fingers. I rub behind her ear gently, "It's ok, you're ok…"

In case you hadn't already noticed, I've never helped a leopard give birth before. So in fact, I have no idea whether Nyota will be ok. Or the baby. The thought makes my stomach twist and panic swell in my gut. I can't lose Nyota. Nor her unborn child. Can she make it through this? Is she strong enough?

"We need you," Evan says, a crease between his brows, "You can't stay here."

Jasmine rushes back, "No one is staying."

We all look at her. She kneels by Nyota's side and pushes me out of the way, "I'll look after her. You all have to go. My disc is gone. The head exploded. Nerezza left us a message. There's only one logical answer. She's coming for the bird. You need to go now," she almost looks angry.

"What about Nyota?" I demand, "Have you ever delivered a baby before?"

"I specialise in learning on the job," she retorts, "I've read enough med books to last me a lifetime. I know what I'm doing."

I look down at my leopard, weak on the floor. My ride, my protector, my friend.

"You promise?" I ask, my voice breaking slightly.

Jasmine pulls her glasses down, "I promise. Now go!"

I stand, and nod to the others. They take the silent command and we rise to our feet. I place a kiss on Nyota's forehead, then follow them to the door. Glancing back, I see the other leopards raise their heads, and howl: a long, mournful, powerful sound. It sends shivers down my spine. But it's not intimidating.

More like a salute.

I nod, once, bravely at them, and open the door. The smell of the fresh forest hits me, the green dizzying. Skye stands to attention, a red aura glowing faintly around her as she comes into her element. Charlie gives me a determined nod. Evan gives me that hint of a sarcastic smile, and Anita winks.

We all look back at the Alchemist's daughter.

"Will we ever see you again?" Anita asks Jasmine.

She looks up, and a small smile flashes on her face, "Not if I can help it."

32
SKY FALLERS

As if the day couldn't get any weirder, the second we step out of the house, it disintegrates. I spin around in panic, but the Alchemist's home is shimmering like a mirage. I soak in the image: the thatched roof, the worn down walls and climbing roses twining around the old wooden door. Like something out of a fairytale. Then it slowly fades away into nothing.

"Hey, Avery? You alright?" Anita nudges me with her shoulder. I smile, albeit probably weakly, "Fine. Are you sure you can do this?"

Anita places a hand on her heart, mock offended, "Are you doubting my abilities, Ms Infinite Magic?"

"Not in the slightest, your majesty Queen of the Winds," I say, bowing slightly.

Anita rubs her hands, though she does look slightly nervous, "I'm sure I can do it. It's not that long of a journey anyway."

But the nervous flicker in her eyes, the stiffening in her shoulders gives her away. I place my hand on her shoulder, and look her in the eye, "Are you sure you can this? There's no pressure, Anita."

Her shoulders slump, "But there is," she whispers, the worry swirling in her eyes, "If I can't get us there in time, Nerezza she—" she takes a shuddering breath, "You're right, there's no pressure."

She shrugs my hand off and forces a smile onto her face. The others are watching the exchange quietly.

"You don't always have to be strong," I say, seriously, "I don't care if we have to walk the way, if it means you're going to be alright. Ok?"

Anita's smile flickers. She takes a long, deep sigh. Her eyes unfocused and for a second she seems slightly lost in thought. Then she nods, "I'm doing it. We're doing this."

I squeeze her hand, "Thank you."

Anita nods and swallows, then clears her throat and addresses the others, "Right, you lot. In a circle, and hold hands."

She offers one hand to me, and the other to Skye. We take them and I offer my hand to Evan. He eyes it warily and I roll my eyes, "Now is not the time, Onceller. I'm not contagious."

"Oh, shut up," he mutters, embarrassed, and takes my hand. I look to Anita, who's humming softly. The sound echoes in the tree, stretching tall around us, into a canopy of emerald.

It takes me a second to realise we're floating. My feet are inches from the ground. Charlie lets out a startled squeak in the back of his throat. I hold my tongue and watch as we rise higher and higher.

That's when I realise the echoes in the trees aren't just a figment of the wind. They are the wind.

Suddenly the ground jolts away from us and we're shooting upwards like comets in the sky. I wince and close my eyes as the canopy drops to meet us, but we burst through the leafy green foliage painlessly. The feeling of the sky stings my cheeks as soar upwards like meteors.

It's breathtaking for about five seconds, before I realise things are going wrong. The air feels harder to suck into my lungs, like trying to breathe in metal.

"Anita...?" Charlie asks slowly over the roar of the wind, "Can we stop rising now? I think I'm losing oxygen."

His skin is so pale is almost has a green tinge. Anita still has her eyes closed, so it seems she hasn't heard him. I'm not in the mood to be killed by air pressure, so I squeeze her hand, "Anita...the guy's got a point."

"One second," she mutters.

"Come on," I urge. It's getting harder to breathe.

"Something's tampering with it," Anita says, a crease appearing on her forehead, "Oh no, this is not good."

"Oh really?" asks Evan sarcastically.

"Now is *not* the time," I snap at him.

Anita keeps her eyes closed, but her expression says it all. We're in trouble now. The winds around us are shaking hard. "Ok, guys, we have two options. Either I try and keep us in the air, but there's a 90 percent chance of...well, um, death. Or I let us go and—"

At that moment, the wind stops. For a second, we hang in the air. Anita's eyes fly open, panicked, "And this happens. Crap."

Crap indeed, I think. For a heartbeat, everything's still. Then we're falling.

Anybody who happened to be looking up would probably see five teenagers screaming their heads off as they plummet from the sky. Anita's fingers get wrenched from mine, and I cling onto Evan's hand so as not to lose him too. The wind is rushing past me so hard it feels like my skin is being ripped off my face. In other words, it's painful.

The ground below us is rising faster and faster, as gravity drags us down like anchors.

"Do something!" Evan cries.

"What do you want me to do?" I yell back.

"I don't know! Make us fly!"

"It's not that simple!" My instincts seem to have abandoned me completely. All I can think about is panicking. I thrust out my free hand and try and summon the tingling feeling, but nothing's coming.

Oh no, I think, *this is how I'm going to die, isn't it? Falling from the sky, holding hands with an idiot. Ugh.*

Nope, another part of my brain shouts, *you are not giving up that easily!*

Then Hiro's voice, from when I was younger: '*I'm here for you*'

I wish he was here now. But the thought of never seeing him again sends a sharp ripple of pain through my chest. I have to make it. For him.

This time, I yank my hand up with as much force as I can muster, and we stop falling. The wind feels less like a cushion, more like concrete. We smack into it hard.

"Ouch," groans Evan, "Maybe something slightly less painful next time?"

"Shut up or I'll drop you," I warn through gritted teeth, focusing on keeping us steady. There's hyperventilating coming from nearby, and Skye's voice, "Breathe in Charlie! Just breathe!"

They're hovering nearby, clutching hands. Charlie's eyes are wide with terror and his breath is coming in uneven, ragged gasps.

"A-Avery," he chokes out, "Put us down p- please!"

I focus all my attention onto that one task. It's harder than it looks. Unlike the other times I've used this power, there feels like a cold presence of darkness pushing down on me. The wind barrier beneath us is trembling unsteadily.

Now I see what Anita meant about the magic being tampered with. If I can't hold this together, we'll all die.

Anita herself has her hands outstretched, taking deep breaths as she faces the ground below. A stupider person might've thought she was meditating to keep herself calm this high up. But I know she's contributing most of her energy into keeping this wind shield up. Without her power, we'd be toast by now.

She catches my eye and I curl two of my fingers in, holding three up. She nods the tiniest inch. Slowly, the darkness clawing at the edges of my vision, I put my fingers down. Then we both plunge our hands in unison.

We drop again, but this time in a controlled way. Well, *controlled* is an overstatement. The wind around us shakes and rattles like we're trapped in a glass cylinder. I keep my eyes pinned on the ground, but the smoky dark presence has almost completely absorbed my vision. I grit my teeth and try and steady my hand, which is shaking nearly as much as the wind around us. The whole world seems to vibrate.

Nerezza's voice flits into my mind, a taunting laugh echoing inside my head. I block it out, clench my jaw, and keep my hand from trembling out of control as best I can. 500 metres, 200 metres...

100 metres...

50 metres...

The ground rushes up to meet us, and the wind chasm breaks. We fall the last 10 or so metres, shrieking all the way. I hit the ground hard, the air knocked out of me as pain stabs through my head and chest. Evan's hand goes momentarily limp and I let go of it, instead feeling along my lungs. Nothing broken. Just a couple of bruises. I try and take a deep breath, ignoring the acidic sensation in my throat and the burning in my eyes, which are watering.

I sit up slowly, one hand feeling along the back of my head, but besides a smallish lump which hurts when I brush my fingers against it, nothing is fractured.

Rubbing my eyes, they slowly focus, and I wince through the pain in my chest. We're lying on the dusty ground near a set of gates.

I need to check the others are ok. The fall wasn't bad enough to kill anyone (I hope) but I'd never forgive myself if they're badly injured. The closest person to me is Evan, who's lying spread eagled on his back, groaning softly.

Placing one hand on my ribs to steady myself, I adjust my position and look down at him. No cuts that I can see, though a purplish bruise is emerging on his hand. He must have landed hard on his wrist. I take it and examine the joints, looking for anything broken.

Miya's teachings come back to me. For a while, she gave med training in case me or one of the others were stranded and injured far away from base.

I test Evan's wrist and he winces, eyes flashing open and darting to me.

"Thanks for the warning," he says weakly.

"Sorry," I mutter, "Was too busy trying not to let you die."

"Now who's being sarcastic?"

"Oh, I'm sorry, who are you talking to?"

"Forgive me your highness," he mumbles, and closes his eyes again.

I tilt my head and raise an eyebrow, "Are you actually that badly hurt or just playing it up for effect?"

"Turns out being thrown from the sky is less fun than it looks," he says, but with a sigh, he sits up slowly.

"Well, your wrist isn't broken," I muse, dropping it, "Do your ribs feel ok?"

He almost smiles, "That's enough, Dr Avery."

I let out an incredulous laugh, "Since when do you have a photographic memory?"

"Since the last couple of days have been *very* memorable," he says, wincing as he runs his fingers down the back of his head.

"I don't know," I mutter under my breath, "When you're in danger every day growing up you kinda get used to it."

If he hears me, he doesn't say anything. I don't turn around to glean his expression, instead pushing myself to my feet. The world swims around me slightly, then steadies. I take a deep breath and stay still for a second. No concussion, hopefully. I'll heal myself if I can. But first order of business is helping the others. Where are they?

As if he can read my thoughts, Charlie's voice calls out, "Over here."

He sounds slightly dazed, but not injured. I frown, "Where?"

As far as I can see, the only life around is the pair of tall wrought iron gates, and a large oak tree. Wait. Hold that thought.

I step up to the tree and squint into the leaves, "How in the world did you get up there?"

33
THE BIGGEST ENEMY LIES AHEAD

My friends are hanging from a tree.

"Hi," Anita chirrups, "So, funny story…"

"You got caught in a net…in a tree," I say, eyeing them. They're wrapped in fine golden thread, so elegant it looks like beads of sunlight. It blends in with the dappled sunlight coming through the leaves. Besides looking a little shocked, they all look unhurt.

"The net stopped our fall," Skye explains, long black hair hiding her face almost completely as she swings upside down, "One problem: we can't get out."

I frown, "Not at all?"

"I've tried," Skye grumbles, "But my arrows aren't having an effect and I'm really getting sick of hanging upside down *again.*"

I almost laugh, then remember our situation and decide the better route. Not only because embarrassing Skye would probably be the last thing I ever did, we have bigger problems. Once we've got them down…well, there's only one place those gates could lead. Sure enough, when I look over my shoulder at the intricate metal frames, I focus on the white skyscrapers peaking just behind them. Adriana's border. Now all we have to do is get in.

I pull out my knife, place the hilt between my teeth like I used to do in Zoriana, and place my hands on the rough bark. The quicker I can get this done, the better.

I move fast, slicing their bonds on the count of three so they have time to catch themselves. The fall isn't far at all, so Skye lands perfectly on her feet. Anita stumbles slightly. Charlie flails around and lands smack on his face.

Skye looks like she's trying not to laugh as she helps him up, "You ok there?"

"Never been better," Charlie says with forced brightness. Skye eyes me, "You on the other hand look a mess. Are you bleeding?"

"Not that I can tell," I say, "Evan's not either, though he still won't get up."

"I heard that," Evan grumbles.

I laugh, then realise that this is somehow one of the most relaxed moments on this crazy up and down mission. Why? When Nerezza could be waiting? When the biggest enemy lies ahead?

Because maybe you're scared, whispers the voice in my head. *These moments could be your last with them all. Savour it.*

Turn back, urges the cowardly part of me. I crush it. There is no room for fear here. We're doing this.

"I'm sorry about the fall guys," Anita sighs. She looks genuinely upset about it. I place a comforting hand on her shoulder, "Hey, it wasn't your fault."

"Whatever Nerezza was doing was really powerful," she shudders, "Before we took off, that's the reason I was so nervous to do it. I didn't want to hurt anyone. And then we nearly died."

"Way to put a damper on the mood," Evan calls over.

"Shut up," me and Anita say in unison. I share a mischievous smile with her and then we're both laughing.

"Come on," I say, "We've got some shadow ass to kick."

Adriana is silent again, which is…weird, to say the least. I study every detail, mind feeling clear again after healing me and Evan. The cold, gleaming chrome streets are silent. No one stirs. An unbidden, but gut-twisting thought flits unbidden into my head: *maybe Nerezza took them.*

What would she do with them? Torture them for information? Kill them? My chest tightens. Heck if I'm going to be responsible for so many dying. We need to take Nerezza down. And fast.

Just when I feel like the silence could last forever, it breaks. Two people run out from a nearby skyscraper, stumbling down the street. They leave behind them a trail of red. It's a girl and a boy, both with red hair.

I rush forward to meet Cecile just as she collapses. Skye grabs her under the arm and drags her to her feet, "What happened?"

Cecile lifts her head, her face lividly white, a scratch marring her cheek, "Shadow th-things," she stammers, "Nerezza, she-she's here."

Callum's clutching his side, "One punched me in the side. Dang, it hurts. You guys need to hurry."

"Wait," I steady him, "What exactly happened?"

"Shadow thingies barged in, locked up most of the servants, and beat up the ones that didn't oblige. That includes us," Callum gestures to himself and his sister, "We made a break for it, but the rest of the staff, guards and all are locked up."

"You two need to get out of here," Skye says roughly. Callum shakes his head, "Nah uh, sister. Not while they're locked up. We're going back, but Ceci needs med care."

"Says the one with a broken rib," I retort, and crouch down to place a hand on Cecile's forehead. The shadow warriors slashed her hard across the cheek. Almost all the blood has drained from her face.

The tingling feeling leaps to my command, my heart leaping with it in triumph. I'm getting pretty good at controlling this one. Since it's most frequently used…which wouldn't happen if I didn't have these powers in the first place.

Full circle of irony.

The colour returns to Cecile's face, and I do the same to Callum. He lets out a small breath of satisfaction as the bruise on his ribs fades, "Ah, the sweet joys of weird magic stuff."

Weird magic stuff. Maybe that's how they see it here. That's certainly how I saw it only a few days ago.

Cecile pushes herself to her feet, "Let's go Callum. We should raid the kitchens on the way there, see if we can get some weapons. Do you still have your penknife?"

They go to run the other direction, but I interrupt, "Wait, one second. Both of you be careful, ok? We've faced these things before. It's not pretty."

"Will do," Callum salutes me, and they run. Soon they've rounded the corner and they're gone.

"Did anyone else realise we probably should've followed them?" Evan asks, "We could've snuck in via the servants entrance."

"That won't be necessary," Charlie says, staring at something ahead with eyes wide. The castle gates are open.

The elegant gates gape wide apart as we approach. To me, this doesn't seem like a big deal, but Evan looks horrified.

"This is not good," he mutters, "These gates are never open. Not even in emergencies. Where's Michelson?"

That prat? I almost say, but don't. Not worth starting an argument. We've got bigger things to worry about. And maybe over fifty people's life on the line.

I break into a run before the others can stop me, pounding

up the path to the huge double doors. I shove them open and pull out my dagger as they give in. But the room beyond isn't full of demons, like I thought. It's silent.

The chandelier hanging from the ceiling catches the golden evening light. The staircases shine with polished oak wood. The floor is inlaid with marble, and not a footprint in sight.

A cold shiver travels down my spine and images of Darkswift flash through my head. The same feeling lingers here. Something bad has happened.

I'm running again just as the others catch up, racing down the nearest corridor and barging through doors. Together, we keep our weapons out.

Then there's a shriek. The goldwing. It's close.

I force myself into a run again, though my legs are burning, and sprint towards a pair of grand, double doors. Pushing them open, I stumble into the room, my friends at my side.

Then I stop dead still. By the throne, the goldwing is chained and shrieking, flapping its wings desperately in an attempt for freedom. The president kneels at the base of the throne, bound and gagged.

And holding a knife to his throat is Nerezza.

34
CHOICE

She lounges on the throne like a queen, elbows resting casually on the armrests as she holds the jagged blade against the president's throat. The president himself is breathing fast, eyes pinned on us in wide fear as the knife edge skims his neck.

Seeing her in real life is even more terrifying than my nightmares. Her face is shrouded by her hood, just her crimson eyes glowing back at me. She wears long back armour and a jagged cloak that moves with the wind and is such a dark black it looks like it was woven from shadow itself. It flourishes behind her like a void, ready to suck us all in. Her hands are ungloved and marble white, flawless, but like all the life has been drained out of them. They don't look real. Her nails are long and crimson. I imagine a raven, long talons reaching for us.

For a beat, nothing moves. I can hardly remind myself to keep breathing. Around the edge of the room, shadow warriors stand to attention, spears raised and black eyes glittering with hate. I wonder if any of these are the scumbags we previously killed, brought back from shadow dust for round two.

At their feet, shadow wolves snarl and growl, low and rumbling. Their feet drip darkness onto the floor.

The late sunlight coming through the window sets the whole room bathed in pure gold. A vivid image enters my mind: darkness and gold, coiling around each other in an interchangeable pattern. The light hits the bird and makes it look like a new sun in itself.

I have to avert my eyes to avoid the blinding light. Even with them pinned on the floor, I can feel Nerezza's gaze searing into my head like she can see right through me.

My heart rate speeds up and a cold sweat breaks on my palms. Just being in this room is making me afraid. The shadows in the corners seem to grow and loom, distorting menacingly, then recoiling against the golden light.

And voila, the voice inside my head sighs, *Another trap. Didn't think this through, did you?*

I mean, I expected Nerezza to be here. Not with an army of killer shadow guards, but here. I guess I hoped…we could get there before her. Seems I was wrong.

Nerezza laughs, and it's just the same as the laugh in my dreams: cold and twisted and bitter. She never releases her gaze on me, or her knife against the president's throat.

When she speaks, it's almost as if she knows exactly what I'm thinking. Her voice is the same, too. It makes my stomach flip in terror every time. It's so full of menace, so full of *darkness*.

"Oh, dear," she drawls, eyes pinned on me, "Too little, too late, as they say. Well, don't say I didn't warn you," she flashes me a sharp-toothed smile.

I say nothing, but a swirl of emotions rises inside of me. Fear, of course, and anger. Just a seed. But growing. Surely.

"All that tampering nonsense," she chuckles, and rolls her crimson eyes, "Like I would let any of you fall to your death. The fun has hardly begun! No, there's use for you all yet."

Her cold eyes scan over all of us, "But a truly smart set of assets would've realised that was my warning. I've been here since that stupid little girl sent you on your way. Waiting for you. I did think you would've steered clear, though," her tone turns thoughtful, "You should've known from the moment you bolted into the sky that I was affecting your magic. But alas, you chose your brash instincts over your intelligence," now her smile becomes cruel, "Fools."

The anger begins to rise, slowly but surely. We are not assets. We are not fools. I continue to stare at Nerezza-or glare, rather, but say nothing. She tilts her head, "Although maybe I should give you more respect. After all, I thought you were all too cowardly for this. Teenagers."

She scoffs, "The phrase 'too young to die' is quite the correct statement here. But not for any of you, no. The younger, the better. The more they scream," her smile widens like a devil's.

This is where I open my mouth, but my tone comes out cool and detached, and hard with anger, "No. You're not killing any of us."

"Don't be pathetic, dear. It's not a good trait for a protégée," Nerezza says, clicking her tongue, "Besides. I could murder any of you weaklings in seconds. It'd be fun."

"If we're weaklings then what do you want with us?" I ask, narrowing my eyes.

"It's not what I want with them," Nerezza says, tone dripping with disdain, "Haven't you realised it's you I want, my dear? They are merely *distractions. Inconveniences.* And possibly bait, since you care about them so much…"

"You got one thing right," I say harshly, "I care about them. So don't hurt them. It's me you want. And I'm willing. As long as you don't hurt them."

Nerezza cackles, "Willing, oh my. My dear, if you knew exactly what I have planned for you, you would not be willing."

I keep my expression detached, "What do you have planned, then?"

"I want you to join me," breathes Nerezza.

"Yeah, and you're totally going the right way about it right now," I retort, "Give me a call back when you're not about to murder my friends, ok?"

"Don't be insolent," Nerezza's eyes flash, "I'll have to train that out of you. Hmm."

"What makes you think I'd join you?" I hiss, heart beating with fear and anger, "Why would I ever help a monster like you?"

"I'm no monster," Nerezza says, "I'm but a victim to this world's cruel scheme. A world which you must surely see the injustice in?"

I hate to let the thought in for a second, but for a tiny moment, I see where she's coming from. It must show on my face, because Nerezza smiles, "Ah. That's struck a nerve, yes? Indeed. I would've thought, after all, growing up in that hole, you would see the way the system is rigged. How come you were left to fend for yourself against freezing nights and firing squads, while the boy to your left was treated to caviar and candy?"

She's talking about Evan. I glance, once at him, to see his eyes on Nerezza, red staining his cheeks and his eyes narrowed in anger.

I turn back to Nerezza, "You don't know what you're saying," she gives me a cool, amused look, and I continue, "You know nothing about my home, and the people in it."

Nerezza laughs incredulously, "You mean your parents you left you to die? Your 'brother' who raised you for what? Taught you nothing about the power you have. You are dangerous Avery…"

Most people would say it with a tremor of fear. Not Nerezza. She sounds awed, greedy. But her words about Hiro make me break, "Don't you dare talk about my brother. He's incredible, and always will be."

My voice rises, and I'm yelling before I know it, a fire lit in me, "Don't try and mind trick me, twist me. I'll never join your side!"

Nerezza smiles, "You're angry. What a spirit…I can use that. Go on, foolish girl. Try and hurt me. The only mind games I'm playing are against your own will. Use it for the true power you have."

I can *feel* the power she's talking about, rising like a storm. I clench my fists, "The only power I have will be used for good. Never for this. Never for you!" I spit the last words.

The dam breaks. The golden light floods out of my hands, reaching for Nerezza. The shadow warriors shriek and hiss. The room goes darker, a freezing wind blowing in. My friends let out choked sounds and stumble away from me.

"Avery!" shouts Anita, panicked, "Stop! She's making you do this!" she sounds genuinely terrified.

I glare down at my hands, "Stop! Stop it!"

And above the goldwing's piercing wail, Nerezza cackles.

With a wave of one of her pale, spider-like hands, the golden light in my fingers vanishes. The room returns to normal. It's a moment before I realise I'm holding my breath. I gasp for air.

Nerezza coos, "Oh, how marvellous. Even more diabolical than I would've thought. I'm impressed, for such a young age…"

I think about the horrified expressions on my friends faces. If Nerezza finds that awe striking, then I want nothing to do with it. A cold wave of shame washes over me.

Nerezza's blood red eyes impale mine, searching their depths, "What powers do you hide? Aren't you curious,

Avery? To see how wonderful and dangerous you truly are?"

"I don't want to be dangerous," I growl, "I never want to be like you!"

"You are *just like me*," Nerezza hisses, "You do not see your true capabilities. Look inside. Find your hate for me. Use it!"

Her words ring around the chamber. I do nothing, heart thudding, hands shaking.

Nerezza tilts her head, "Or has that woman made you soft? Your oh so precious lady Tempest. And her school of cowards. She's using you."

"She's not," I manage to say.

"Oh, but she is," Nerezza chuckles, "Like a lamb to the slaughter."

I shake my head, trying to keep it clear, "You're using me. Not her. I'll never join your side!"

Now it's Nerezza's turn to say nothing, but she stares at me with a slow, lazy smile, "You will. Oh, you will. When I've destroyed everything you love, oh, you will."

"What?" ice cold fear washes over me.

Nerezza smiles even wider, knowing how scared I truly am though I hide it, "Oh yes. That pathetic city you love so much. Imagine it destroyed. Nothing but ash," she snaps her fingers, and black smoke billows from them, forming shapes. I see Zoriana. Burning.

I swallow, "You're lying."

"Am I? Or are you too scared to face the truth?" Nerezza taunts. The smoke takes on other shapes. I see dead bodies. Bile rises in my throat.

"That's right," hisses Nerezza, "All those you know and care about. Imagine them dead. Gone. I can do horrible things to you, Avery."

Her words come out sharp and piercing now. A threat. She narrows her red eyes to slits, "Or I can make you adored. You'll have everything you ever wanted."

"All I ever wanted was a family," I say, voice breaking slightly, "And you want to take it from me."

"No," Nerezza says, "You are the only one who can destroy your family."

The words are cryptic. I frown, "You're talking in riddles."

"You'll learn one day," Nerezza says with a Cheshire Cat smile, "But I'm offering you a choice. Right here, right now, you can take my side. Take control of darkness. Take control of the world. Or you can be destroyed. Your choice."

Your choice. The world seems to zero in to just me and her. It's my choice. If I take her side, do my friends live? Or will she kill them without a thought? The latter, it has to be. Nerezza's just using me. Tricking me.

"You're right," I say, oddly calm, "It is. And I choose to understand," I step forward, even as the shadow warriors hiss and the wolves growl. Even as the shadow smoke in Nerezza's hand reaches for me in long, coiling black tendrils.

"What are you doing this for?" I ask her.

Silence. Stunned, silence. Nerezza pretends to think, "Hmm. I would've thought a smart girl like you would remember. Money, power, to be adored. The needs of the great."

"That's not it," I shake my head, "You're telling me to look deeper at my own power, but what about you? What do you want? Why are you doing this?"

I search her crimson eyes for a hint of the girl from the vision. I think I know who she is now. The goodness. The human soul left in Nerezza. Who she was before. And she snuffed her out like a candle.

Nothing shows in Nerezza's eyes, not a hint of anger, emotion, anything. Just cold, searing numbness.

And very smoothly, she smiles, baring her sharp white teeth at me, "Revenge."

35
ERUPTION

She snaps her fingers once. Immediately, shadow warriors surround us. I draw my dagger and stab one, but a wolf leaps at me, claws raking my chest before Nerezza whistles. It backs down, and the demons stand to attention, forcing us into a tight circle. I back up against the others. Out of the corner of my eye, I can see them, shaking, but standing. Standing with...me.

Nerezza stands up, all playfulness gone. Her dress is long and coils with darkness. At her feet, tendrils of shadow wrap around the president, binding him. Nerezza fingers the sharp edge of her knife, sighing, "My deepest apologies, Avery. You had a choice, I did warn you. So this is your last chance," her scarlet eyes flash, "What will it be?"

"Never," I spit, pain stabbing through my chest, as spots of red hit the floor. Nothing fatal. Luckily that beast didn't get near my heart, "I'll never join your side."

Nerezza's smile vanishes. Her eyes fill with hate, and her voice is cold, "Then you will die."

She raises a hand to the ceiling, but at that moment, I run at the shadow warrior nearest me. It raises its weapon, and anger crashes inside me like a wave. A burst of golden light disintegrates it. Nerezza falters. Just a heartbeat. Just enough.

I sprint for the throne, vault myself to the very top, and grab the goldwing. It shrieks in protest, and, almost as if they're jolted out of their trance by the sound, shadow warriors rush me. I dodge and duck between them, stabbing as many as I can. Two grab my arms and wrench them behind my back. Just before it slips out of my grasp, I slash the goldwing's chains with my knife. The bird shoots up like a golden comet, straight through the glass ceiling, as Nerezza screams, "No!"

I feel like shouting with triumph. The feeling doesn't last long.

Another shadow warrior punches me hard in the face, and one more presses a knife to my throat, turning to their mistress for the order to kill me. My knife is kicked away across the marble floor.

"Avery!" yells a voice. Evan's holding a blade. I lock eyes with him and he throws it, "catch!"

"Foolish boy," Nerezza sends him flying backwards against the wall with a burst of black, sparking electricity. Evan slumps down, eyes fluttering closed. The knife lands a few metres short. I stare at it.

Nerezza's breathing heavily, "You...you dare to try and defeat me?" she cackles, "So be it. Hold fire," she orders the shadow warriors surrounding me, "I have something planned for these ones."

She stamps her foot, hard, and a jagged crack appears, cutting through the air with its sound.

Oh no.

I lock eyes with Charlie, stunned. His face dawns with slow terror. *The volcano.*

Nerezza stamps again, and two more huge cracks appear. Then the floor splits, right down the middle. The air seems to be pulled towards the chasm. A few rocks skitter off the edge.

Then comes the rumble. Like something ancient and powerful is roaring, far, far below. And the ground starts to shake, tremoring so hard it nearly knocks me off my feet.

"Have fun," Nerezza sing-songs. Then, in a black lightning flash, she vanishes. And the room starts to collapse.

My instincts kick in and I kick at the shadow warriors holding me. Startled, they let go, and I dive for the knife. One kicks me in the back of legs and I practically collapse on top of it. Grabbing the hilt, I swing it at my oncoming attackers.

Across the rift, my friends are fighting the shadow demons around them. Charlie unlatches a grenade and vaporises three before a wolf claws his arm. A shadow warrior clocks Skye in the side, but she hits them around the head with her bow, before impaling another with a silver tipped arrow. Her red aura is flickering. Anita is somewhere in midair, fighting off dozens of the things flying at her. That's all I can see before I'm attacked from all sides.

I fight back, even as I feel a wolf's teeth sink into arm. Spinning and pushing myself to my feet, I slash and stab more shadow warriors. One wolf drags its claw across my leg, and I kick it hard before stabbing it through the head. Two more demons attempt to grab me, and I elbow them hard, before bringing my leg up to knee one. All the fighting techniques Hiro's taught me come back to me, every sweat soaked lesson I ended with bruises on my knuckles, every time he barked commands and pushed my endurance. It's what's made me.

I stab another and whirl to hit one, when the air is suddenly knocked out of my lungs. I fall to the floor as a shadow warrior raises its weapon: a club, to hit me again. I roll out of the way and press my face hard into the cool concrete as the club smashes down inches away.

There's another earthquake beneath our feet, and a marble column starts to lean across the rift. Towards my friends.

"Watch out!" I scream. The shadow warrior kicks me in the mouth and I taste blood. As another grabs my arms, I yank myself up and head butt it hard. The world seems to be tilting.

Suddenly there's a huge gust of wind and the column stops its descent. I hear Anita's scream and whirl to try and see her, but all I can see are shadow warriors surrounding her in the air.

A huge chunk of the glass ceiling falls in and shatters. I feel millions of tiny shards embed themselves in my hands. I use the distraction to my advantage and slash a shadow warrior on the left, then fend off another wolf as it leaps at me, jaws yawning.

The quicker I kill them, the quicker even more are coming at me, black eyes full of rage and shrieks ear-piercing. With a grunt, I high kick one of the shadow warriors and punch another hard. Stunned, it stumbles for a minute, before a falling piece of marble crushes it. I stare upwards for a split second in horror. It's like it's raining, but with a high chance of death. I dodge a piece of falling marble and let out a yell of pain as another shadow warrior hits me in the face. Stars flash momentarily in my vision.

I hear an explosion across the chasm and look over to see Evan fighting three at once, jacket ripped and blood staining his trouser leg form where a wolf's got him. On the floor at his feet is Charlie, groaning. Evan stabs another shadow warrior as I watch, then pulls him to his feet and says something to him. Charlie nods in determination and they bump fists, before Charlie runs to help Skye, who's facing three wolves. Evan continues the fight.

The world almost goes black as another shadow warrior hits me in the jaw. I somehow manage to keep myself conscious, fighting off the ringing in my ears, but the momentary distraction doesn't work to my advantage this time. The piece of floor I'm standing on tilts, and I slip on the smooth marble. Slowly, it begins to crack. I can't stop myself from sliding, and then somehow I'm hanging off the edge of the floor, the abyss gaping beneath me. Lava has begun to rise, staining the shadowy room red and orange. A geyser shoots up and I recoil away from the heat.

The shadow warriors hiss and shriek, but turn their attention to my friends, obviously deciding I'm done. The wolves, on the other hand, seem to fancy a barbecued meal, because they slink forward, growling, jaws snapping. One lunges at me and I duck with a shout, slipping even further. I'm only hanging one by one hand now. The wolf barrels over my head and falls into the lava with a screech. It gives me little condolence. I'm going to be next in about two seconds.

"Help!" I scream, my voice finally working. It's probably impossible to hear over the cacophony of hissing, screeching, and deafening rumbling. Pain shoots through my chest and fear rises in me. My fingers are beginning to slip, ever so slowly. I stab my other hand up, reaching for the side, but the second I get a hold on the ridge, more crumbles away beneath my fingers.

I try to keep my breathing coming in steady breaths. It's impossible.

"Someone help!" I yell again, before trying to summon the tingling in my hands. Nothing. Nada. The only tingling I can feel is my straining fingers and the pain of my nerves where the glass hit me.

"Come on," I whisper under my breath, "Now or never!"

But nothing's coming. The ringing in my ears gets louder. The heat becomes sweltering. The room is beginning to fill with smoke, small pieces of lava spitting out of the abyss and leaving charred spots and in extreme cases, small fires. My vision blurs.

My fingers slip and I fall down…down…down-

Someone catches my hands and pulls me upwards, away from the cesspit. I gulp in the cold air and blink the blurriness away from my vision. Anita is pulling me up slowly, the wind carrying us both. Her face is tense with concentration.

"Thank you!" I manage to choke out. Anita grins.
Two shadow warriors come at us and she hesitates. The wind

breaks. I tumble to the floor, but my head is clear enough to remember my training. The fall nearly doesn't hurt. Emphasis on the 'nearly'.

I stand back up just as an arrow grazes my jaw. I spin around to see a shadow warrior, bow aimed at me. I dodge as another arrow hits the wall behind me, and glance up in time to see Skye stab the shadow warrior from behind using her bow. She winks at me, even though she's got a black eye, then turns, red aura blazing, to fight another demon.

Glancing across what's fast becoming a cesspit of fire and shadows, I see Evan, back turned as he fights off a wolf that's leapt at him. Behind his back, a shadow warrior lunges for him, eyes glowing with malicious fury. Somehow I sprint over there and stab the demon just as it bares down on my friend.

My friend. Since when did I become friends with Evan Onceller?

"Thanks," Evan says breathlessly, eyes frantic.

"No problem," I manage to reply, "You owe me one, ok?"

He grins, "Oh sure…"

I roll my eyes, then get distracted as another demon hurls themselves at me, shrieking. I impale them and brush off the shadow dust, kicking away another wolf that draws close.

"Hey, not sure if this was your plan," Evan says, "But how about running soon?"

"Not a bad idea," I say. Evan looks up and his eyes go the size of marbles, "Watch out!"

We both throw ourselves to the ground to avoid getting crushed by a falling piece of marble. Glancing at the rift, I see it's nearly overflowing with lava, the fiery liquid shooting into the area and alighting anything it touches. Soon this place will be an inferno. We have to get out.

I pull myself to my feet and whistle hard through my teeth. From their various states of fighting, my friends glance over.

I point at the door. I think they get the point. We sprint for the doors and wrench them open. The destruction has not yet reached the corridor outside. Smoke fills my vision, making my eyes sting and water. I hurtle through the doors and pull Charlie through, then slam the doors shut behind us. The frantic yowls of the wolves and the shadow warriors follow us. Then the ground shakes again, sending picture frames and marble shattering across the floor.

I look at the others. Their faces are ghost white and smeared with soot.

And we run.

36
THE CHASE THROUGH THE INFERNO

And, would you look at that? I'm running for my life. Again.

For a weird moment, I don't see the stretching corridor of shattered glass and crumbling walls ahead. I see Zoriana. The side alleys, Hiro's silhouette ahead in the oil lamps. Parker behind me, neck and neck as we race through the labyrinth. The image vanishes as quickly as it came, leaving behind the same burning feeling of adrenaline. The knowledge that I could die any second, and I can't let that happen.

Halfway through, Skye lets out a cry of pain and sinks to her knees. I stop, panic flaring, and turn back to rush to her side. Charlie reaches her first. He kneels by her side, gently taking her shoulders, "Skye? Can you hear me? Where does it hurt?"

His voice sounds soothing. Skye, breathing heavily, shifts slightly. Her right leg is drenched in blood. The wolves must have got her. I crouch down and press a hand to the wound, blood soaking into my fingers. I ignore it, focusing all my energy on my magic, on healing Skye.

"No," Skye croaks, "Avery, don't. You need that magic more than I do."

"You can't move," I shoot back, "Let me do this. We have to get out of here."

As I say it, the corridor gives a great groan. Behind us, half the wall falls in, creating a kind of makeshift blockade with a judder that shakes my bones. At least it might hold back the shadow warriors. I can already hear the wolves barking and roaring behind the rocks.

The tingling feeling sputters into life, like a flickering candle. I can feel my energy draining with it. The colour is just beginning to return to Skye's face when a rock falls from the ceiling, blotting out the sunlight.

"Look out!" Charlie yells, pushing me out of the way and throwing himself into the firing line. The jagged rock grazes his shoulder and he lets out a long hiss through his teeth. As he stands, shaking hard, Skye does too, her face set and her leg trembling. I push myself to my feet to try again, but Skye protests, "No. Don't. I can run. Heal Charlie."

I turn my attention to Charlie, who's wincing. He stops my hand, "I'm f-fine. We have to g-go, ok?"

I shake my head, "Not a chance—"

Behind us, the rock wall shatters and the shadow warriors burst forth in a rolling wave of darkness. A tidal wave of wind crashes into them, sending them crashing backwards with shrieks. I turn to see Anita, hand outstretched. Evan is next to her, drawing something. He lifts it, and I realise what it is.

He aims the metal cylinder at the sky and fires the thing. A red burst of light shoots upwards through the cracked ceiling, high, high into the grey sky that's rapidly filling with ash. It lights up the darkness like a firework.

"A flare," he explains, "A shout for help. I can't promise anything. We might be on our own from here," his face is grave. I'm amazed he can still stand, what with the blood rapidly staining his trouser leg. My legs are threatening to give way and my lungs burn.

"No," I say, "We're not on our own."

Maybe they don't understand what I mean. Maybe they do. I just hope they understand that they're my family now. And I'd run through this inferno for them.

I grab Anita's hand, then Skye's, "Come on!"

And we're running again. My legs scream at me, but I don't stop. I can't.

The doors at the end of the corridor are gone, nothing but splinters now. I vault over the kindling and into the cavernous hall beyond. The floor here is shattered, cracked in so many places that I can't see the marble anymore, just the yawning fire below. The walls are trembling like a leaf in a storm. I can hardly keep myself on my feet.

I press my hands into the cool banister and lean over the edge for a better view. Behind me, my friends clear the shattered doorway and hesitate, breathing heavily. Then shadow warriors fly at us again and the chaos begins again. A wolf barrels at me and I kick it hard in the gut. Screeching, it dissipates. I back against the balcony and glance over my shoulder. The walls are unsteady and threaten to cave in, but there's a line of broken marble busts created a kind of jagged pathway to the door. If we can just get there. It probably won't get the distance we need from the shadow warriors, but it might be enough.

A rush of wind hits me and I have to fight to keep myself from tumbling over the edge. Anita has her hands outstretched towards the doors, pushing the shadows back with the same kind of wind shield we used to stop our fall. Her breathing is loud and laboured, and she's shaking, but the wind holds.

"Come on!" I yell at the others, then stand on the balcony edge. My feet can't get a good grip. I feel like a tightrope walker.

"What are you about to do?" asks Charlie, looking horrified.

"Jump," I say, zeroing my attention on the nearest bust.

"Are you crazy?" asks Evan, "You'll never make it."

"Am I crazy? Yes," I say, "Anita's wind barrier won't hold forever. We've got to go."

Another marble column falls across the chasm and breaks into a million tiny pieces on impact. I swallow. If I'm not careful, that'll be me.

Evan grabs my wrist, "There's got to be another way. What if you can't leap all the way?"

I know he's being serious (for once). His eyes are panicked. Instead of reassuring words, which die on my tongue, I smirk at him, "Are you doubting my abilities, good sir?"

He doesn't roll his eyes, "Just be careful—"

Another crash rings across the chamber. The wall behind Anita crumbles and she hurls herself out of the way with a scream. The shadow warriors surge forward and are crushed under the weight of the marble. *That won't hold them for long,* I think. Anita sprints towards us, "Go!"

I take her advice and jump. The air around me judders under the weight of the collapsing building, but I don't think about it. I try to shut off my thoughts, just focus on the marble ledge. My hands stretch…then my stomach scrapes the ledge and I claw at it, pulling myself up onto the statue's shoulders. Their expression is one of serenity. Well, the lucky beggar can't feel anything even if the place does fall down, can he?

My heart does a drum beat inside my chest and I keep muttering nonsense reassurances to myself in an attempt to stay calm. All my efforts are wiped out as a huge chunk of deadly sharp marble misses me by an inch. I glance down at the dizzying drop below into roiling lava, and my head spins. I gulp and force my legs to stop shaking as I stand up. The next marble column looks so far away. What if I can't make the jump?

Shut up and stop thinking about it, I tell myself, *just do it. Your friends' lives depend on this.*

So I do. And somehow I reach far enough, because I smack into the second marble column like I've been thrown. Groaning, I pull myself up and make the jump to the next one. It's like the most dangerous game of stepping stones ever.

Every leap leaves my heart feeling like it's run a marathon. I

315

glance over my shoulder at the others, who have started the dangerous journey, following me. Charlie's hyperventilating.

Then there's shouting and I'm forced to look away. My gaze snaps to the double doors, where two people are standing, cloths over their mouths and waving at me frantically.

"Callum? Cecile?" I gasp, too afraid to move.

"What's happening?" Cecile yells back. Or at least that's what I think she says. The rumble of the volcano beneath the floor is deafening. Any minute now, it'll erupt.

"The volcano's erupting! You've got to get the civilians out of here now!" I shout, my voice hoarse. Cecile nods, red hair swinging, then she grabs Callum's arm and they turn to run. I stare at the spot they were, trying to work up the courage. The marble statues have run out. There's only one thing for it.

I grit my teeth, and, ignoring the shouts of the others, I jump.

Time slows. The heat of the lava penetrates my lungs as I fall, and for one horrible heartbeat I think I'm about to fall into the lava and die. But instead, somehow, my fingers catch on the edge of the marble floor and I cling on. Blood drips from my wounds. The world's fuzzy. I pull myself, arms screaming in pain, over the edge and lie there, shaking and coughing on the cool marble. Then there's a shout, and my name, "Avery!"

I look up at the others. The shadow warriors are swarming towards them from where they've somehow materialised through the smoke. The room is so full of ash now I can hardly see three paces in front of me.

I catch a glimpse of Evan's blue tipped hair and Skye's acid green eyes, then nothing. Yelling. Panic. The roar of the lava. I summon all my remaining energy, drag myself to my feet, and thrust out both my hands, imagining some kind of lasso. To bring my friends down before they're killed.

Nothing's coming. There's no time-then all of a sudden the wind rushes to my command, the effort weighing me down like concrete. I drag my hands back towards me, and with screams, four people coming hurtling out from the ash. I stop my hands just in time for my friends to collapse, panting, onto the marble floor. Anita coughs out blood.

Slowly, they rise, Skye helping Charlie up, Anita wheezing and gasping as she does so. I wrap them all in a quick hug, my arms burning, "We have to go."

My voice gets whipped away by the deafening rumble coming from deep within the earth as the very ground shifts.

We have to go.

So we do, sprinting as fast as we can, out the shredded double doors, down the path that's scattered with broken marble and glass like sparkling glitter thrown over everything. Out the wide open gates into the empty city of white, shadows chasing us all the way.

And behind us, the sky lights on fire.

37
THE LAST HOPE

The impact hits me. I'm thrown to the ground, stunned, and for a second, half conscious. The world drifts in and out of blackness, smoke in my eyes and my mouth and my nose, clogging my senses. Driving me crazy. I cough and sputter, my lungs desperately trying to reach air. Through the thick, dark, glutinous smoke, I can see what remains of the sky. It's painted with orange and red and gold as lava shoots upwards in a terrifying eruption. *Air. Air. Air.*

And there's screaming. Maybe from my friends or other innocent people. Maybe someone's hurt. Every protector instinct inside me rises and I want to stand, to shield them, to do *something*, but I can't move. My lungs are on fire. Everything's burning. Somehow one of my bloodied, bruised hands finds my ribs and I clutch my chest as if I'm falling apart.

Then there's a ringing sound in my ears. My body drags itself back into consciousness and a wave of pain hits me. I blink back the tears stinging my eyes and curl my fingers around the closest thing I can find, to hold onto reality before I fall unconscious again. It works. My grip on whatever it is anchoring me to the present. I'm alive. Somehow, I'm breathing. *Breathe,* I think, *Focus.* Next to me lies my knife blade, my hand wrapped tightly around the hilt. I stare at the woven patterns as they blur. Heck, even tilting my head hurts. But slowly, everything comes back into focus. My instincts come screaming back and my first one is to check for fatal injuries. My head hurts, but nothing's bleeding, miraculously. My ribs aren't broken. My heartbeat is strong. I can hear it in my ears.

I'm not dead. Now the next step is moving. Even pushing my hand into the ground sends pain up my arm, but somehow I work my way into a seating position. Around me is smoke and fire. I can't see anyone, just shadows. Then one of them is right next to me, and a voice is saying my name, weakly, but surely, "Avery?"

Anita comes into clearer focus as I take a rasping breath. She looks worried, "Someone get over here!"

There's footsteps and shouting and my other friends appear through the fire. Charlie and Skye are leaning on each other. Anita holds out a hand to Evan and he practically collapses down next to us, "What's wrong with her?"

"I'm right here," I manage to get out. The pain in me lessens slightly. Anita blows cool wind into my face, and it feels like crystalline clouds. I breathe it in and blink, slowly. My eyes still sting, but I can see properly.

Evan hardly smiles, but the corner of his mouth twitches at my sarcasm. I could swear he looks really relieved, "She's ok."

"She's not ok," Anita rounds on him, "You shallow nitwit! She could be in shock! Heaven knows she took that impact harder than the rest of us! Don't you—"

"Anita," I interrupt. My voice feels clearer, "I'm ok. Well, maybe I've been better but," I cough out smoke, "I can move. We need to get out of here."

"Good point!" says Charlie weakly, wide green eyes pinned upwards. Flaming pieces of ash are falling like meteorites. We could still get cindered if we stay.

I jump to my feet and turn towards the wreckage. My eyes water at the sight. Where a gleaming white castle once was there's a blur of fire and smoke. Charred black wreckage gapes like a haunted skeleton. Once so beautiful. Strange how it fell apart so easily.

Suddenly there's hissing and screeching, and shadows swarm from the ashes, fire glowing in their coal black eyes. With angry shrieks, they head straight for us, claws bared. We've destroyed every step of their plan. We were meant to be incinerated in that volcano. Nice and neat and tidy.

Well, I think, *that's never been my specialty, now has it?*

And we run. I don't even know where I'm going, just letting my screaming legs take me away. The best route will be the high way. The rooftops. There, we have coverage from the merciless ash and the shadow warriors will find it harder to catch us. My logic is probably pretty flawed, but hey, I don't see a better option.

I vault myself at the nearest wall, clawing at the bricks and pulling myself upward, blinking through the smoke at the last pieces of sunset. The clouds. The first stars. If I can get there…

And somehow I do, pulling myself onto the rooftops. Every movement is almost robotic, practiced from years of instincts ingrained in me. My fighting is at my very core. I've never had to run like this before, though.

I help up Anita, then Evan. Skye and Charlie help each other up. For a second, in this crazy messed up situation, I see how perfect they are for each other. Then we jump to our feet and we're running again. Somehow my fumbling fingers find my knife and I grasp it, sweat making the hilt slick and hard to keep a hold on.

A shadow warrior attacks me from the side, rabid with rage. I slice it down in one smooth motion. We've reached the edge of the first rooftop. I can hardly see the gap between the next one. Easy to misjudge. The smoke is too thick.

I blink my distraction away and grit my teeth, preparing for the jump. I clear the roof easily, but every muscle spasms as I land. My nerves are so frayed. They can't take much more.

The others stop short, and Evan pulls something out of his pocket. A pen. I watch him close his eyes and utter what looks like a silent prayer. When he opens them, a faint gold aura glows around him. The pen moves through the air, leaving behind a trail of golden liquid that flows and creates a shape. A rectangle. A bridge.

His hand is shaking, but somehow Evan finishes the bridge and holds his hand forward. Obeying his command, the shape solidifies into a wooden plank and he catches it, neatly laying one edge on the rooftop. My reflexes kick in and I catch the other side before it drops, holding it in place over the roof. A barrage of arrows misses the others by inches and Skye counters with her own, the silver tips glinting in the hellish fire. Evan gestures them across. Interesting. Wouldn't he have usually put himself first? Maybe...maybe I've actually underestimated him this whole time. But there's no time to dwell now.

The board shudders, but the others make it across. I'm

standing up, the adrenaline rushing again, ready to go-suddenly a whirlpool of darkness seems to descend on us. Claws whip across my one uninjured cheek. I press a hand into the wound and stumble backwards, bumping into someone. Anita meets my eyes, her own terrified. The darkness clears, the slightest bit, but we're surrounded. The shadows crawl closer and closer. Forcing us backwards.

There's no way out. I look up at the inferno above. Raging fire seems to be falling right for us. The world starts to tilt.

My injuries are catching up to me. I fall to my knees first, the smoke blocking my vision, my lungs spasming in pain. I can't see anything. There's just fire.

I could swear I hear a familiar shout on the wind. Hiro's voice, "Avery!"

But it's nothing. He's not here. He's far away. I'll never see him again. I attempt to stand again, but my struggles are in vain. The cold rooftop makes my knees sting.

Through my rapidly darkening vision, I soak in the image of my friends. They're all facing the shadows. Evan's face is milky white, but his jaw is set. In his shaking hand, the pen trembles, dripping golden ink onto the roof. Anita has one hand on her chest, the other raised. In her eyes I can see the firelight and darkness reflected. Skye and Charlie are holding trembling hands. As I watch, Skye murmurs something in his ear and kisses him softly on the cheek. Charlie almost smiles. They lean against each other, and all of us somehow lock eyes. Anita salutes me. Then Evan does the same. Slowly, my quest team, my friends raise their hands and salute.

I do the same. But not in honour of me. In honour of them. I can't speak, can hardly see, but I hope they know everything they mean to me. If we're going down like this, we're going down together. For one second, nothing moves. Then the shadows descend on us and I squeeze my eyes tight shut-

The pain never comes. Instead, shouting rings across the roof. The clack of weapons, the angry hissing of shadow warriors. I daren't open my eyes. Something warm touches the back of my raised hand, and, slowly, my eyes open a tiny crack. A flash of silver. The shadow warriors are being battered back, screeching. And fighting them... I gasp, eyes flying wide open. It's my gang.

I recognise Parker's dark curls as he taunts one of the demons, laughing and kicking ass at the same time. Jade moves like a cat, her silver knife flashing as she slices the demon. Hope rises in me like a storm. My family. They're here. It's not over. We're alive.

I tilt my head. The thing nuzzling me is Nyota, golden eyes sparkling. I let out a crazy, joyous laugh, and throw my aching arms around her. She rises and practically drags me to my feet, but the spark is relit in me. We're alive. We're fighting. We can do this. I stand, slowly, hand on Nyota's silver back, and search the crowd of fighters for a familiar face. Then I see him.

Hiro runs towards me, looking horrified, "Avery? Avery can you hear me? Are you alright? Can you breathe? Oh damn-Miya get over here!"

I stop him, stunned, "You came."

The words are enough. He smiles, "I always will."

"How did you-?" I start to ask, but there's no time for questions. A demon comes at us. Hiro slashes it down easily.

I grin up at him, "Not bad."

He shakes his head, "Stay here. Don't fight, ok? You're hurt—"

I interrupt with a determined grin, "Let's do this."

The next few minutes are a blur. My gang and my friends fight together, weapons flashing as we drive the shadow warriors back. The air around us is clearing, ever so slowly. Evan and Parker work together: Evan sketching, Parker punching. Jade and Anita fight side by side, Jade's white blonde hair swinging as she gives Anita an appraising look. Anita seems to glow with her very own golden aura, the wind bending to her will and smashing into the shadow warriors. Driving them back.

The leopards move like blurs between the fighters, pouncing on the shadows and dissipating them with growls. And comfortably wrapped around Nyota's front leg is a tiny silver cub, mewling a high pitched war cry. The sight of it makes me want to laugh and gasp and cry at the same time.

And me and Hiro fight back to back, knife and knife. The shadow warriors don't stand a chance. For every one that appears, we destroy twenty more. I can hardly see my blade, it's moving so fast. A new tingling rises in me. Maybe my Archery magic is kicking in. Maybe…maybe I've got my own glowing aura.

When I look down at my hands, they're enveloped in a faint golden glow. I resist a smile and whirl to hit another demon, fire coursing through me.

An arrow soars past me and I see Skye pull back another in

her bow, green eyes pinned ahead and full of light. Behind her there's an explosion and Charlie runs out from the smoke, grinning, grenade in each hand. As Skye aims her bow, Charlie throws the grenade, and together they wipe out a squadron of shadow warriors.

The sun glints off the surface of the roof, sending rays of gold everywhere. Wherever they hit the shadow warriors, the darkness melts. The smoke seems to wash out of the sky, leaving behind a fiesta of pink and dusky purple.

The final shadow warrior hisses as we approach. Hiro gives me a nod. I feel a surge of pride. Once upon a time he trained me for the world. Now it's paid off. I meet my friends' eyes, but they all nod at me as well. I turn to the shadow warrior, "I think you and I got off on the wrong foot."

Then I stab it to dust.

The wind settles. We all stop for a second. My muscles relax. I've got to say, I'm stunned. I'm alive. It's over. Just like that, it's over. Or…or is it?

A cold prickling feeling creeps up the back of my neck and I turn, already knowing exactly what'll I'll see. And there she is. Nerezza.

Her dress is torn and peppered with holes, as if the damage to so many of her minions has affected her. I feel a surge of anger and cruel satisfaction at that. Her crimson red eyes, however, glow just as strongly.

"Very good," she muses, her voice a thin, husky rasp. The smoke and smouldering fire behind her seems to twine around her, melting into the shadows in her dress. She's breathing heavily. In her hands glints the silver knife, jagged edge wickedly sharp. It's pointed right at me.

I glance at my friends. No one moves. Skye takes a step forward, looking murderous, and I shake my head frantically at her. Slowly, I turn back to Nerezza.

"Oh, this?" I ask, and shrug slowly, "Cakewalk."

It's the wrong thing to say. Looking back now, maybe I could've stopped what happened next. Damn, I wish I could've. I wish with everything inside me that I could've. Because, blood red eyes as cold as glaciers, smile even colder, Nerezza raises her jagged knife. And aims at me.

"No!" A weight crushes into me, pushing me out of the way. I fall to the floor, pain shooting through me as the world tilts. My injuries scream bloody mercy. Then there's a thud. A sickening sound. I lift my head.

No.

Nerezza has gone, vanished in a flash of black light. Slowly, very slowly, hardly daring to breath, I look at Hiro.

The knife in his heart.

38
SIX YEARS EARLIER

It was a cold night. The wind bit at my cheeks and blew my hair away from my face as I followed Hiro up the smooth steel fire escape. I'd never been up here. It was open air, so the railing was like ice beneath my fingers.

"Where are we going?" I asked curiously.

Hiro looked over his shoulder and grinned. His brown hair was messy, like a raven's nest, and his eyes were young, "You'll see."

"I hate surprises," I complained, "Can we go back inside? I'm freezing!"

"You'll want to see this, I promise," Hiro said sincerely. I stopped and crossed my arms, scrunching my nose up like I did whenever I was annoyed, "I don't want to. It's too cold."

Hiro stopped, and thought for a second. Then he hopped down the fire escape, boots clattering, and knelt in front of me so we were eye level. He took my hands, and his were warm and soft.

"Avery," he said seriously, "When have I ever broken a promise?"

"Lots of times," I say indignantly. Hiro just raises an amused eyebrow. I falter, "Ok, maybe not lots of times, but…you do!"

Hiro laughs, "Well, if you're so sure, then you can hop back down these stairs and help Miya sew tonight."

I pouted, sticking my bottom lip out, "Sewing's boring. It hurts my fingers."

"Then I can't help you, little one," he shrugged.

"Are you coming back down?" I asked him.

He grinned mischievously, "Oh, heck no. I wouldn't miss this view for the world."

I thought over it for a second, eyes narrowed at him. Then I stuck my chin up, "Well, if you're going, I'm going."

"That's more like it," he ruffled my hair affectionately, "Now come on. I want you to see this before it gets dark."

And together we raced up the fire escape, into the frigid evening. As we bounded up the last steps and onto the roof, I gasped.

There are sunsets, and then there are sunsets. This was one like I've never seen before. The sky seemed to glow with beautiful pink and orange and fiery red. The sun was a raging ball of fire sinking into the horizon, leaving a fiesta behind it. It glinted golden off the skyscraper's smooth surfaces, and cast huge looming shadows over the streets.

The roof was unremarkable, except for one thing. A bare tree, growing right out of the concrete, its roots tangled. Its branches were dark and leafless. It curved and bent like it had stood there for centuries. I wondered just how old it was.

Hiro took my hand and led me over, then hoisted me into the branches. Already advanced at scrambling up buildings, I pulled myself into a comfortable position in the tree and waited for Hiro to ascend as well. He settled himself next to me and for long moment we just sat there, staring at the sunset.

"Pretty impressive, huh?" Hiro sighed, eyes pinned on the setting sun. I nodded, awestruck, "It's so…beautiful."

Beauty was hard to find here. You had to be very determined, and very lucky. If you fought hard to see the beauty in the little things, it appeared all around you. And if you were lucky, you'd get a night just like this.

The air was crisp and dry. The sun felt warm against my face. I closed my eyes and nestled into Hiro. The rough bark of the tree scraped against my fingers, and I opened one eye, "Hiro?"

"Yeah?"

"Why do things have to die?"

He tilted his head to look at me, "Why'd you ask?"

I stroked the tree, "I mean, why can't things live forever? Why can't everything be perfect?"

He chuckled softly, "Oh, Avery. The world is far, far from perfect," his eyes took on a slightly glazed look for a moment. He never told me his story, and I never asked, but I assumed he must have felt pain before.

Hiro continued, "And things, I'm afraid, have to end. That's why sunset is my favourite time of day."

329

I wrinkled my nose again, "Why? If the sunset marks the end of something, how could it be a happy time?"

Hiro squeezed my hand, "Maybe not happy. Maybe sometimes sad, or painful. Sunset does mark the end of a cycle. But it's a normal part of life. Everything has to end. The day has to let the night come. The dark is part of the light. It's a part of the world," he takes a deep breath, "But it's not the end. The sunset lets the night come, but then the sun rises again, see? The next morning, there's a new beginning."

"But why does the night have to come?" I asked, "Why can't the sun just stay up?"

Hiro smiled sadly, "If only it were that simple. But I love the sunset, because it doesn't just symbolise the end, you know? It symbolises the start. New life. A new dawn. New possibilities."

I was quiet for a moment, just watching the setting sun. Hiro looked down at me, "What are you thinking?"

"I just wish," I began, then hesitated, "That I could freeze time. And the night would never have to come."

"Sometimes I wish that too," Hiro said, "But, if we didn't have the night, what about the stars? Where would that leave us?"

I pondered it, "Maybe the stars would shine in the day. And everything would be perfect."

Hiro sighed, "If only."

He didn't speak again for a long while. I huddled into him as the cold crept into me. The sun cast the warm orange on everything. If I squinted at the sky, I could just see the stars, beginning to shyly emerge.

Then I whispered, "Hiro? Are you awake?"

"Yeah. Why?"

"Will you promise me something?"

"I thought you said I broke my promises," he teased gently.

"That was before," I correct, "And I was lying. I know you too well."

"Ok then," he said, "What is it?"

"Will you promise to never leave me?" I whispered the question into the sunset. Hiro didn't answer straight away.

When he did, his voice was grave, "I can't make that promise, Avery."

"Why?" I pressed, "Are you leaving?"

"Not soon," Hiro answered, "But one day. And when that happens, I want you to look at the sunset, ok? And remember something. The sun rises and falls, day after day, but when the night comes, it doesn't stop. It's still there. Just waiting. And every day, it blazes a new trail of fire in the sky. You get it?"

I nodded slowly, "I-I think so. Are you saying that I have to go on?"

"That's exactly what I'm saying," Hiro said softly, "No matter what happens to me, blaze your own trail, ok? Do it for me."

"But," I shook my head, "You're right here. You're not going anywhere…Right?"

Hiro smiled faintly, "Not now, little one. I'm right here."

I settled into him, contented. The stars above us became brighter, sparkling and twinkling like little jewels. Maybe they were smiling fondly down.

My eyelids started to grow heavy, and I yawned as I nestled into Hiro. I fell asleep like that, nestled against him.

Watching the sunset.

39
SUNDOWN

I'm running before I even know what's happening, rushing to Hiro's side as he falls, seemingly in slow motion. His legs crumple and I catch his torso just before he hits the ground. *No, no, no, no, no, no, no.* My mind is screaming at me. I have to do something. *I have to do something.*

There's so much blood. I lay my hands on his wound, somehow trying to staunch it, my breath coming in ragged gasps, my lungs rejecting oxygen. Hiro's face is contorted in pain, chest spasming as he convulses slightly. Words are pouring from my mouth, "No, no, Hiro, can you hear me? Stay with me, Ok? You're going to be ok. I can fix this, I promise, I can, I can fix this."

My voice breaks, "I can fix this, I swear. I just need to—"

I squeeze my eyes shut as the first tear trickles out, summoning the tingling. An onslaught of pain and horror seems to be pressing on me, but I shut the feelings out, focusing on this. I need to help him. But nothing's coming. Not a single feeling. I open my eyes and press my hands harder into his wound, blood drenching my hands, desperately trying to stop the flow of blood. The marble around us is stained with red. Hiro's grey eyes find mine, weak and pained. He's trying to say something. My breath comes quicker, rushed and panicked. I can't seem to get air in properly. My throat is constricting in pain, and my voice comes out shrill and panicked, "It's not working. Oh, heck, someone. Hiro, I'm so sorry—" this is where the tears come, and my voice cracks, "I can fix this. I can stop this. I can do something. I can—"

"Avery," my name comes out a rasp. His grey eyes are flickering, "There's nothing you can do."

His words break the barrier. I start to cry then, properly, the tears falling before I can stop them, but I shake my head, "No. no, no, no. Don't say that. You're going to be ok, I can—"

My crying takes over. There's nothing coming. My magic has abandoned me now, when my brother, the person I love most in the world, is dying. Hiro's chest is rising and falling raggedly beneath my fingers. His heartbeat is sporadic and faint. The blood is everywhere.

No, no, no, no, no, no. This can't be happening. My movements become rushed and frantic, and I'm trying to find any way to get air into his lungs, to stop the blood. It's so vividly red. *No, no, no, no, no.*

Hiro's hands find mine, and he grasps them weakly. His movements are jerky, as he says, "I need to tell you something."

I nod through the crying and the pain, "Anything."

"Go on," his voice is hardly a whisper, "You have to. I'm not gone. I'm there, on the other side. Someday I'll see you again."

"Don't say that," I say, voice hoarse with pain and grief, "Don't. You're not going to die. You *can't,*" my voice drops and the tears take over again, trickling down my face and splashing onto our intertwined hands. I bow my head, sobs racking my entire body.

Hiro's soft fingers cup my cheek and he tilts it up, "Look at me."

His movements are growing weak, his body shaking with the effort to keep speaking, "I will always love you. Go save the world for me, ok?"

His face is kind, his eyes full of sadness and flickering with life. *Go save the world for me, ok?* The same thing he said to me in Zoriana. I nod numbly, "I will. I promise."

The blood is wet on my fingers. It's everywhere. The full force of everything seems to drag me down into darkness. Another sob racks my body, and my voice is almost gone, full of pain, "I love you too. I promise I'll destroy her. I'll save the world. I'll save our home. I promise, Hiro."

The tears blur my vision. Hiro's heart stutters and he coughs, the colour all gone from his face. His eyes are fading in and out of focus. The sight of him, everything in my whole world, about to fade away forever breaks my heart. I press my forehead against his, crying so hard I think I'm being hollowed out inside.

335

"I promise I'll do good for the world," I whisper, "I promise I'll, I'll make you proud." A gulping sob leaves my lips. I can't speak through the pain.

"Avery," Hiro's voice is the faintest whisper. I lift my head to look at him. A faint smile curves his lips, and his eyes fill with tears, "I am proud."

His body stills. His hands fall away from my face limply. The light in his eyes goes out and they turn glassy, reflecting the glow of the sunset. His heartbeat fades to nothing. For a second I just stare at him, a thousand memories flashing through my head, words I can never now say to him. Then the grief hits me and my mind curls in on itself, and I'm crying again, ear pressed against his chest as if his heart will somehow beat again.

A primal scream rips from somewhere deep within me as I sob over his still body, my lungs screaming, tears flowing down my cheeks. He's gone. He's gone.

The darkness presses in on me. I whisper his name over and over, but no reply. Sobs jolt my body. All the pain comes flooding out and I cry.

And over the skyline, the last traces of the sun slip behind the horizon, plunging the world into endless darkness.

40
THE REFLECTING POOLS

I'm standing at the crest of a hill, overlooking a sunset that paints the sky red. Reflecting pools in the shapes of moons are like still glass, the golden sunlight refracting off them. The clear water sparkles like crystal. The sun is a heart of fire. It's probably the most beautiful thing I've ever seen. *No,* I think bitterly, *The most beautiful thing I've ever seen was that night with Hiro, the sunset.*

And now he's gone. Every part of my body feels numb, but sometimes it hurts so bad that I can't help but start to cry again. Like right now. A cold tear curves its way down my cheek. I don't stop its descent.

It's been two days. Travelling here, for the funeral. This place has a name in the ancient languages, according to Hiro's will. *Reflexionis Amora.* Reflected sunset.

Hiro's will. I never knew he wrote one, but…it makes sense. He always knew he might die. He always knew any one of us might. And he left me a legacy. The tears threaten to spill over again. When I found his will I cried, long and hard, the letter pressed to my chest.

And he said he wanted to be buried here, at the foot of this very hill. So that's what we're doing.

Nobody else is up here. Nobody else is awake. Just me, and the ever present pain that accompanies thoughts of him. *It gets better,* Anita had said. *I don't know if it will,* I'd whispered, *I don't know anything anymore.*

The cold wind seems to knife into me, but I don't feel it, just a strange detachment. I wish he was here. If I'd stopped Nerezza quicker, if I'd somehow stopped the knife-I close my eyes, another tear trickling out. I can't go there. It's too painful.

Over in the distance, I can see the towers of Zoriana, like distant silhouettes. There was nowhere there we could've buried his body where it wouldn't have gotten stolen. And then we found the letter, and so we came here.

Hiro never told me this place existed. I get the feeling that not a lot of people know about it. He certainly never took me here. It's too far from home. But maybe for him this was home. It could be something from his past, before the gang, before me. And I'll never know.

I swallow hard and let out a shaky breath. The sun paints everything awash with gold. The wind rustles the grass ever so gently, whispering reassurances. I'd trade this, I'd trade anything, for Hiro to be here with me right now.

There's the faint sound of footsteps and I close my eyes again. I don't want to see who it is. But whoever they are, they don't speak. Instead, a rough pink tongue caresses my hand. I open my eyes to see Nyota, looking up at me with sadness in her big golden eyes. I stroke her head, rubbing behind her velvet soft ears. Her fur is so, so, so soft and warm. There's a little war-cry mew, and I look down at my foot to see the cub attempting to climb my leg like a tree. I laugh softly and bend to pick it up, "I don't think that's a very good idea, little one."

Little one. Hiro's nickname for me when I was tiny. I blink back the memories, the tears and hug the little cub tight as it mewls into my ear, tiny little nose quivering against my cheek. It's so small. So delicate. So fragile. So beautiful. I glance down at Nyota and smile, a hint of sadness in it, "She's gorgeous."

Nyota butts my leg with a low, comforting purr. She seems to know exactly what I'm feeling. I let out another sigh and return my eyes to the sunset, not really seeing it. I'm still lost in memories.

The silence seems to stretch forever. Then there's more footsteps. This time, I turn. Standing there are my friends, hovering anxiously. They're still in quest uniform, as per Infino tradition, but clean. I haven't properly talked to them since Hiro's death. Everything passed in a blur. I briefly spoke to Anita, remember Skye giving me a cup of something warm. Apart from that, the last couple of days could have been a dream. Or a nightmare.

Now I gently put the cub down, where Nyota picks her up between her teeth to try and clean her, and look at them all. I've been crying, they can see it. But they don't say anything. Instead, Anita walks forward and gives me a tight hug. My hands trembling slightly, I hug her back.

"I'm sorry," I whisper.

"Don't be," Skye says fiercely, walking over and putting her arms around me as well, "Don't even say it. Ok?"

She sounds really determined, adamant. I just nod and close my eyes again, not wanting to look any of them. If I do, then I have to return to the real world, the one where Hiro is dead.

But the world can't stop, and it won't, though it feels like it might. I have to keep going. *Go on,* Hiro's voice whispers in my head, *you have to.*

He's right. This is my chance to honour him. To say a proper, final goodbye. There are more dangers out there. I can't lose any of my friends, not again. Nerezza is still alive. Feeding off my grief. Trying to twist me with darkness and pain.

She won't, I think determinedly, *I won't let her.*

I step away from Anita and Skye, "Is it time?"

Anita nods silently, and takes my hand, "I think so. Are you ready?"

I tilt my chin up, "I'll be fine."

"You don't have to do this," Skye says softly.

"She's right," Charlie adds gently, "We can call it off. Just say the word."

"No," I say, shaking my head, "No. I-I have to do this."

Evan's watching us with his dark eyes. Charlie pushes his glasses up his nose like he does when he's nervous, and says,

"We're here for you, Avery. We always will be. We're a team now. And," he hesitates, "Just remember we're here. You're not alone."

You're not alone. It sure damn feels like it right now. I nod and swallow back the emotion that rises in my voice, "Yeah. Ok."

There's only a few people gathered at the bottom of the hill, where the soft grass makes way for the first glassy pool. I see the gang, talking quietly. They all look worse for wear. Jade's usually flawless demeanour is gone. She just looks like a scared teenage girl now. Parker has lost all his levity, just nudging a stone with his foot and staring at the ground. Miya and Bianca have their arms around each other. And Jodi is talking to a tall, graceful, willowy woman with long silky brown hair.

"Lady Tempest," I blurt out. She looks up, smiling when she sees me, "Avery."

Gently taking Jodi's hand, she approaches me, "My dear, I am *so sorry,"* her eyes are full of sympathy and sadness, "If I had known the stakes that would rise, I would never have brought you into this."

I just nod, because the part of me that's looking for someone to blame really wants to blame Tempest right now.

Tempest watches my expression carefully, then continues, "It seems you weren't the only one born with magic in your gang back in Zoriana," she squeezes Jodi's hand.

I give Jodi a smile, "I thought not. Are you feeling better?"

Jodi nods shyly. She does *look* better. Her cheeks are faintly pink and her skin has brightened, no longer waxy and pale.

Her little shoulders aren't hunched with cold, instead she holds herself taller, if a little nervously.

Her smile fades, "I'm sorry about Hiro. I miss him too," she looks at me with a nervous, doe-eyed look, as if she's worried I might start crying again.

"I know," I sigh, and hold out my arms, "You want a hug?"

Jodi releases Tempest and wraps her little arms around me. They don't feel like matchsticks anymore.

"You're still so light," I tease her, and lift her off her feet to prove it. She squeals and squirms, "What are you doing? Oh my gosh, put me down!"

But she's laughing, and the delighted look on her face makes me smile too. This must've been how Hiro used to play with me. I squeeze Jodi tighter and lift her higher, much to her surprise and more squeaking. As long as I'm alive, Jodi will always have a home, and she will always have me.

Me and Jodi never used to talk a lot. We all babied her, true. And we were a family, even if we didn't have time for small talk. Without words, I know anyone in my gang would run to the ends of the earth for me. I would do the same.

Hiro would, the voice in my head whispers. This time, I let it speak. It's true, Hiro would've done anything for us. And now, his legacy is mine. Jodi's squeals have reached ear piercing volumes, so, laughing, I put her down. She gasps for breath and beams up at me, this time the smile not hesitant at all.

"I'm starting at your magic school," she says, rocking on the balls of her feet.

"That's great," I say warmly, "You nervous?"

"A bit," Jodi shrugs, "Actually…a lot."

"Don't worry," I take her hand, "I'll be there."

"Aren't you going home to Zoriana?" she asks, surprised.

This makes me freeze. Shame wells up in me. It crossed my mind, it did. But I can't.

I look at Tempest, torn. I could go back to Zoriana, my home, and raise the gang. Continue Hiro's legacy. But then Nerezza might destroy everything I love. And I can't let that happen.

Tempest gives me a serene, serious look. *It's your choice,* her eyes seem to say, *it's your decision.*

A choice. Nerezza offered me a choice as well. Before she killed my brother. I swallow back the anger, the emotion, and clear my throat, "I-well—"

At that moment a hush falls on the gathered people, and I automatically turn to the raised ground, where Evan is standing, one hand raised for attention. Slowly, everything falls silent. He meets my eyes, and nods calmly. My cue.

I step up to where he's standing, every step making my legs tremble. The part of me that wants to run and hide is tugging at my conscience. But I grit my teeth and push it down. Instead, I force my hands to steady. Evan steps aside.

"Your floor," he whispers, giving me a serious look.

"Thank you," I say, and turn to the waiting cluster of people. My friends, my gang, Lady Tempest.

"Hiro Gayle," I say, my voice ringing out over the pools, "Where to begin? He was… he was my everything. He was a guardian. A protector, to all those he knew."

You could cut the silence with a knife. My gang shuffles closer together, some of them putting their arms around each other. A silent show of support. I continue, "He was a teacher. I wouldn't be who I am today without his guidance. In fact, I wouldn't be here at all," I take a deep breath, "Hiro saved my life. Multiple times. He taught me so much about the world. This crazy world, that will swallow us whole if we let it," I shake my head, "I won't. I won't let it. Hiro wouldn't have. And his footsteps leave the pathway for the rest of us."

Something distracts me out of the corner of my eye. On a nearby tree, a flash of gold. The goldwing. I blink, stunned. It lifts its elegant, pure gold head, and meets my gaze with its own piercing one.

I blink out of my distraction and return my attention to the audience, "Hiro isn't gone. He lives inside all of us who knew him. He sacrificed himself for my sake," my voice trembles, "He sacrificed himself for the sake of everyone."

Not a soul moves. My voice hardens, "So now, I ask you to join me in the death of a hero, a brother, a martyr, and a friend. And salute Hiro Gayle."

I salute then, standing to attention. Slowly the crowd does the same. Anita has tears in her eyes. Even Skye's eyes look bright. They all salute, turning to face the one sight I've been avoiding: a beautiful white marble coffin, lying at the water's edge. I take a shaky breath, "Goodbye, Hiro. And thank you.

For everything."

As the coffin gently lowers into the water with a splash, a lone tear trickles down my face. I wipe it away and muster another deep breath. The coffin vanishes beneath the surface of the lake, leaving the smoothest surface, not a ripple. The sunset turns the water to sparkling molten gold. It feels warm on my face.

And in the tree, the goldwing lifts its head, and starts to sing.

41

A BAND OF THIEVES AND HEROES

After the funeral, Jade approaches me. She almost looks nervous, which is something I've never seen happen to Jade before.

"Yo, Avery," she says, sticking her hands in her pockets, "I-I'm sorry about Hiro."

She avoids my eye contact, "He was a great guy. We all miss him."

She gestures with her coat at the rest of the gang, who are talking in low voices a couple of paces away. Parker looks stressed, running a hand through his hair over and over while he argues with Bianca about something. I feel a pang of homesickness, and a stab of pain at the mention of Hiro.

"I know he meant a lot to everyone," I say, looking at the ground, "Were you two ever-?"

Stupid question. Hiro and Jade had a crush on each other since forever. Jade's cheeks colour slightly, "No. No, we uh, we were just friends," she clears her throat, "So, um, where are you going after this?"

I sigh and drag a hand through my hair, "I honestly don't know."

Jade watches me awkwardly, "You know if you come back with us, I know Hiro would've wanted you as his second in command. The positions yours, if you, uh, if you want it."

"Oh," I look down, stunned. Leader? Me? Only a week or so before now I would've balked. I was happy just spending every day stealing with Parker. But now, everything is different. I have a duty. But is it to my gang, or is it to Infino?

I wish Hiro was here. My chest constricts slightly at the thought. He would've known exactly what to do. He always did.

Go save the world for me, ok? His words to me. I've grown beyond a scrappy girl on the streets of Zoriana. I have a quest team, a place. The prophecy was written *about me*. It's impossibly huge to imagine that I could ever play an important in the future of the universe, let alone be the deciding factor between its existence. I'm part of something bigger than me now. I don't think I can walk away from my magic, from my friends.

My magic. The same magic that wouldn't come to my control while Hiro died. Sadness wells up in me again, and anger. How could I be a part of something that reminds me so much of him?

But I promised him. I'd said it over and over. *I promise.* I'm bound by that. Hiro's death won't be for nothing. I look up at Jade, hoping she can't see that I'm scared, "I can't. I'm sorry, but my place is here, at Infino."

Jade nods. Disappointment flickers in her eyes. Even though we always pretended we hated each other, Jade does care.

"What are you going to do?" I ask her carefully.

Jade frowns slightly, a tight, pained look on her face, "I don't know. We need a new leader now Hiro's—yeah."

"You should do it," I say.

Jade's head snaps up, "What?" her eyes are wide with shock. I smile faintly, "I couldn't think of a better leader. I think…it's what Hiro would've wanted."

Jade looks lost for words. She splutters for a second, struggling to find the right words, "But, I, are you sure?"

I nod, "Certain. You're perfect for this. You know that."

A tear pricks Jade's eye, "Thank you."

I hold out my hand, "Any day, Fencer. Any day."

Fencer. Jade's last name.

She shakes her head, still looking shocked, "You're probably making a huge mistake putting me in charge."

"Don't," I say, rolling my eyes, "You'll be great."

Jade says nothing, just looking at me for a second. Then she grasps my hand and shakes it, "Good luck. You stay safe, ok?"

I manage a smile, "Not my specialty."

Jade steps back and gives me a quick salute, "Keep fighting. Don't give up, ok? Not for anyone. Look after Jodi."

"I will," I say, watching her go. She turns, standing straighter, and walks back to the gang, presumably to tell them the news. Parker looks over at me. I wave at him. Even though his face is pained, he somehow smiles and nods. I can see the message in his eyes: *don't go.*

I have to, I think. He's my friend. He'll understand that.

The gang help each other up onto the leopards, besides Nyota, who's meandered over to me while I was distracted. She butts her head into my hand and I look down at her, a small smile tugging at my lips.

The leopards take off into the sunlight. I wave as they vanish into the horizon. All too soon, they're out of sight.

"You ok?" Charlie's voice says from behind me. I turn around to see all of them watching me, Tempest just behind them.

I shake my head, "No. But I will be."

Skye puts her arm around my shoulders and leads me away from the reflecting pools. I glance over my shoulder one last time, imagining Hiro standing at the water's edge, hands in his pockets, grinning at me. The thought makes me want to laugh and cry.

The next hours? Days? Whatever, they blur. We arrive back

at Infino. Students are waiting. They clap. I remember muttering to Tempest, "I can't do this right now."

She just nods. The door swings open and I walk right out, while she addresses the curious masses. I just let my feet carry me, not really sure where I'm going. The funeral, everything feels slightly unreal.

It's night. The towers are light up gold. The warm light bathes everything in a faint golden glow. Light pours across the darkened courtyard from the windows of the towers.

Somehow I end up in the rafters of one of the towers. Maybe Artistry. The walls are covered in artwork. The floor ripples with a hologram that shifts like golden ink. It's wide and spacious, like an artist's studio. The window gives a perfect view of the stars. Almost as good as in Zoriana.

Hiro's really gone. It's sinking in. The pain is still there, though. Maybe it won't go away. The thought makes me sad.

Physically, I'm not injured. Anatomy students healed me and the others when we returned. But every time I think of Hiro, which is a lot, I feel like crying again.

I hardly cried as a child at all. And in the past few days, that's changed.

I'm so distracted I don't notice someone sitting next to me. When they speak I jump out of my skin and whirl to look at them. They hold their hands up in surrender, "Sorry. Didn't mean to startle you."

It's Evan. I can just about see him in the dark. I didn't recognise his voice because he wasn't being sarcastic.

"Oh," I exhale, looking away, "It's just you."

"Do you want me to leave?" He almost sounds uncertain.

"No, it's fine," I sigh, "This is your tower anyway."

"Why did you come here?"

"I don't know," I shrug, "Just looking for somewhere to hide."

Then there's silence. Evan says softly, "I'm really sorry about what happened to Hiro. You know it wasn't your fault."

I freeze, letting his words sink in. The part of me that blames me rebels against them, wanting to disagree. But he's right. I couldn't have done anything. If only my magic had *worked*…

"There are some things even Anatomy magic can't heal," Evan goes on quietly, watching my expression. Like he knows exactly what I was thinking.

I look at him. His dark eyes reflect the starlight. In the darkness, like this, he's not 'Evan Onceller' a huge pain in the neck. He's just Evan, my friend. My friend. It's weird, and unfamiliar, but…maybe we are friends now. The atmosphere is different.

"I know," I say, "But I'm sorry. I should never have agreed to do this quest, or brought any of you. Everything's so messed up and dangerous now—"

"Don't apologise," Evan says stiffly, shaking his head, "You've really changed us all for better. I know the others feel the same."

The thought warms me inside. "Thank you," I whisper.

There's another silence. My hand shifts slightly, almost of its own accord, towards his.

"Do you still hate me?" Evan asks. I pull back slightly, stunned, "What?"

He smiles, "Is that a yes?"

I shake my head, shocked, "What? After everything we just went through and you think I *hate you?*"

Oh my gosh he's annoying. That's his question?

He shrugs, "Honest question. Because, I mean," he swallows, "I don't hate you."

"Neither do I," I say simply. It's true. I don't hate him. I never really did.

He almost looks relieved, "Ok."

I can tell there's more he wants to say, but whatever it is, he doesn't. I look at the starry sky, not really seeing it, just images of Hiro. Suddenly a golden glow flares up near my hand. I look down, surprised, to Evan tracing something on the wood between our hands, the outline glowing golden. I tilt my head curiously and shift to see it better. Evan taps a finger against it and it springs to life, startling me.

It's a butterfly, golden wings flapping gently as it spirals around. It's so intricate, tiny little swirls patterning its wings. So small. So delicate.

It flutters towards me and I shy away slightly, but it's so

pretty, so elegant that I hold still and let it land on my shoulder. It's so light I can't even feel it, just the breeze as it bats its soft wings.

"It's beautiful," I say, my voice hardly a whisper in case the butterfly disintegrates. Evan smiles softly, "I hoped you'd like it."
The urge to open up to him is strong. I swallow and look down at the rafters, "I really miss him."

We both know who I'm talking about. Evan nods after a long while, giving me a sideways glance, "Is there anything I can do?"

I don't answer. Honestly, I don't know. Everything is so messed up now. Instead, I reach over and give him a hug. Evan freezes under my touch, then gingerly hugs me back, ever so gently. In his arms, I let loose the emotions I've been feeling. What's the harm in crying?

I use to hug Hiro when I was upset. But with Evan it feels different. My heart skips a beat.

We stay like that for a while. Eventually we pull away and Evan stands, "I think I've got to go. Curfew, and, well, Tempest will not be happy, so, um, yeah. Bye."

He gives me a final wave and climbs down from the rafters. I watch him go, fingers tracing the outline of the butterfly, which has faded from my shoulder but still carved into the wood.

It's beautiful.

I hoped you'd like it.

I'm certain I underestimated Evan Onceller. Turns out underneath the sarcastic demeanour, there's someone else. Someone I'd like to get to know. And maybe I will. But right now, I turn my gaze back to the stars outside, still not really seeing. Hiro's smile is imprinted behind my eyelids. He's gone. And I really miss him.

That night I just sit there, watching the stars.

42
HER NAME WAS AZEKI

I'm standing in a corridor, paused just outside a wooden door. The sun streams cheerfully through the windows along this corridor, which is carpeted in white and elegant. The door is simple but seems to tremble with magic. Carved into it is an infinity symbol. The crest of Infino.

I hesitate as I raise my hand to knock. Do I want to be doing this? But Tempest requested to talk to me specifically. And I think, now, I know I need answers. I don't have the full story. Tempest can give me it.

What I do know: The first part of the prophecy may have been fulfilled. Undoubtedly Hiro was a hero. The two birds? The goldwing must be one. My powers have begun to show themselves, though I certainly don't have control of them. Nerezza is back for vengeance, with a plan to build the Blade Of Gold and Shadows. Now that she doesn't have the goldwing, which followed me here curiously and now flutters around the Hall, she'll be trying to find another way.

355

And we have to stop her first. More specifically, I have to stop her. But there's still things I don't understand. And to stop Nerezza, I need to understand.

But if I understand…do I want to understand? There's a part of me that wants to brush it under the rug, to turn and hide. And Hiro's death still hurts. Really bad. Can I face his murderer?

Yes, a furious voice whispers inside me, *Don't you dare think about hiding.*

I grit my teeth and knock once on the door. As footsteps grow louder on the other side, I can feel myself trembling. I force myself to stop.

It's been a week. A long week of crying and missing Hiro and trying to figure out what to do next. Finding the quietest places in the towers and just sitting there, thinking. For the first few nights I didn't sleep. Eventually I let hand drawn guards give me fresh clothes, washed my face, showered, dressed. But I kept my jacket. It's a piece of Hiro, one that I'm not letting go of.

Right now I've dressed in black trousers and a plain shirt, tucked in to my waist and smartly. I didn't want to approach Tempest in my tattered quest uniform. I pull the sleeves of my jacket over my knuckles, running my thumb along the soft cuffs, seeking Hiro's quiet strength. On some level, I don't want to learn about Nerezza's past. It makes her more human.

On a different note, there's also the elephant in the room. The seventh power. I think I've figured it out. Maybe I'm almost able to control it. I resist a shudder. Heck if I want to control it. *The cursed seventh magic.* It's called that for a reason. It's the part of myself I'm afraid of.

To succeed you must be afraid of one thing. Yourself.

Another reason I need to understand. So I can learn to not be afraid. So I don't become like Nerezza.

The door opens, and there's Tempest, looking serene as always, long dark hair swishing down her back, grey eyes calm, "Avery?"

I bow slightly stiffly, "A word if I may, ma'am."

"No need for that," says Tempest, waving a hand casually, but she's smiling in amusement, "To what do I owe this honour?"

I look her straight on, "I have some questions."

There's a weight in my words. Tempest seems to sense it. She nods, a solemn look sweeping across her features, "Come in."

I notice she didn't give me an answer. *Always avoiding the question,* I think. *Why?*

The office is exactly how I remember it, the sun as radiant as ever, pouring in generously through the glass windows, golden fingers lazily stretching across the furniture. Tempest sits at the desk and looks at me expectantly. I work my jaw for a second. Standing is more intimidating. But this isn't an interrogation, is it? And Tempest doesn't deserve my coldness…right?

She hasn't done anything. *Except start this whole thing,* I think

357

to myself, *maybe without her Hiro would be alive.*

I shake myself out of it. What ifs just make me dwell on the past. And Hiro…nothing can bring him back. He's gone. The thought brings a lump to my throat, and I swallow it. I pull the chair out robotically and slump down, trying to make my position casual. In reality I'm watching her reactions like a hawk.

Tempest smiles gently, "What do you need to know?"

Need to know. Not *want* to know. Maybe it was just a choice of words. I clear my throat awkwardly, "Nerezza."

Tempest's face falls slightly, "Ah. I'm sorry, my dear. You must've thought it inhuman of me to send you off like that without warning you."

"Actually yeah," I say, "That was annoying. But that's not my point."

I lean forwards, "I want to know more about her. And you're the person to ask."

Tempest raises an eyebrow, "Am I now?"

"You know her," I say calmly, "That's for sure," Tempest leans onto her elbows, one eyebrow raised, interested. I continue, "Three things gave it away. One, the way Nerezza talks about you. Two, the way you look when I talk about her. And three," I sit back slightly, holding the silence. This is my master play, "It was you in that vision."

Tempest says nothing. We hold each other's gazes, grey against blue and green. She doesn't flinch or look away like some people. I tilt my head, "I'm right."

Tempest finally nods. Something changes on her face, a flash of pride, a flash of memories.

"Yes," she says quietly, "you are."

"So," I sit forward, "I have questions, and you have answers. And I'd like to finally *get* those answers," my voice has a sharp edge to it. Tempest hears it, and sighs, massaging the bridge of her nose.

I wait. Eventually she says, "You're angry. I understand it. You deserve answers that I haven't given you. What do you want to know?"

There it is. Want to know. I let myself relax slightly, "My visions. Every time I touched a scroll, I hallucinated. Flashes of fire. Glimpses of Nerezza. I had dreams about her as well," I grimace, "Ok, more like nightmares. My question is *why*?"

Tempest ponders this, "There's no clear answer, but Nerezza is to fault for those visions. She's trying to mess with your mind, manipulate you into joining her."

"Well that didn't work out for her very well," I say, "So what now? She'll try and destroy me?"

Tempest nods, "I'm afraid so. Nerezza is on the warpath. She won't stop until you and those you love are dead."

I clench my fists, "I won't let that happen."

Tempest smiles slightly, "I know. I've said it before, you have spirit Avery. Nerezza fears that."

I try not to let the hint of fear flicker on my face. Nerezza wants to kill me. She won't stop until she has. This could be bad.

Tempest goes on, "What else?"
It feels like Twenty Questions. I continue, "Darkswift. It's destroyed. Did Nerezza do it? Did Nerezza grow up there? Who lived there?" Now the questions are tumbling out, "What was her name? Who was that shadowy figure in the clearing? What is this cursed seventh magic? Why can't I control it?"

I take a deep breath as Tempest looks at me gravely. She nods, "I have a story to tell you. It should explain. Firstly," she hesitates, "The seventh magic. I think you've figured it out?"

I nod. What I say next comes as a whisper, "Stealing other people's magic. That's the seventh branch."

Tempest nods, "Absorbability, they call it. The ability to take other people's powers. Once you have, they become part of your power. Some absorbability sorcerers are very, very dangerous. Nerezza was one of these," she takes a deep breath, her face darkening with a memory, "But to understand her, you need to understand who she was. Before she was twisted by shadow."

She looks straight at me, "Long ago, when people feared magic, when a magical child was born, they'd take them to a coven of witches known as the Darkswift witches. They lived in a hidden town in the forest known as Darkswift. It was a very powerful place. The witches did good," she pauses, "Mostly. Parents would be thankful for the witches help in ridding their children of magic. But some witches didn't stop there. They became greedy, selfish, took more than they should. Fled the village to pursue their own dark paths."

Tempest sighs, "I grew up in Darkswift. I knew Nerezza, before she was what she is now. She had a different name then. They called her Azeki."

Azeki. Of course. What the alchemist nearly called her. Did she know him? I lean forward, curious, as Tempest goes on.

"Azeki was my age, there about. Kind. Talented. Ambitious. A little protégée. Everyone loved her," Tempest's face falls, "It didn't last. Azeki grew older, more closed off. She wasn't telling us things. She associated herself with the outside world too much. Rumours say she fell in love with a young man who stole her heart and died tragically. Either way, she began to pursue darkness. As for the lady in the clearing," she shrugs helplessly, "I don't know."

"Years went on. One night, Azeki turned completely. I remember it," she shuddered, "Fire. Terrible, raging fire. She'd destroyed the entire village. I pleaded with her, begged her to see reason. It was too late. She had abandoned herself completely. There was nothing of Azeki left. Next thing I know, I had woken up in the forest far away. Darkswift was obliterated. No survivors."

Cold fear settles in my gut, "And then what?"

Tempest sighed, "I travelled. I learnt. The Alchemist was dead at Nerezza's hand, but I ensured that Jasmine's automaton parents were activated. I visited the cities, taught myself the ways of the outside world I once feared. Then I started Infino. I went to Jasmine, now older and wiser, and asked for her help, which she gave. I gave her the seeing disc, knowing that one day it would help someone who truly needed answers. Like you," she smiles sadly at me, "And here you are. Still so new to your powers."

She leans forward, suddenly serious. Her hand grasps mine, "Nerezza will try and trick you. Make you angry. Use you. You must remember who your enemy is, and what you are trying to achieve. Don't let your emotions blind you. Nerezza feeds on those."

"Why? She has none," I growl, anger rising. Nerezza. It doesn't matter who she once was. She's nothing but a murderer now. The girl in the vision, the ghost? That must've been the human soul left in her. And she snuffed it out like a candle.

Tempest nods bitterly, "I wish I could say differently. Nerezza thinks weakness and emotion are the same. Only hate is power to her. Don't let her way of thinking change you, Avery," her voice is urgent, "For the sake of our world."

I look down at the table, a new weight in my chest. So much pressure. What if I let everyone down?

"What if I can't," I whisper, "What if I become like her?"

Tempest shakes her head, grey eyes stormy and fierce, "You won't. You're different from Azeki in one key way, Avery. You're *selfless.*"

Selfless? It's my fault Hiro's dead. It's my fault my gang are mourning. It's my fault. How can Tempest think I'm selfless?

"You are," Tempest says, as if she can read my mind, "You put your friends, your family above everything. For a girl whose parents abandoned her, that's very difficult to do. I believe in you, Avery."

362

It sounds like something Hiro would say. I feel a pang of sadness. If he were here, everything would make more sense.

Tempest watches me, then says calmly, "Your name. A unique one. You know what it means?"

I shake my head. Tempest smiles softly, "Avery. Ruler of the elves."

"So I should go find a load of elves?"

She shakes her head, "You were born to be magical, and born to rule."

I hold her gaze, "So what should I do?"

A smile creases her eyes, "So fly."

43
UNTIL NEXT TIME

The next days flash by. I must've taken part in this whole crazy quest really late in the year, because according to Tempest, it's time for term to end. After the summer, the students will return for another year. Not me. I'm staying here, training myself. Tempest arranged for me to have a dorm in Archery.

And it's weirdly…ok. Maybe this summer I can find more than just new skills. Maybe I can find peace.

I'm perched on the edge of the fountain, leaning back with my hand against the cool marble. Behind me, I can hear the comforting trickle of the water. It fills the pool, shockingly blue and glinting gold in the sunlight.

The sky above me is a warm blue, and fluffy white clouds drift lazily across. The wind is cool but not crisp, just enough to ruffle my hair and keep the sun from being sweltering. Perfect summer weather.

Summers in Zoriana were never like this. We'd get a few sweltering days when the concrete and skyscrapers felt like a prison, but aside from that, mostly thunderstorms.

Here, though, the summer feels like a cloud: lightweight and pretty, settling over everything like a ray of sunshine. I trace my fingers along the marble and tilt my head back, eyes closed, soaking it in.

My hair almost touches my hands when I tilt my head back like this. I'm not used to it being so clean and soft. It caresses my fingertips and I smile despite myself.

Around me, other students' laughter and chatter fills the air as they say goodbye, promise to meet up, to keep writing to each other throughout the holiday. The carefree, excited atmosphere is infectious. Normally a crowd like this would put me on edge. I don't know, but maybe I really am getting used to this place.

I wonder where the others are. My eyes open at that thought and I scan the clusters of students around the courtyard for my friends. No sign of them yet.

That's really the only reason I decided to come down here and be amongst the students. I want to say goodbye before they have to leave. Although…it's actually not too bad here on the fountain. I don't have to watch my back constantly. The weight that's followed me around since Hiro's death seems lighter, somehow.

"Avery!" I spot Anita's wild dark curls as she skips through the crowd, patterned bag slung over one shoulder and dressed in a colourful patterned summer dress. We all had to wear mandatory black and gold robes for the end of term assembly, which I suffered through (it's a glass hall and the sun was shining. Go figure) but afterwards the students rushed to change into something more comfortable. I did the same: I'm in jeans and a t-shirt. My old jacket is folded neatly by my side: the piece of Hiro I have left.

Anita reaches me and grins, "I hoped I'd catch you."

She perches on the ledge next to me, "You alright?"

I shrug, "Surprisingly…yeah. I am," I grin at her, and she gives my shoulders a squeeze, "Looking forward to summer?" I ask her.

Anita's eyes light up, "Definitely. I can't wait to be back home and see my brothers and sisters again."

"You have brothers and sisters?" I ask, surprised, "How have I never known that about you?"

"I have five," Anita laughs, "There's not a moment of silence in my house. But, you know, it's home, and I could certainly use home after this year!"

"True," I say. My voice peters out.

"What are we going to do about," Anita hesitates, "Nerezza? Are you in danger?"

I shake my head, "Tempest has promised to keep us safe for the summer. She says we can worry about Nerezza's plan once term starts again."

Anita still looks doubtful, "Will Nerezza wait that long?"

I grimace, "She needs to lick her wounds. Tempest bets we'll be fine. Besides," I nudge her, "We're fourteen. Even we need a *little* time to relax, right?"

I'm making light of the situation and we both know it. Thankfully, Anita lets the subject drop.

Coco bounds over, multicoloured hair bouncing, "Anita! We've been looking everywhere," she pulls her up, "Lacy needs to talk to you about those books she borrowed…"

Anita looks over her shoulder at me worriedly and I give her a smirk, casually saluting.

"Don't worry," Coco tells me, "I'll return her in one piece."

"No problem," I tell her, and Coco drags Anita away into the crowd. I watch them vanish, fingers idly dancing over the concrete. Golden ink spools from them and creates loose shapes in the air. I don't try and stop it: Tempest said that the stronger the magic, the less good it is to contain it. For me, having infinite magic, containing it could be disastrous. So I just watch the golden threads of ink dance in the air, loosely moving my fingers to create a wobbly heart. I've never been the sentimental type, but hey, magic training. I gotta start somewhere, right?

"Hey," a voice startles me and I look up, the golden ink dissipating. Standing awkwardly, hands in his pockets, is Evan. In jeans and a t shirt, he looks like a normal teenager. The thought makes me want to laugh, but that would be cruel, so I don't.

He pushes his blue-tipped hair out of his face, "Anita said you were here."

I shrug, "Just chilling. Practicing magic stuff."

"I saw. Try extending your fingers," Evan advises, a small smile on his face as he demonstrates. The golden ink bends magnificently to his will. I roll my eyes, "Show off."

"Alas, I admit it," he says with a smirk, "So…I've got to head to the station in ten minutes or something."

I clear my throat, "Yeah. Uh, ok."

He watches me awkwardly. Today feels different to the night in Artistry, even from when we were on a quest.

I bite my lip, unsure of myself, which is something as a rule I never accept. Eventually I look up at Evan, and stand up. He takes a step back, confused. I hold out my hand, "Friends?"

He blinks, shocked. I raise an eyebrow, "I don't bite."

He glances down at my fingers and then back at me, a smile building on his face, "I'm taking this as a sign that you don't hate me?"

I roll my eyes, "Are you going to shake my hand or not?"

"Fine," he holds out his hand, and we shake, "Friends."

I pull away, my fingers tingling. I hope this doesn't mean I'm going to suddenly start a hurricane or something.

"Excuse me!" a voice says, and we both turn to see Charlie making his way through the crowd, "Oh, sorry, thank you. Excuse me-!"

Eventually he reaches us, glasses askew, "That was painful."

"You have got a lot of luggage," I point out. It's true. Charlie's got three large suitcases at his feet. He turns red, "They're my chemistry sets."

"Very large chemistry sets," Evan comments. Charlie glares at him, and Evan claps him on the back, smiling, "Missed you, mate."

For a little bit of context here, none of us have seen each other for over a week, besides me and Evan. We've all been sleeping off the quest and I have no doubt the others have been answering a ton of questions from curious students.

Evan and Charlie laugh and launch into some kind of teenager boy thing where there's a lot of slapping and hugging and whatnot. I turn and scan the crowd for Anita, pausing when I see her rushing back towards us. She doubles over when she reaches me, "Ugh, sorry about that. Is Skye here?"

"Not yet," I shrug, "She probably has to learn to manage a bow in a suitcase, right?"

There's a cough behind us. Everyone turns. Skye's there, dressed casually in black ripped jeans and a black t-shirt, long dark hair swinging. Her acid green eyes are pinned on Charlie, who immediately turns bright pink.

I step back slightly. If these two haven't spoken to each other in a week, since they *kissed*...this'll be fun.

Skye marches forward and Evan steps back from Charlie. We lock eyes and I shrug. Skye pauses right in front of Charlie, and for a second I think she's going to hit him. Instead, she leans forward and kisses him hard on the lips.

Anita lets out a squeal and shakes my shoulders. I have to fight down a laugh. Evan has his eyebrows raised. Neither Charlie nor Skye seem to care.

Eventually, the two break apart. Skye scowls, "If you ever try and nearly die again, I'll kill you myself. Understood?"

Charlie nods, smiling cheekily, "It's nice to see you too."

Skye rolls her eyes and throws her arms around his neck. Me and Anita exchange nods and in unison say, "Awwwwwwwww!"

Skye glares at us, "Not one word."

This makes us do it even louder. Skye looks like she wants to kill us.

Evan interrupts, "I've got to go in like five minutes, so…"

"Oh!" Anita jumps up, "Group hug! Group hug everybody!"

And we all gather together, arms around each other. I close my eyes and let the feeling of happiness stay with me, wrapping around me like a comforting blanket. My friends. No matter where it goes from here, we'll always have each other.

"I'm gonna miss you guys," Anita whispers.

"Me too," Charlie says.

"Yeah," I agree, "This has really changed my life. …thank you, I guess. For everything."

"Remember we'll always have each other's backs, right?" Evan asks, "Things could get messy from here."

"No doubt," Skye says, "But I think we'll be alright."

Eventually, we pull apart.

"Time to go," Evan sighs, and we watch the students slowly head for the gates in a steady trickle of laughter. I look up at the golden spires overhead in the clear blue sky, catching the light. Winking at me. I take a deep breath and soak in the pure sunlight, the cool breeze, the soft green grass beneath my feet. The babble of the fountain behind me, the sight of my friends around me.

A goodbye is never the end. That's for sure.

ABOUT THE AUTHOR

Inspired by her teachers, supporters and favourite books to a love of English, Sula started writing outside of the classroom from a very young age. This, her first book was written when she was 12 years old. She lives in rainy but beautiful northern England, where she plans to write many more novels.